Also by Nicole St. John

The Medici Ring
Wychwood

Guinever's Gift

Guinever's Gift

Nicole St. John

Random House
New York

Library of Congress Cataloging in Publication Data

St. John, Nicole.
Guinever's gift.

I.   Title.
PZ4.J7233Gu   1977   [PS3560.03897]   813'.5'4   77–6008
ISBN 0–394–41167–6

Manufactured in the United States of America

24689753

First Edition

Guinever's Gift

1

What happened to me at Avalon was doubly strange, for I knew quite well I had no cradle gifts. If I ever had any illusions on that score, my father in a few brief sentences had disabused me.

"You are not, my dear Lydian, the darling of the gods. You will have fortune neither in your face nor in your purse. I would advise you learn how to be useful." He had smiled thinly, caressing the narrow bronze dagger he employed as a paper knife between his artist's fingers, even as the careless cruelty of his words stabbed at my heart.

I was twelve then. I am twice that now, yet I can close my eyes and still recall each phrase, each nuance of tone, the austere purity of his profile silhouetted in the pale light that filtered through the oriel window of his study. Father. Ason Wentworth. Scholar. Classicist. Connoisseur of the rare, the beautiful. He had spent his life in the quest of absolute perfection and it was, no doubt, inevitable that I should prove a disappointment to him. At the age of twelve a daughter does not always understand such things. Especially when her mother, who was the archetype of grace and beauty, had died tragically, too long ago to leave even a memory to emulate. I had said,

"Yes, Father," and "I shall surely try," and had crept into my own private corner. And that was the night the dreams began.

Those dreams of my childhood, of mist and cliffs and a strange alien landscape, of lurking, overpowering emotions too great to bear . . . how they had terrified me, and how distasteful they had been to Ason. I early learned to hide their effect upon me, for I strove hard to please him. I can still remember their irrational power, and, too, I can remember the exact moment when I at last stopped saying "Yes" to Father.

It was a Tuesday in the early April of 1906. The hansom cab that was carrying me to the Savoy Hotel clip-clopped through a London that was illumined by the warm yellow glow of an English morning. Strange, how moments of emotion are crystallized, encapsulated for me in qualities of light. That pale remembered coolness of Father's Massachusetts study. The sharp, almost chilling brightness of the Greek mountainside where Father had died alone, pursuing his long-dreamed-of excavations while I, unknowing, reveled in the hitherto-impossible delights of London sightseeing and shopping. The looming, threatening twilight of the Balkans, through which a train had hurtled me, shocked and despairing, to claim my father's body and to bury him, as he would have wanted, on his Grecian hill—the closeness to his beloved Mycenaeans would have mattered more to him than would a daughter's cemetery visits. I had stood there, committing him to the earth, in the company of his three laborers and an Orthodox priest who spoke no English, with the hot white sun burning my fair skin. And now again London, the kinder northern light filtering through the grimy window of the cab, and what I felt in my heart was not grief, not even sorrow, but an empty numbness that was worse than pain.

Father would have approved, I thought, my cool control. Would he have cared, I wondered, that it masked not feeling but its absence, a kind of walking death? Of course he would, for in his own way he had loved me deeply. Had he not, my shortcomings could not have so grievously disappointed him. Even in his dying I had failed him.

Traffic slowed my cab next to a lorry at the curb. Its black-painted sides formed a mirror-backing for the cab window, reflecting my own face with cruel harshness. Pale, drawn, overpowered by the heavy fashionable hat all plumes and flowers. I had not had time to do more than order mourning before I left for Greece.

I had been purchasing this hat while Father died.

That had been my first flicker of selfhood, of rebellion—my unreasoning and, to Ason, incredible determination to remain in London a few weeks, sightseeing and shopping, while he went on to Greece. London, inexplicably, had made Ason uneasy; he had paid a few visits to the British Museum and that was all. But for me—it was as if some daemon had laid hold upon me when I first set foot on English soil. Something as yet unnamed I had not known was within me stirred to life. I wanted the lovely city, wanted teas and calls and shopping, all things familiar by custom to other young women my age but not to me. I wanted, too, what Ason would have understood even less—a sense of touching roots, not with my own heritage but with one I longed for. England, the England of myth and history and literature, was my secret vice; I drank of it, drugged myself with it in secret, for to Ason no antiquity was worth serious consideration save that of Greece.

Always in the past my private wishes—my longing for the society of other children, my young enthusiasm for the Arthurian legends Ason considered quite inferior aberration from true myth—had withered in the first faint chill of Ason's look of scorn. But this time it was different. Perhaps it was the awareness that it was my money, my inheritance, that had made possible this trip, made me secure for once in the knowledge that I was giving and not only taking. I had shown, to Ason's distaste, a reflection of his own silent determination. Ason could go on ahead to Greece, and I would follow. Funds were available for him to hire the type of trained assistants he had always needed. So he had gone, in the cool, quiet disapproving way that had the power to freeze my heart.

I would never forget that I had been shopping on Bond Street when it happened. Father on a Mycenaean mountaintop, a thin elegant figure bending over the white stones in the burning sun. I in a shop all cool gray and silver, trying on toques, picture hats, embroidered mulls. Seeking something that would touch

5

me at last with beauty, would kindle for once in Ason's eyes the approval that must have been there when he saw my mother. I would be meeting some of my father's important colleagues in Greece; if his expedition was successful it would bring him public recognition to match all dreams, and I longed at that time to be a credit to him.

I had selected this hat, this tailleur of pale-gray linen-wool to travel in. And I had turned, and seen upon a dressmaker's form the stuff of dreams. Silk velvet, soft as breath, lighter than cobwebs, the color of sea-water at high tide. A *robe de style* for tea—I had no place nor time for such a garment, but it called to me in the language of my heart.

"If Madame would like to slip into it?" The saleswoman had unerringly noted my unspoken longing. I had followed her silently into the dressing room, stood wraith-still as she dropped the lovely folds upon my shoulders, had moved as in a spell out before the pier glass to stand there seeing not myself but a world long gone, a world known to me only in reading and in atavistic dreams. This was a gown suited to Arthur's queen.

"Does Madame wish to order it?" I bowed my head, assenting. Just then the clock struck the hour.

At that same moment, half a continent away, my father fell. If he had had some seconds of consciousness between the first pain of heart attack and last oblivion, he must have been gratified to know he was expiring in the land that was his soul's true home. And I had at least the satisfaction of knowing I had made it possible, through that large unexpected legacy from an unknown British relative of my lost mother. Poor Father, he had never forgiven Schliemann for discovering Mycenae and ancient Troy ahead of him, had never reconciled himself to the lack of funds that had doomed him to teaching at a Massachusetts college. He had never quite recovered from that early, rarely-spoken-of field expedition from which the financial backing had suddenly, disastrously been withdrawn after my lovely mother died. When my legacy had come, I eagerly, gratefully, laid it at my father's feet; I was at last proving useful to him. I at least had that. But I had not been beside him as he wanted, and I would carry that knowledge with me to my own death.

I would never wear the fatal, memory-laden velvet gown.

6

Was it guilt, I wondered, the burden of never having been able to be to Ason what he had deserved, that caused this numbness and held back weeping? My cabdriver lurched ahead, shattering my reflected image. I closed my tearless eyes, and in the dim labyrinths of memory, pictures formed.

A shy girl with hair the color of parched wheat, too thin, running eagerly into a still house on a warm June afternoon. "Father, look what Miss Mason from the Sunday School just gave me! *Idylls of the King!* It's a splendid poem."

Father, setting down his pen with the faintest, the merest hint of irritation. "My dear Lydian, is it too much to ask that you remember my labors suffer from the slightest interruption? We'll speak no further of it, I know that you are sorry." Surveying my beloved new possession with a lifted brow. "Sentimental versifying on an unworthy subject: that is the level of taste I would expect from the bucolic Mason. I would have hoped that you, at least . . . however!"

A year turned round . . . that girl eleven now. Climbing, in search of a stray kitten Ason tolerated, to a forbidden attic. Finding treasure: a small, fat volume, dark blue, leather-bound. *Morte d'Arthur*, by Sir Thomas Malory . . . this the second of what was to become a recurring pattern of Arthurian myth to touch my dreams. And on the flyleaf, making it doubly precious, words in a distinctive, regular hand. *To Virgilia, who has all the Gifts. From C.* My mother's name, my mother's book. I had never before had anything that belonged to her.

That was why I recklessly, unwisely, hid the book in the pocket of my pinafore and carried it downstairs. I devoured it avidly, compulsively, in private, becoming hopelessly fascinated by its magical world. From then on, Arthur Guinever his queen, Galahad and Lancelot were the companions of my dreams.

A winter evening, the girl who ought to have known better lingering over the haunting pages. Until Ason had come upstairs with his silent tread to find why I was late for dinner, had opened the door to my bedroom without knocking. The guilty expression on my face must have prompted some suspicions— of what, I do not know. But nothing could have aroused more shocking reaction than his discovery of that little book. His face went white with a passion I had not known he could feel. He had snatched it from me, broken its back, ripped it asunder and flung it on the fire—Father, who valued books as living things. His voice when he spoke had been shaking and almost inaudible.

"I will not have you befouling whatever mind you have with such worthless trash! Do you understand?"

I, in a still, dead tone I did not recognize as my own replying, "That was my mother's book."

He closed his eyes as if to steel himself, and a shudder ran through him. He looked so vulnerable, in that moment of unsuppressed emotion, that I ached for him, for all he was missing that I could never give. Perhaps that was why I dared ask, in a breathless whisper, "Father, what was she like, my mother? How did she die?"

He turned away, turned to stone, and when he looked at me again he was the old Ason, emotionless, austere. "You must realize you are speaking of a subject too painful to be borne. I beg of you not to mention it again."

I never did. But after that I tried harder than ever to fill my mother's shoes, knowing with aching emptiness that I could never be but a pale copy of her. It was then that Ason's advice on learning to be useful came, and the nightmares began. Even now, in this London carriage in broad daylight, remembering them could make a clammy mist brush against my neck. I willed my tired eyes resolutely open, but still they came, those waking pictures . . . a girl no longer quite a child, flinging herself bolt upright in a blackened room, crying out in sick, shamed panic. Ason, striving with difficulty to restrain himself, pointing out that dreams were the harmless products of an idle brain, that a night light at my age was childish self-indulgence. Even with the lamps lit—as now, here years later in a city carriage—those visions of cliffs, of water, could press with terrifying force at the edge of consciousness. With what effort had I learned to hold back my cries, to ride the crest of the waves of terror until they left me exhausted on the shores of sleep! But now, even now, after I had faced real tragedy on the peaks of Greece, those remembered dreams still had more power to move me.

And one dark related vision that was not a dream at all.

Myself, still twelve, as shy and lanky as a woodland creature, helping our housekeeper "turn the house out" for its seasonal cleaning. Finding, in a corner, a painting wrapped in paper. Unfinished, yet filled with urgency and a driving strength. A woman standing on wild cliffs, looking out at a storm-swept sea.

"Father, look what I've found behind an attic trunk! It's beautiful!"

Ason not even looking up, his voice dry and cold. "Burn it."

"But, Father—"

"I said burn it."

It never occurred to me to disobey. But I realized, as I watched the flames devour the curling canvas, that Ason did not want the picture, or the book, yet nonetheless had kept them all those years. The woman in the picture was my mother. And—this was what caught at my throat, made me prod the canvas more deeply into the fire—the painting had been an image out of my own dreams.

Why did I never ask about it afterward—was it thoughtfulness, diplomacy? Or fear?

Ason was gone now, and I would never know the painting's story.

I was given too much to dreaming, that was one of the things about me Ason so deplored. My cab had arrived at the Savoy; the doorman sprang forward to help me down, and I still sat dazedly.

"Welcome back to London again, Miss Wentworth." His eyes were kind. I had told no one but the concierge and Rose, my maid, the reason for my departure, yet such was the servants' grapevine that by now they all knew of my bereavement. "If you'll allow me, ma'am, I'll attend to the cabman for you while you go on in. Rose will be waiting for you in your rooms."

I was grateful for the solicitude which I did not deserve. The concierge spoke in welcome, the liftman sprang to serve me, the cheerful maid who had attended me on my earlier stay was standing in the open doorway of my suite. I moved into the baroque rooms like a sleepwalker, allowing her to unpin my hat and take my cloak.

9

"There's mail come, miss, and the clothes you sent for. I've hung them in the wardrobe, very careful."

That would be the mourning I had ordered. I ought to don it, to sit down at my desk and commence answering the business and condolence correspondence that had been accumulating. Ason valued prompt and meticulous attention to detail, and he had trained me well. But suddenly I felt too weary even to attempt it. Rose moved toward me, her pretty face puckering with concern. "Lor', Miss Lydian, you take those traveling things off and lay right down. I'll run a hot bath for you and ring for breakfast."

I was not used to having such attention, but it was an exquisite relief not to have to think. I submitted gratefully, scarcely noticing. The bath water was fragrant with lavender salts she had procured from somewhere; they were another luxury to which I was not accustomed. But afterwards, to Rose's disapproval, I insisted on donning the black gabardine basque and skirt; on turning, after the bun and coffee I could scarce choke down, to the voluminous heap of envelopes she reluctantly produced. It was better having some mechanical work that I had to do; I dared not yet face the emptiness that would stretch before me when these few tasks were done.

I had been Ason Wentworth's assistant; what was I now? "Study to be useful"—but to whom? I had neither sufficient training nor the proper scientific discipline of mind to be an archaeologist in my own right. It came to me suddenly that I was indeed alone, that one is ten times lonely when one has no purpose to fulfill. This great pile of mail—it was so gratifying to discover that Ason's work, in his small corner of America, had been known and valued by scholars the whole world around. But they were his friends, not mine. And not really friends— colleagues, acquaintances, or not even that, for Ason had always been a man to hold humanity aloof.

But I was not. The thought welled unbidden from my innermost being, startling me with a wave of astonishment and guilt. Astonishment, for I had never had the chance to know whether I responded to human warmth or not. And guilt because at this moment I should be thinking of myself.

I pushed back my chair and went to stand at the long window, looking toward the river. On the far shore a cockney girl of Rose's age leaned from a window shaking out a cloth, her work impeded by the young man nuzzling at her ear. I envied her, brisk and busy and alive. Rose came in; she must have been loitering in the hall outside, waiting to hear some sound. I rejected her suggestion that I go for a nice walk along the river and have a restaurant lunch—she had, in the interim of my funeral trip, adopted the familiarity of close family servant, and I found it oddly comforting. It was easier to acquiesce to the luncheon she ordered than convince her I did not wish to eat. When the tray came, though, I dismissed her, and after a few forkfuls, the food as well. I went back to the desk and stared at letters but could not see their words; picked up pen and paper but could not write. What was it our own Amherst poetess had said? *After great pain a formal feeling comes.*

I could at least unpack. Rose had tended to my personal luggage, but I had not permitted her to touch the bag containing my father's things, the journal, record-book and papers I had thought too precious to trust to packing crates and trains. To look at Ason's careful script recording the meticulous notes I had not been there to take would be a lance in my heart, but anything was better than this deadness.

The dog-eared copies of Aeschylus and Sophocles, valuable to Ason not for their soaring poetry but for historical clues . . . the account books of daily wages paid his diggers, photographs, picture postcards he had purchased not for unnecessary correspondence but for reference . . . The air of the room took on a faint mustiness as of old tombs, and for a moment I could almost feel my father there beside me. Ason's journal.

Ason's journal. Was it a need to know what I had missed, a need to punish myself for my absence, or a predestined fate that drew me to it? I shall never know. I did not want to read it, yet my hands reached for the small leather-covered book. It fell open—again by fate?—to the very page on which he had last been writing.

March 22. Lydian still not here. I must confess
I am grateful for that small boon. At least for these

*few weeks I have been spared the burden of that calf-like
eagerness, the clumsy futile efforts to be of use . . .*

Even as my head moved faintly in a numb negation, my
disbelieving eyes raced on.

*Unbelievable by all laws of science that the child can be
so unlike the mother. I have been saddled with a Greek
ironic fate. Ironic, too, that I must now be grateful even
to her for my being here. That is indeed the hemlock mixed
with gall. Had it been, not this non-child, but the Other . . .*

And then the last crucial, damning words. *What a pity it
was not she that died.*

I sat as one turned to stone. Time passed, and I neither saw
nor heard. The light filtering through the river windows turned
from brightness to cool afternoon. A coldness grew along my
spine. My fingers stiffened, and Ason's book slipped from their
numbness and fell to the floor with a dry little crack.

The spell was broken.

I rose dumbly, dazedly, my mind aching as though sensation
was returning to limbs just released from a long imprisonment in
ice.

Ason had not loved me. My lodestar and the source of all my
guilt was gone. I stared with a sort of incredulous horror down
the long corridor of years, at the child I once had been; trying so
desperately, despairingly to please, because the idolized father's
disappointment in me was doubled by the fact he cared for
me.

He hadn't cared. He had never cared, and all those empty
days, with that faint cruel smile upon his lips, he had let me go
on trying. Allowed? Nay, goaded. Always, with the cold, emotionless rejection of my efforts, had been the never-voiced but
always implicit suggestion that I try again. A cat toying with a
helpless mouse. Oh, I had been so blind.

How many nights I had crept to bed, my pillow wet with
shameful tears because I had not been able to be the daughter
he deserved? How I had labored in the never-ending effort to be
useful, to quell the poetry and yearning in my soul, to discipline

myself to that scientific objectivity in which I never could succeed. Ason had not wanted me to succeed. He had wanted me as an object of contempt.

He had wanted me not even to exist.

What a pity it was not she that died.

I turned, still numb, and saw as a stranger my own reflection in the cheval glass. A slender, pale-haired woman with sea-colored eyes, whose pallor had no glow. Who in the robes of mourning had a look too early old; whose simplicity was not enhanced by the hairdresser's attempt at a fashionable pompadour. I heard Ason's voice, in that dry emotionless tone that was like acid, saying. "Your mother in black was all Persephone, triumphant over death."

And suddenly my own voice, shattering the silence of the empty room, said, *"No!"* I would not be the ghost of Persephone. I, who had not pleased my father in his lifetime, would not doom myself to that futile effort in his death. As an archaeologist, as a scholar, I honored and admired him; as a father, I knew quite suddenly and completely, I despised him. I had to break into life, break from this confinement to which Ason, dead as when quick, still held me. My fingers were scrabbling at the hooks of the high tight collar, ripping open the black rigid bodice with its whalebone stays that were like the bars of a cage, tearing ruthlessly at the fabric of the stiff new skirt. The garments of false mourning fell from me like the halves of a confining shell. I stood looking at the mirrored image of a pale vestal, her bosom heaving in unaccustomed passion beneath the thin white chemise. There was a look in the eyes I was not used to seeing there, of life awakening from the drowned depths of the sea.

> . . . the Lady of the Lake,
> who knows a subtler magic than his own—
> Clothed in white samite, mystic, wonderful . . .

The words swam upward from somewhere deep within me. Then my head cleared, and memory returned. Tennyson; Tennyson and The Coming of Arthur over which my young heart had wept and thrilled, and which Ason had so scorned.

That a daughter of his should be so dull, so unscholarly as to think Arthur, the once and future king, as worthy of study as his beloved Greeks.

Arthur, the once and future king . . .

In that dazzling moment of clarity I knew what it was that I was going to do. The ultimate heresy. I was a rich woman, with no claims upon me, totally independent and with leisure to employ as I would. Very well; I would follow my irrational girlhood interests, focus those skills in which Ason had drilled me upon the trail of Arthur. If I could prove that the legendary British king had once existed, then Ason Wentworth was not infallible, and I would be free forever of the dark spell he had cast upon me.

I rang the bell-pull to summon Rose.

She appeared almost at once. "Oh, miss, I was just coming," she began. Then stopped, eyes widening, taking in my torn garments, my breathless altered face. "La, miss, are you all right? Is something wrong?"

I laughed aloud. "No, Rose, everything is blessedly, perfectly all right! You can send in some tea for me if you will, and make up the bed. And Rose, I should like to send you to Hatchards' bookshop in Piccadilly to fetch something for me. Is that possible?"

"Oh, quite likely! Mr. Hawtree, he's particular about us not going off the premises while we're on duty, but for you it'll be different. What can I get, miss?"

I reached for my purse. "Get me the *Collected Works* by Lord Tennyson—make sure it contains *The Idylls of the King*; and a copy of Malory's *Morte d'Arthur*. Here, I'll write it down for you. And here's a pound note; you can go there and back in a cab, that will keep Mr. Hawtree from being deprived of your services for too long."

"Oh, yes, miss!" Rose's face sparkled at the thought of this unaccustomed treat. "And I'm near forgetting! This just came for you, in th' afternoon mail."

She extended a creamy envelope on a silver salver. There was a black border drawn carefully upon it. Another letter of condolence; the last thing that I wished to look at. So it was that carelessly, unknowingly, I put it aside, dismissed Rose on her

14

errand, bathed and put on the pale-green robe I so inexplicably had ordered. Tea arrived, and I sat down by the window to partake of it, and all the while the letter that was my destiny waited.

I finished my tea. Rose had not yet returned. The light, angling through the tall window, struck the silver salver she had left. And I thought, I will read that letter, will reply to it and all the others in one fell swoop, and then I will have done with Ason Wentworth.

I opened the envelope, and there was no drumming in my temples, no pounding in my veins to tell me that this, next to Ason's journal, was to be the most significant communication I would ever read. The crest on the letter paper was unknown to me and so was the name of the writer: Lord Charles Ransome. No doubt some member of the aristocracy Ason had come across at one time in his search for archaeological funding. I forced my eyes to focus on what I knew would be conventional condolences for a grief I could not feel. Then the reply address struck me with the force of light.

Avalon.

Avalon, the mystic land to which the slumbering Arthur was reputedly taken.

My eyes raced over the paper with a growing, breathless wonder.

I was once quite close to both your parents, and though our paths have led in separate ways, I have never forgotten them, and I owe them much. You do not know me, yet it occurs to me that now, stranger in a strange land at a time of loss, you may need time and place apart to gather strength.

How did he know?

In that I can serve you, if you will allow me. I put my home and servants at your disposal. Come here to Avalon for your time of mourning. The house is large, and I am much engaged in my own labours, so you need not fear I shall intrude upon your solitude unless you wish . . .

15

Come here to Avalon. It struck me like an affirmation of some second sight.

> ". . . *the island-valley of Avilion;*
> *Where falls not hail, or rain, or any snow,*
> *Nor ever wind blows loudly; but it lies*
> *Deep-meadow'd, happy, fair with orchard lawns*
> *And bowery hollows crown'd with summer sea,*
> *Where I will heal me of my grievous wound."*

Sanctuary. A place to seek my own vision, find my dream. The words spoke to me now as they had spoken to that young enchanted reader long ago. *Come,* said Charles Ransome's words upon the paper, and the voices in my own inner emptiness echoed *Come,* and that fantastic impulse I had felt earlier crystallized into resolution.

I would go to this house so prophetically, so strangely named. I would use the resources offered by my father's friend as my father had used mine; would go, as those knights of old went, on a quest. A search into the past, for King Arthur—and myself. In finding the roots of a real, historical Arthur behind the myths—as Schliemann had found Troy and Agamemnon's city—I would find my own.

I sat down, and with strange, compulsive speed wrote my reply. Then I read the letter yet again, and all the while an odd irrational familiarity grew and grew, as though I had read these words, this writing, long before. The pieces of a picture began to form a complete pattern, rising from the depths of my unconscious mind.

It was childhood memory, brief but deep, which spoke, and the vision it conjured was of something long since burned in Ason's fire. I had no tangible proof, and yet I knew. The hand that had penned this letter, offering me sanctuary, offering hope, was the same which once, in a distant time, had written the dedication in my mother's copy of *Morte d'Arthur.*

So I went down to Avalon. To Avalon, my destiny, the citadel
of my soul. Went like some Celtic princess to set in motion that
which I understood too late and could not stop.

I had responded to Lord Ransome's letter not with my head
but with my heart, yet that was inward only—the cool classical
façade of my father's training was not so easily torn off as robes
of mourning. It was the proper New Englander who penned a
formal reply to the condolence offered, thanking Lord Ransome
for his sympathy, inviting him to call. Several days passed before I heard again from Somerset, and in those days I engaged
in many things. Dealt with the masses of funereal correspondence, held a business conference with my banker here and sent
instructions to my lawyer in the States. The picture I had already surmised was made more clear: a woman young, compara-
tively wealthy, devoid of family or friends, too much an intel-
lectual to be content with aimless drifting, too little trained to
be of use to anyone at all.

I caught a glimpse of myself in a shop window, while returning from my appointment at the bank, which brought the image
home with double force. I looked old. I looked drab. I had, as
Ason said, no fire. Then suddenly, superimposed upon that vision in my mind's eye, was that other reflected, secret self—a

naiad in seafoam velvet, passionate with life. I knew not why, but my step quickened; I hurried back along the Strand alive with spring.

"Have there been any calls?" I inquired of the concierge. But the answer was, as always, none. Irrational that I should have thought there would be; unlikely after all that Lord Charles Ransome would contact me again. His offer of hospitality had been only a conventional, kindly gesture to the unknown daughter of a former friend. My sedate reply had not conveyed anything to warrant a further step.

I dined alone, rather drearily, in my suite, and that night I dreamed a dream. It had none of the attributes of my childhood nightmares—no cliffs, no running, no sound of pounding sea. Yet I awoke in the dark solitude of the night in that old cold panic, with the same rapid heartbeat, the same thundering of my own pulse in my ears. Gradually the sense of terror faded to a strange and bleak despair. Perhaps if I wrote awhile . . . Ason had trained me in the journal-keeping habit, and I had long since learned it could serve to compose my mind. I lit the lamp and wrapped a robe around me, yet when I picked up pen and book an odd lassitude assailed me. What did it matter? There was no one now I had to strive to please by disciplining the wandering of my thoughts. I closed my eyes and let the words come what way they would, and when at last the broken Gramophone record in my mind was stilled, I fell asleep.

The next morning when Rose arrived with early tea, she brought a letter propped against the bud-vase on the tray. I recognized at once the distinctive writing and the crest.

I ought to have explained I am able to travel seldom, if at all, and that is why I did not wait upon you in person to express my sympathy and offer aid. Dear Miss Wentworth—Lydian— may I call you that, presuming on old family friendship? You will think this strange, but pardon it in one who, you will find, is already noted for more than his fair share of eccentricity. Something is telling me so strongly that you must come here. In the name of old debts, let me put my home at your disposal. I pray you, cable what train you will arrive upon and come at once.

I sent Rose to fetch a telegraph blank and see about trains.

It was not like me, not at all like the careful Lydian Wentworth I had been at home. Something had changed, irrevocably; my inner self was breaking through the mirror-image, and I followed wheresoever she led. Not till after I had bid Rose send the telegram, pack my bags, did it occur to me to look up my prospective host's identity in *Burke's Peerage*, and what I found there sent me straight to the nearest reference library, my heart again pounding.

Lord Charles Ransome was an Arthurian scholar. Scholar, artist, writer, literary critic—all the things that were the antithesis of my own father, that made me wonder strangely at their one-time friendship, made me conjure, rather, a picture of the father I had longed to have. Lord Charles Ransome was a recluse artist whose work was highly valued but very rare. A younger son in a titled Somerset family, he had been at the height of social and artistic fame when without warning, twenty years ago, he had withdrawn to the country house he renamed Avalon.

When I had finished the last reference volume in the library I put the book down, dazed. *Eccentricity*, he had said. Lord Charles Ransome was not so much an eccentric as he was a legend. Long ago, when I was scarcely more than an infant, he had cut himself off abruptly and completely from all friends, all contacts. He worked meticulously, brilliantly I gathered, in that citadel from which, at too-rare intervals, issued magnificent paintings, exquisite books, learned treatises on Celtic and early British mythology. And now he had broken custom to reach across the barrier of the years to offer comfort to the daughter of a friend. His pattern was breaking, even as my own.

I went down that afternoon, on the designated train, to Glastonbury. From long habit, when settled on the train, I took out my journal and began to make a record of the trip, but I soon closed it. Let the dead past bury its dead. I took out instead the copy of Tennyson that Rose had bought me and turned once more to the Arthurian poems, and if this was a childlike defiance of old ghosts, I trust that the woman I am may be forgiven.

Perhaps it was this small symbolic gesture, perhaps it was the strangeness of the landscape through which I traveled, but as time passed I felt the layers of protective imprisonment falling from me. The Arthurian saga enthralled me; I was saddened to discover that to my adult, discriminating eyes the poetry did seem somewhat forced and precious, but nonetheless the power of myth itself still worked its spell. I was a girl again, devouring my mother's old copy of Malory, trembling beneath the covers. My mother's book, which my soon-to-be-host had given her . . .

"Glastonbury!"

The conductor's voice cut through my magic daze and I looked out, startled, into an enchanted world.

How can I describe that strange, skewed landscape which stirred me so oddly, so completely? Avalon—Glastonbury—cannot be caught in words; it can only be experienced. Optically, in some weird subtle way beyond explanation, it was a world beautifully, gently distorted, as though what one saw was not reality but its reflection, seen through mist and water. Perhaps this effect was magnified by my arrival just at sunset. The carriage that had been sent for me rolled past green acres of reclaimed marsh, blanketed with mist. Beyond loomed the hills, also green and bare, their outlines silhouetted against the glory of the setting sun. I felt as though I were entering into a primeval land embodying some ultimate secret of creation. Creation and fall . . . I do not know why that association suddenly struck my mind like a blow, and yet it did.

To my left, barely visible as masses are when caught at a particular angle of the dying light, misshapen dark forms loomed against the glowing sky. And then the carriage turned inward through great gates, and I forgot completely whatever lay without their walls.

Avalon, the enchanted isle. On the outside it was a conventional Somerset mansion of gables, oriel windows and pale stone. But inside . . . The door swung open, a servant, who had introduced himself as "Hodge," leaped to help me from the carriage, and as my eyes for the first time beheld the great baronial hall, my senses reeled. Purple velvet curtains stirred, and a wave of scent—cinnamon, sandalwood, vetiver—assailed me. Flames leaped from a central firepit to touch darting fingers of light upon bronze shields, swords, battle axes hanging on the walls. Stone benches were spread with cushions and rugs of gray wolf, red fox, sable. Tapestries, which even at that moment I knew were of incalculable value, loomed in the shadows.

The servant relieved me of my wraps and vanished silently. I was to learn, later, that this was a house of stillness. I was alone, wondering, dazzled. Then there came an awareness of a sound—faint, faraway, but growing ever closer, like the twittering of alien birds.

A door had opened somewhere in the far reaches of that endless room. The heraldic banners, extending in serried ranks out from the high walls, stirred, and even the light from the stained-glass windows far above seemed to change. Approaching me, slowly and then gradually faster, down the long hall came a figure out of unknown, archaic myth. The fantastic oaken chair could have been a king's throne but had been converted, with wheels, for an invalid—so that was the secret of his mysterious withdrawal from the world—but I had only a moment for a stab of compassionate pity, only a moment to notice the dark youth with sullen eyes who propelled him.

"Lydian! My dear Lydian. I may say that, may I?"

For an electric instant I had seen in Charles Ransome's face that same startled shock of irrational recognition I knew was in my own. Then the beautiful voice had spoken, and he was extending welcoming hands. Lord Charles Ransome, with his pointed golden beard, velvet jacket and lap-robe of dark fur, made me think of John of Gaunt, and the imprisoned Richard II. I had expected an older man and he could be old, anywhere between forty-five and eternity. In the pain-ridden face burned the unquenchable eyes of a saint, a rebel, a fanatical dreamer. And we dreamed the same dreams. We both had known it, in that time-stopped moment before our fingers touched.

Our fingers touched, and then we both were laughing. And I was sitting on a red foxskin on the firepit ledge, and Charles was saying, "You felt it, didn't you?"

"Felt what?" All my old instinct for self-protection, for survival, leaped within me.

"The atmosphere. I knew you would." His voice was warm and kind. He had seen that flare of panic, could not have missed it, but the only notice he took, if it could be called that, was to rest his fingertips upon my wrist, and my pulses stilled. "We are next door to Glastonbury's ruins, you know. And Glastonbury is strong magic, and not dead."

". . . Glastonbury?" I had a need to keep up a breathless effort at casual conversation.

Charles Ransome smiled. "I forget you are American and do not know our English legends. The abbey was once the premier church of England; the current ruins date from the twelfth century and are the result of Henry VIII's notorious seizure of its financial assets. But the original church, according to myth, was founded by Joseph of Arimathea, he of the Gethsemane tomb, who supposedly walked from Palestine across all Europe, crossed the Channel, and planted his thorn staff on Wearyall Hill, where it promptly flowered. You shall see the thorn tree; it puts forth blooms dutifully at Christmas and Eastertide. And of course, Chalice Well, supposed to be the repository of the Holy Grail."

I looked at him, frowning slightly. "You are teasing me."

"Not at all, I am quite serious. This is Grail country. I have spent years proving that all the literary accounts of Round Table knights' quests for the holy chalice precisely match the history and geography of the Glastonbury area in the fifth century." His eyes twinkled. "Of course, it is far more likely the legends are Christianized accounts of old pagan pilgrimages than of any true Grail quest. The Cauldron of Wisdom, that mystical vessel of light and knowledge, has always been considered the prime source of the special magic at Avalon. Which is no doubt precisely what drew Arthur here."

The room was growing very warm. "You are not saying you —believe in the actual existence of King Arthur—"

"I surely do. Or at least *an* Arthur; the body of a fifth-century warrior thus labeled was discovered by the monks during the twelfth century, buried again by Edward the Confessor with all high honors, and then, during the dissolution of the monasteries, lost from sight."

In the cold vision behind my eyes was Ason's image, Ason's voice saying, "Inferior aberrations on true myth." And here was Lord Charles Ransome, rational, sane, a reputable authority, taking my childhood fantasies and clothing them with the garb of possible truth. His face was still, his smile had vanished; he was gazing into the flames with an intensity that I recognized as the concentration of the true scholar. He was worlds away, and I was intruding. Then, as if sensing my withdrawal, he turned to me, becoming once more warm and human. "Forgive me. You are your father's daughter, and no doubt think my preoccupation with the Matter of Britain a quixotic fancy. Your myths will be of Diana and Apollo, not King Arthur."

I felt as if I had been staring too long into a great light, and there was a drumming in my ears. "I—know of him. I have read of him—in my mother's book."

"Your mother was an exceptional woman, able to appreciate and reconcile many disparate strains of thought. What am I thinking of? You have just arrived, and must be longing for rest and tea. If you will pull that bell-cord there, someone will see you to your room."

It was a quiet, kind, but definite dismissal. He was growing tired; there were signs of strain and age now around those splendid eyes. I rose.

"You cannot know how I appreciated your invitation. I hope my presence is not an imposition, an intrusion."

"You must never think that."

"Lord Ransome—"

"Charles! Please. We have come that far already, have we not, across a swift-cross'd bridge? We need not stand on ceremony here."

"Charles . . . where did you know my father?"

"Our paths crossed, long ago. And went our separate ways, but what had been cannot be undone. Which you're too young to know, yet. Here is Hodge. He will show you to your apartment, and tea will be up directly. We dine at eight."

Twice in as many minutes he had warned me off the territory of the past, and was it fancy only that I sensed a look cross his face that was almost fear? A chill touched my neck, yet in the long room nothing stirred.

My room was in a tower. The great bed, with its high Tudor baluster, was draped with cloth of silver, and pale-blue velvet hung by windows looking out toward the ruined abbey. On a dark oak table in the oriel window two tall gold altar candlesticks flanked a mirror intricately framed with gilt and gems. My suitcases had been unpacked and my garments hung; a softfooted manservant appeared presently with tea in a beautiful Queen Anne silver teapot, and a porcelain cup. This was, apparently, a house of men.

The servant poured tea and built up the fire in efficient silence. Then he was gone, and I was left alone to peace and twilight. I needed that. The force of this house, of its owner's presence, was too strong—my senses all were drugged.

I sat in that tranquil dimness, sipping tea, gazing into the fitful flames as the myth unrolled before me like jewel-colored figures on an illuminated scroll. Arthur the mysteriously begotten, child of Uther Pendragon and Ygraine. Born at Tintagel; raised by the wizard Merlin. King by right of wresting the sword from out the stone. Creator of a united Britain, creator of the Table Round—a circle of peerless knights bound together by morality, religion, honor. Galahad the pure, Gawaine the virtuous, Lancelot the perfect knight . . . the names marched from the scroll of childhood memory, pure and shining. Upholders of the right, defenders of the faith, helpers of the helpless, seekers of the Holy Grail.

Arthur, the greatest of them all. Wedded to Guinever, the queen of love and beauty. Plunged into tragedy when Guinever, whom he adored, and Lancelot, who was to him as a son, were caught helplessly in a web of fatal passion. The three of them locked for years into a triangle of mutual love and torment.

"The concept of Camelot, of achievable perfection, proves the British myth inferior," I could hear the voice of Ason saying. "The Greeks were realists; they did not seek an impossible return to such a lost Eden." For of course, Camelot's dream had fallen. Maintaining absolute altruism had been a strain too great to bear. The other knights had found Lancelot and Guinever together; she had been imprisoned, charged with adultery and treason, condemned to burn. The triangle had been broken; Arthur and Lancelot were forced to fight on opposite sides. The Round Table had fallen; and Arthur in his old age, his strength and power failing, had fallen too, struck down at the Battle of Camlann by Modred, his dark opposite, who the legends said could have been his son. Arthur, dying, borne off in an other-worldly boat by shining queens to the fabled Isle of Avalon—from whence he would come again on the apocalyptic day when the world had need of him. Arthur, the once and future king.

Oh, Ason had been wrong, these myths were potent. I looked into the yellow flames and I saw visions. But the future I saw, coming toward me, as down the corridor of my life, was Lord Charles Ransome.

I ought not to be sitting here this way. It was near time for dinner, and I had much need of reality. I pulled myself up like a swimmer surfacing through depths of water. Hodge, unbe-knownst to me, had laid out what he had deemed suitable for me to wear. The sea-green velvet gown. Heaven knew why I had bought it, why I'd brought it. Then I thought, Why not? Its suits me, suits this house. We would be alone for dinner, as I under-stood, and certainly Charles Ransome was not one to stand upon the ceremony of convention.

I donned the velvet gown, and forsaking attempt at fash-ion, coiled my hair in the old way, at the nape, with a few great pins. It had a will of its own tonight, would not go smooth, insisted on falling into a softer shape than it was my custom to wear. Bare-throated, for I owned no jewels, feeling as if I had stepped back in time, I went through the dark shadows of the endless upper corridor to the great staircase.

The flames leaped high in the great firepit far below, and torches burned at intervals along the walls. From this perspec-tive, the scene took on a curious distorted quality, much as had the landscape I had glimpsed from the train and carriage win-dows. I had a sense of looking through a kind of time-telescope such as might have been invented by the novelist H. G. Wells. Then from the great throne-chair on the dining platform at the far end of the room I saw Charles Ransome lifting a golden goblet in a toast to me, beckoning me down. And all sense of separation vanished, never to return.

I cannot write much of that magic night, could not have even immediately afterward. I had lost such scholarly detachment as I once possessed; the memories I had were sensory, not fact, coming in circular patterns and not straight lines.

We ate celestial food, which I could not remember; we drank

what must have been the wine of gods. Or were we growing drunk on our own senses, that Dionysiac intoxication Plato had written of but which Ason, speaking to me of it, had not been able to comprehend. *Eros is a daemon*, Plato had said, referring to the fact that some energy, some life force we might not know was in us could be at the same time both infernal and divine. I was beginning at last to understand.

We dined; we returned to the firepit, and we talked. Told all; told nothing; opened our secret visions to one another.

"Tell me of your work," I said to Charles, and he wove me a living tapestry of a creative life. Fetched exquisitely bound books to show me; collections of etchings, scholarly monographs. Gradually, the nature of his work grew clear to me, and with it a sense of rising exhilaration.

Charles was indeed attempting to prove that there had been a historic Arthur, the tribal leader whose bones had been discovered in the abbey, and that not only had a few of the earliest exploits attributed to him actually taken place, but that there was reason and purpose worthy of study in the body of earlier and later myth that had, as if by some divine plan, attached itself to him.

"The Arthur of the myths embodies not only a pre-Saxon reality, but something infinitely more important—the unconscious needs, fears, aspirations of the British people. Or of all people; the Celtic tales and superstitions reflect very clearly a kinship with the Vedas of the East. What we have in the Matter of Britain, I believe, is some kind of collective memory of our heritage which has much to teach us of the nature of ourselves."

"And you seek to prove this?"

"That, exactly." Charles's face was lighted from within by his enthusiasm. "Precisely, what I hope to find is the coffin of that *quondam* Arthur which has been lost from sight these past four hundred years. Reportedly there are hidden passages, deep beneath Glastonbury's ruins, which lead to other early buildings in the neighborhood, and this is one. The coffin could easily have been hidden by monks at the time of the dissolution. The church of the British Isles does not like to own it, but there are many far earlier primitive mysteries embodied in its customs and superstitions. I know that coffin does exist, and I mean to

26

find it. It will give me great satisfaction to prove at last that the Matter of Britain is worthy of scientific study."

I looked at him, and we both knew we thought of Ason.

"Where did you know him?" I asked abruptly, and this time he answered.

"Twenty years ago, in London, when for a time we were able to share a common vision."

"*Ason* was studying the Arthurian myth?"

"He never told you? I am not surprised. Ason never liked to confront his failures. You are not wearing black, I see. You're wise. You ought always to wear dull blues and greens and reds, medieval colors. They become you."

"My mother wore black." I was surprised by my own *non sequitur*, but Charles merely nodded.

"Your mother was one of the shining ones. You are familiar with the Celtic belief in the Sidh, those beings, either human or purely spirit, that embody the halfway state between this world and another, who bear the aura of supernatural power. It was your mother who first made me perceive that perhaps they could exist. They are said to be of two kinds: the tall shining ones and the opalescents, who were lit from within. Your mother was the former, you the latter."

I could not speak; I had a sense of being carried too fast by a rushing wind.

"You have the look of her, you know," Charles said. "Your mother. Her coloring and, I suspect, her gifts. Ason never told you that, did he? I thought as much." He looked at me as though he could read my soul. "Lydian, Ason Wentworth was my great friend, my idol. He was also a life-drainer, a devourer. He cannibalized your mother. You must not allow him to do the same to you, however much you love and honor him."

"I think I hate him!" The words burst from me, shocking me not only with their passion but with their present tense.

"Those who hate greatly can also greatly love," Charles said quietly. And then, "His ghost still walks for you, doesn't it? For your own health and sanity, not to say your future, you must lay that ghost to rest. You must exorcise him."

"I think I have already set foot on the way of that, by coming here."

Charles laughed somberly. "The invisible Sidh are watching us—and I think they smile."

He spoke quietly, but the atmosphere in the hall had become too intense for me to bear. Instinctively, defensively, I pulled the talk back to a measurable reality. "You seek Arthur then, and do research. Do you think it will be long before your theory achieves scholarly recognition?"

Charles shrugged. "My synthesizing history, psychology, literature into a larger truth is not fashionable intellectually. Oh, I am called often to give lectures, but that is mostly on the strength of my—curiosity appeal. I have no wish to be one of their rarer monsters." Involuntarily he glanced for a moment at his legs. It was the only reference he had made so far to his incapacity, and though I longed to know the cause of it, I could not ask. Then his head lifted, and he went on with greater strength.

"And of course, I paint. I have not had a gallery show for some four years now, and my London dealer is understandably becoming restless. But my efforts have been concentrated on a series of paintings that are not for sale. The entire Arthurian cycle; a portrayal of every significant scene in the whole body of the myth. You shall see them. They are not complete, but I do hope— There is a major archaeological symposium in Winchester this September, and if I am able to complete certain aspects of my research in time to submit a paper, I may then also allow the paintings to be put on public view."

His voice had taken on a curious kind of urgency, but he checked it abruptly and closed his eyes. He was growing very tired. I rose, and at the same moment the surly youth appeared. He was intent on hustling Charles off to bed, but Charles waved him away. "Lydian, this is Barrett Doffman, my nurse-companion, who means so well but despite his yearnings to be a painter does not understand the artist's mind. Go to bed, young Doff, and let me be. And Lydian, stay! This talk is bread and wine to me, and worth the price!"

Doff shot Charles an angry, troubled look and vanished, and after a moment I resumed my seat. I do not think I could have left to save my soul. We talked the night through, our excitement ranging from Arthurian England to classic Greece, to the

Grail legends, to the Glastonbury Lake Villages where there had been some early Christian proselytizing—"the source," Charles explained, "of that curious commingling of pagan psychological truths with Christian spiritual ones, a mirror-image of ourselves of which we are much afraid. That, of course, explains why ascetic scholars are so threatened by the reality of a past or future Arthurian Age. It confronts them too strongly with their own daemons."

"Why, then, do you think the myth has persevered so long?"

Charles made a gesture. "Why did the myth of Agamemnon live, though disbelieved, until your father came along, and Schliemann? Because myths hand down to the future the realities of the past. In symbolic fashion, to be sure. And because there is more truth to myth than its historic roots alone. Myths transcend human reality and become the embodiment of our true nature, our culture's values and ideals. They are our what-ought-to-have-been, what-yet-may-be, given form and substance. And our world needs that. Oh, how it needs it now!"

Charles's face took on an almost mystic light; his eyes gazed far off. I dared not speak. "A world of grace and beauty, where right is might, where Theseus and not Hercules is the king. Where the philosophers, the artists, the strivers after truth and justice are the heroes. Where the true gentle man stands strong and tall, clothed in the armor of light. And"—he held out his hand to me and, as though hypnotized, I placed mine in it—"the woman also, wholly free, wholly conscious and responsible for all her gifts. Neither one behind, nor yet before, but side by side."

I said shakily, "That seems like an exceptionally modern notion."

"Not at all. Read your old Celtic myths. It was only the classical Greco-Romans who found such ideas threatening. That's why they so fanatically stamped the old ways out. But the great British heroines—Guinever, Iseult, Grainne—are all prototypes of the Immortal Mother." Charles chuckled. "I wonder if Ason found that threatening. Something in him drove him always to dominate, to be repelled by the thought of need, especially for women."

We were silent then, lost in our separate memories and shadows. In the pit beside me a log broke, sending up a shower of sparks.

"You had your mother's Malory," Charles said abruptly. "You saw the dedication."

"Yes. But I did not understand it all."

"Virgilia Wentworth was kind enough to take a maternal interest in a very young and searching boy. I was quite vulnerable to influence in those days. She was for me a . . . an antidote to Ason's dispassionate, skeptical detachment; she taught me the true nature of the classic Golden Mean, not nonfeeling, but the rational balance for an irrational lust for life that feels too much. She personified and explained to me the true magic of the Sidh, the gifts of all those magnificent women in the Celtic tales."

I was silent, and after some moments, he went on. "I told you what I hope to find in Glastonbury's ruins. Will find, when I am at last able to persuade its hereditary owner to have done with outdated traditions and sell to me. There are tales dealing with the interment of Arthur and his queen, you know, recounted in rare old manuscripts that I've managed to obtain. According to them, Guinever's body and her dower gifts were buried with Arthur, and their nature, in the light of the old myths of Celtic woman, is significant. Jewelry, of course, as was the custom. Two major pieces. A golden chalice—perhaps *the* Grail, perhaps the cup or cauldron symbolic of woman in all old tales. And a golden torque or necklace—a circle, symbolizing continuity, union, wholeness. Together, the synthesis in one being of flesh and spirit, ordinary reality and a higher one. It was this gift of transcendent wholeness, the attribute of the Sidh, which was the characteristic of all ancient Celtic goddesses and women. And it was Guinever's chief gift, much misunderstood—even by her husband—which brought about their fall. Lord, Lord, if the world will ever learn!"

"You sound almost as if it were Guinever, and not Arthur, who has bewitched you."

Charles did not answer.

A pale-blue light was beginning to filter through the great panels of stained glass high above us. Charles stirred himself and smiled. "I have kept you the whole night invoking my visions for you. You must forgive me. This is an opportunity I rarely have. But you must rest now, and I as well, for I shall commence my work again in a few hours."

"I ought not to have kept you up—I am so sorry—"

"Pray do not be. I find the man I am now needs little sleep. But I have exhausted you. I have poured too much out to you too rapidly, and you must rest. There are violet shadows underneath your eyes."

I rose and at his bidding rang the bell that would summon Doffman to his aid. As I turned to leave, Charles called me back quietly, holding out his hands for me to take.

"You understand now, I think, what I referred to as your mother's gifts. Remember them, and when the ghost of Ason comes to haunt you, recall they too are a part of your inheritance. You can claim them whenever you will. All you need is to seek the way, and find the courage."

I went upstairs slowly. I was exhausted, but I stood for several moments leaning against the window, looking out at the haunting ruins of Glastonbury Abbey. And I knew that if I had had any self-protective stirrings toward flight, it was now too late. I was spellbound, not only by Avalon, but by its master.

It was dawn when I fell asleep; it was noon before I again arose and went downstairs. The house was very still. The courteous, soft-spoken butler met me, showed me into a separate dining room, served me one of those delicious English breakfasts that was really luncheon. I was alone and I was grateful, for I had much to think on.

The Great Hall was deserted. Only the ashes spoke of last night's fire, and from the roof vent and the stained-glass windows came streams of light. Charles was not there, but Barrett Doffman was. He had about him an air of shambling clumsiness that was at variance with his deft movements. A guard dog, defending his master and his treasures against intruders—of which I was one; the youth's abrasive manner made that quite clear.

"His lordship's not up. He usually works all morning, but he can't when he wastes his energy talking through the night. He's not got strength to fritter away like that. As it is, his work demands more than he has to give, and his work's the whole world to him."

"I know. We spoke of it." Why was I justifying myself to this rude young man? "Please tell Lord Ransome I am quite content to be left to my own devices. I, too, have studies to pursue."

I smiled impersonally, dismissing him, which only seemed to make him angrier. "You're to be driven round Glastonbury Tor and past the ruins. He's ordered the carriage, and I'm to go with you if you want, to show you round."

"Pray do not trouble yourself." I looked at him coolly. "I'm sure you have duties here, and I am quite accustomed to being my own companion."

The day was sunny, filled with the warm promise only England in the spring could have. As the open carriage clip-clopped gently past orchards green with April, my heart rose within me, and all the sensation I had had last night of time and events rushing like a too-rapid river fell away.

Even more markedly than before, as we climbed the rise of Glastonbury Tor and looked down at the little city, I had a sense of a landscape touched with a very special magic. The spire of the cathedral, the sun-touched shell of the ruined abbey were minuscule against the background of rolling hills patch-worked in velvet greens. The clouds were so white and even the air, I thought, was different here. There was a tangible sensation of moving in another state of reality, another world and time. There was nothing threatening or alarming to it; rather, I was filled and brimming over with a positive and energizing peace.

We rode over the Tor; past the Chalice Well with its wooden cover intricately bound with scrolls of iron; round the marsh-lands that had once been water surrounding Glastonbury—"island of glass," home of the glass-blowing lake villagers of prehistory.

The driver turned to me. "Abbey's on private ground of course, and the gate on High Street tight shut and locked, but the wall separating it from Avalon is not so dreadful high." His eyes twinkled at me.

I smiled back. "Let us see that wall."

It was, of course, reprehensible, the notion of invading another's private land. But Charles had told me the abbey's present owner was an absentee, and I had been too long exposed to Ason's doctrine that places of ancient importance and beauty ought to be open to all who had the wisdom to appreciate. The right of knowledge over the right of property was of dubious legality, but well-espoused in the world of archaeologists and

33

scholars. And I had been trained by Ason better than I knew—Oh, no, I could not blame this on my father, I thought, laughing. The truth was, I was half mad by now to see those ruins.

The wall was not high and my elderly driver, his eyes amused, gave me a boost across. "Take your time. I'll be here waiting," he advised.

I found myself in an enchanted land. Sanctuary indeed, but not in the cloistered sense of old churches, of Avalon's Great Hall. This serene landscape throbbed and pulsed with life. If there was any sense of sadness to the buildings it was only owing to the waste of their being ruins; the glowing stone, the very land itself, was vibrant.

The breeze caressed, the sun was filtered gold. I wandered, drinking in the beauty; sat down on a low foundation wall of stone where wildflowers were already poking up among the rocks. To my left loomed the shell of the abbey church, with the two masses, copper-flushed, that had once been the frame of the main arch. Far to my right, above the apple trees, I saw the crenellated edge of a small tower—my own room at Avalon.

I must be getting back, for Charles would wonder. I was troubled, too, that the intoxicating wine of that all-night conversation had been too much for him. Beneath the vital blaze of his personality Charles Ransome was not strong. I did not need to be told that, but I wished I knew the nature of his illness. One thing was certain; I would not ask Doff.

I returned to the wall, was helped over by my driver, who had been enjoying a pipe placidly in the sun. We returned to Avalon, where Doff was waiting.

"*He's* painting and is not to be disturbed. I have been delegated to guide you through the gallery. If you'll come this way, please."

I gathered, as Doff unlocked the heavy carved cathedral doors opening off the front corridor, that I was being granted a rare privilege of which he did not approve. This gallery was a closed passage running along the right side of the Great Hall, and as I stepped across the threshold I gasped. There were no windows, and the low roof was arched; the whole gave the impression of an endless cave. Iron torches, in reality cunningly contrived gas jets, flared along the walls. The floor was ancient, uneven, stone-cobbled. And everywhere, everywhere were the pictures . . . enormous, mysterious, brooding; they had the same curious magic as old tapestries, that strange darkness suddenly lit with glowing reds and creams and golds.

They were all scenes from the Arthurian myths, portrayed not with the romanticized trappings of traditional sentimentalism, but as they might actually have been lived in the fifth century. Swords were crude; the soldiers' armor was of leather; palace floors were littered with discarded bones over which dogs and rodents wrangled. Mutilated bodies showed congealing blood. Women did not wear medieval houppelandes and hennins but woolen robes and hair in long cord-bound braids. I cannot describe the force, the brooding power of those pictures. They were haunting, deeply disturbing; works of genius.

Involuntarily I turned to Doff. "Did he do all these before—"

"He's been working on them steadily, the past fifteen years. He paints every day, in spite of what it puts him through, so long as he's not kept from it by interfering fools."

This was clearly what Doff considered me. But as we moved slowly down the corridor, pausing now and then as a detail caught me, I became uncomfortably conscious that he perceived me in another way as well. He lingered too closely, contriving to brush against me as if by chance. Once he put his hand upon my elbow, to steer me toward a particular object he wanted me to see, and his fingers lingered. I moved off immediately and he followed.

"What is the matter? Are you uncomfortable with me in here?"

"The air is very close."

"It wasn't too close for you before, breathing the smoke from that open hearth all night."

I walked away hastily, but he followed. "If you really want to concentrate on the paintings, have a look at this. The technique used to depict the stonework is remarkable." He met my startled glance with proud, angry eyes. "Oh, yes, the serf is knowledgeable. I paint—but my *own* visions, not monuments to a dead past."

"It must be helpful to you, working for Lord Ransome."

"Lord Ransome is not interested in any talent but his own. Especially mine. He finds me useful. I'm what's keeping him alive, and he does know that."

The question of Charles's illness hovered on the verge of speech. Then was stilled, as a deferential voice spoke from the doorway.

"His lordship wishes assistance in preparing for his tea." It was the footman. Doff looked irresolute.

"I must go. He needs me." It was clear he wanted me to leave as well, but I stood my ground, merely nodding in dismissal. They left, the oak door shutting behind them to close me into this subterranean world. For a moment I looked back at the doorway, frowning.

I did not care for Barrett Doffman, did not care for him at all. He clearly had a very specific view of women and was quite likely to present a problem. I could always, of course, refer that to Charles Ransome, but hoped I would not have to. What *was* Doff's position in this household, anyway? Much more than servant, yet somehow less than friend. He seemed too young to have gone through hospital training, yet it had been clear, even in the limited time I had seen him with Charles, that he had a gift for nursing. Moreover, he adored his patient, I knew that without having to be told. But that was understandable, was it not? I felt my skin flushing.

I turned hastily back to the paintings, grateful to be left alone with them. They hung, unframed, enormous, along the walls, spaced at odd intervals by some inconsistent, organic pattern of their own. I dropped down on a bench; the spell of art and setting began to commingle and work a magic on me. The air was so close, so still; the pictures shimmered and almost seemed to move. Viewed from here, in one long sweep, they began to reveal their secret to me. They represented the key encounter moments in the whole body of Arthurian myth, and the empty spaces came where scenes still remained to be painted. A knight knelt in vigil before a tournament; rode back from it in triumph with his lady's favor; only bare stone indicated the scene between. King Uther Pendragon, disguised, climbed stealthily up rock steps to a forbidding castle; the painting that should have depicted his arrival missing; his departure in a kind of obscene triumph while behind him, her face hidden, a woman sobbed by the edge of the rocky cliff.

I could almost taste the salt spray that mingled with her tears, could feel the wrench of anguish in her body. This was art, as Charles had said, that tapped the hidden current of the daemonic. Lord God, the man could paint.

Or was it more than that . . . I was unable to sit still any longer. Unable to walk forward except with halting steps that drew me nearer, nearer to the brooding cliffs. My heart began to pound, my senses blurred, I was overpowered by a totally irrational fear. Irrational? By an enormous effort of will, my vision cleared. I stared at the looming canvases and understood. The distorted landscape of the paintings was the landscape of my own nightmares.

And of the hidden picture . . . I whirled round, and saw that the painting on the far wall was an enormous duplication of the haunting scene I had found long ago in an Amherst attic. Which Ason, in cold anger, had ordered burned. Why had I never connected my nightmares with that picture? Because something within both must have gripped at me with a bone-deep terror, and because the dreams had not sprung from the picture but had begun before, before . . .

It was that same terror, evoked overpoweringly by the painting, which paralyzed me now. But past association did not explain why my fear was not of remembered panic but of present danger. I knew it was ridiculous, but I knew too that I needed to leave this room at once, and that to force my feet to retrace their steps would take all the courage I could muster. The skin on my neck prickled; somehow, in this sealed gallery, I was being watched.

Down the corridor ahead of me, light flooded in. Ordinary daylight. A door at the far end had been opened, letting in fresh air. I took a great breath of it, and my head cleared. My feet were freed. I moved toward the open doorway as toward a source of life.

Then I saw him, watching me from a niche, so still that but

for his modern workman's clothes I would have taken him to be a statue. Involuntarily I recoiled, and he gave a short laugh and came toward me.

"I'm sorry. I might have known you'd be alarmed." His manner seemed to indicate he expected little better of my sex. "I'm Lawrence Stearns. Resident archaeologist and Lord Ransome's research assistant, in case it never occurred to him to tell you so."

I nodded shortly, tucking in a stray end of hair that had fallen loose, my fingers trembling. With his human presence, my panic had been converted into anger. I felt, uncomfortably, as if I had been observed while bathing; I was at a disadvantage, and I did not like it.

"And you are the mysterious guest whose coming has thrown this well-ordered household into quiet turmoil. You are as much a surprise to me as I to you, you know. In my two-year stay, no one has been admitted that I remember except Meriel, Lady Spenser, and she's a relation. We had expected at the very least a distinguished scholar. I did not think old Charles had the wit nor interest to entertain a girl."

"I find his work quite sufficient entertainment."

His eyebrows rose. "Don't tell me scholarly monographs and plans for digs amuse that pretty head." He was not tall, but there was a lithe power to him. There was a dark Mediterranean look as well; his hair was burnished black and his beard was close-cut; the impenetrable depths of his inspecting eyes were very brown.

"The thought of an Arthurian dig particularly interests me. I am not unfamiliar with the process. I'm Lydian Wentworth."

The look in Stearns's eyes changed and he whistled softly. "*A son* Wentworth's daughter?"

"You've heard of him?"

"Enough to know he was Charles's mentor, much as Charles is mine. Charles never speaks of him, but it's obvious your father had a great influence on him. Allow me to extend my sympathies on your bereavement."

"Thank you. Are you working with Lord Ransome on the proposed tomb search?"

"He told you of that, did he? He must think well of you." His

38

tone was much the same, though something in his manner had imperceptibly softened, and he accepted my change of subject smoothly, as though sensing Ason Wentworth was for me as well as Charles a forbidden subject. He began walking with me toward the far door, pointing out details Charles's research into the Dark Ages had led him to incorporate in the paintings.

"That drinking bowl is adapted from a description in *Perceval*."

"The likeness to the work coming out of Mycenae is remarkable."

Stearns shot me a startled look. "You really are interested in history, and not just the romantic myth?"

"Is there necessarily a contradiction? Myths, after all, are abstract truths, not falsehoods. And the word *romantic*, correctly used, means visionary, subordinating form to theme, not melodrama." I did not need to glance in his direction to know that I had scored. My use of words had been more precise than his. And moreover, if he had seen my vulnerability earlier, I had now seen his. He mistrusted myth, and Charles Ransome did not like that.

I did not like his glibness, and I dared a further thrust. "Do you think it likely there could be a chalice buried with the Arthurian remains? As you point out, drinking bowls and horn cups are far more likely. I am rather surprised, considering your bias, that you are interested in pursuing here what is, after all, a quest for a mythic hero."

"I am intrigued by the human beings behind the myths. And by those the myths intrigue. Surely you know there *are* stemmed goblets dating from the fifth century?"

I had dangerously underestimated him. Who was he, anyway, with his sharp historian's brain so at variance with his laborer's clothes? And what work did he do for Charles that caused such calluses on his hands? I turned away, pretending interest in a painting, on guard lest I betray further the limits of my knowledge. Ason was right, I *had* been undertrained, and the fault was his. But I am a quick study, I thought grimly. I can read. I shall not soon be caught again.

Behind me I heard my companion laugh. "Shall we call it a draw? We've tested out each other's *bona fides*. And I was not fair; I'm well aware the area of your father's research, and no doubt your own, was Greco-Roman. Come along while I lock this far door, and I'll walk you back for tea. Charles won't much like it if we keep him waiting."

He shut and bolted the thick wooden door, saying that it was important always to keep the house well locked, since Charles feared thieves. "He has so many artifacts and curios of great value. And of course there's always a market for stolen paintings. Charles exhibits so seldom that the few pieces he's willing to sell always fetch high prices, and possessing one gives its owner great cachet. There are collectors who value his work so highly they would snap it up quickly without asking questions. He hoards most of his paintings like a miser, for his own pleasure. It's quite a tribute, you know, his wanting you to see them. Do you know his work? I don't believe there is any of it in the States."

"I have seen one painting." Some instinct held me back from saying more. I felt his eyes on me, but with that tact he had displayed before, he began talking of Charles's quixotic sense of humor, of the subtle touches incorporated into small details of the paintings.

"You see this picture of a knight offering a jewel to his beloved? Look in the lower corner. See the squirrel offering his mate a nut formed in the same shape as the jewel? The female squirrel's eyes have the exact 'coax me a little' expression of the noble lady's."

He continued to speak as we moved down the corridor.

"I heard somewhere that in his early days Charles once got a series of bad reviews from critics who could not understand his style. It was all over the front pages of the papers, of course, because of his social fame. Some of the wording was much more clever than it was kind. Charles seemed to take no notice, but in his next exhibit all the small animals seen in lower foregrounds wore the critics' faces."

"No!"

"Truth," he said. "At least, Lady Meriel says so, and Charles does not deny it. That's the fey side of Charles you may not have seen yet."

"You make him sound like a dual personality."

"Charles is many persons. Perhaps that's his magic. Look, see this storm scene? You can almost feel the spray."

We were standing before the painting of my nightmare, but I felt no terror now. The sense of stepping back into an earlier time was gone. Lawrence Stearns's presence, though I hated to admit it, was regenerating, and so was the shared excitement of archaeological talk that sprang up between us, spurred by our simultaneous recognition of various Great Hall furnishings Charles had incorporated into the paintings. I was light-headed, I think, from release from that earlier fear. We began to play "Who Spots It First," searching the backgrounds for recognizable details.

By the time we reached the oak door to the front passageway, we were laughing, and our laughter spilled before us into the Great Hall.

Charles was waiting. He was sitting in his throne-chair by the fire, tea table beside him, and he looked as if he had been there for an immemorial time.

I do not know why, but our laughter stilled. Charles watched as we approached, his eyes going from one to the other, and it was as if a shutter closed somewhere within him. I felt a wave of embarrassment, then of faint anger. I was not a girl, but a young woman accustomed to making her way alone, and surely there was no impropriety in my viewing the art gallery in his own house with his own assistant. Then my vision altered and I saw, not Charles, but Lawrence Stearns and myself as he must have seen us. Young. Laughing. *Walking.* How terrible for Charles, to be so gifted and at the same time so imprisoned. For Lawrence and me to be weaving a shared experience of *his* work, *his* art, without his being a part of it was doubly cruel.

I went forward quickly, holding out my hands. "Mr. Stearns was kind enough to guide me through your gallery. Charles, they're magnificent! They take my breath away!"

"You like them?" The shadow that had been across Charles's face was wiped away, replaced by a sparkling countenance and twinkling eyes. "The critics won't. They'll think them too pagan. Not a bit appropriate from an old academician. It will be interesting to see what the press will make of them."

"Charles," Lawrence said slowly, "do my ears deceive me?

41

Have you made up your mind to accept that exhibition?"

"Old Warminster at the gallery has been plaguing me to exasperation. Best way to make him desist is to give him what he wants. It will mean much work, of course, but the book on Glastonbury history comes out in June, and the publishers are after the extra publicity." Charles was all innocence, but that special vitality of his was fizzing like champagne. "Well, what say you, Lydian? The paintings of the Arthurian cycle are not for sale, but will it pleasure you to see the nobs and swells of London Town vie to see them?"

I started to say I would have to return to my own country long before that. Then I looked at Charles, vibrant with enthusiasm, and remembered how he had been a few moments ago with that blaze unkindled. And I held my tongue. Yet surely that invalid chair need not be such a prison. Someone should care enough to find a way round that fierce pride—and I caught my breath. It was like a light blazing, this insight flooding me at once with tremulous excitement and a kind of terror. An instinct deep within was telling me so strongly that *I* could be the key.

Lawrence Stearns and Barrett Doffman joined us that night for dinner, and to my surprise there was another guest as well. I was taken unawares, as I hurried to the Great Hall, by the sound of rich contralto laughter. Then I saw them, at the far end of the firepit, Charles with his head bent forward, lifting a sparkling glass in toast to the woman who sat where I had, only the night before.

Was that all it was, one night? In twenty-four hours to have come so far away from my known self that now, watching, an emotion I refused to name was like a knot of ice within me. I felt as if I was hurtling back through time to the child who so often had thought to please and so often had been rejected. Then my head lifted with a confidence I did not feel, and I went forward firmly, the slight train of my gray silk rustling softly. Charles turned, holding out his hand, and the light of him warmed me.

"Lydian! We have received an unexpected pleasure. Come meet Lady Meriel Spenser, who's motored down from Bath."

She wore black, magnificently. A parure of garnets in a perfect setting was displayed against her dazzling throat. Behind their kindness, the dark eyes inspected me with a measuring glance, but she was very gracious.

"So you are Ason Wentworth's daughter. This is a pleasure."

"Did you know my father?"

Lady Meriel laughed, and her hand rested for a moment carelessly on Charles's. "I am no archaeologist, but one cannot be exposed as long as I have been to Charles's enthusiasms and not be aware of all his idols. As I imagine he has neglected to tell you, I'm his cousin."

That irrational tightness within me eased, but only slightly.

" 'A little more than kin, and less than kind,' " Charles quoted bitingly, and she chuckled, murmuring something inaudible in reply. They were encircled by an almost tangible ring of shared associations, and I sat on a straight carved chair, sipping the wine the footman brought me.

How old was she? I could not tell. Younger than Charles, perhaps, but far older than I. Beside her I felt naïve, giftless, new grapes compared to vintage wine.

It was not the most perfect evening of my life, and I was disturbed to find it so great a disappointment. Throughout the exquisite dinner I kept looking involuntarily in her direction. More than once our glances met, and it was I who looked away, feeling hot, feeling caught in some embarrassing impropriety. I ought not to have come here. I had deliberately sought to open Pandora's box, and I had. What was the ultimate treasure that box was supposed to have contained? Hope, at once both the greatest blessing and the greatest curse.

If I had any sense, after dinner I would pack my bags and go back to London, back to America. Even as my thought shaped this firm resolve, I knew I would not do so.

I made mechanical conversation, drawing on my small store of social repartee. But I knew too well that whatever light Charles Ransome had seen in me the night before was gone. He did not notice, thank God; he was wrapped in the excitement of his own enthusiasm, discoursing at length on his sudden plans for the gallery exhibition.

Lady Meriel's eyes had widened when she first heard the news; she began to stare at me with such curious concentration

43

that I began to shrink from the nameless, heavy undercurrent of the air. Across the table Lawrence Stearns ate in silence, watching us. Stearns had a look upon his face I knew so well from Ason—the maddening, detached amusement of the scientist to whom the interactions of emotions are like the movement of strange creatures performing for his benefit beneath the lens of a microscope.

"Let us take our brandy over by the firepit," Charles said genially.

It was better there. We did not gather where we had sat before, and Charles, bless him, took over the situation, sending Doff for the galleys of his latest book. Neither Stearns nor Lady Meriel had yet seen it, and neither was a part of publishing, so it was Charles and I who now shared a common world. At length Lady Meriel excused herself; shortly afterward Stearns took himself off as well. So it was Charles and I, as before, who sat with our heads together in shared excitement. It was I who caught two or three printer's errors, and Charles who looked at me, exclaiming, "Would you be good enough to proofread this for me tomorrow? You would not mind? Now I begin to understand why Ason insisted on keeping you beside him all those years. He might not have admitted it even to himself, but the help you gave him must have been invaluable!"

It gave me great pleasure to spend the next day proofreading the Glastonbury book. I had the leisure for it, for as Charles had promised in his letter, I was left totally to my own devices. Lady Meriel breakfasted in her room and, shortly after, went away on some occupation of her own. Charles was painting, as was his invariable practice in the morning when he was not under the pressure of a writing deadline.

"Are you working on another of the Arthurian cycle paintings? I should so like to see it."

Charles smiled brilliantly. "When it is completed, and hung with all the others. Please forgive me, and humor my peccadilloes! I allow no one in my studio; I find it inhibits my work."

"You must find that inconvenient when you work with models."

"I use no models." Charles's face, unaccountably, had gone rigid and I changed the subject quickly.

44

"And your archaeological research? Are you still engaged in searching through manuscripts or have you been able to commence any actual field work yet? If I could be of use—"

"Stearns handles that, at my direction," Charles said shortly. "To make any disclosures now would be premature." He stopped, looked at me, and with what seemed deliberate effort relaxed his tone. "I have been rude again. Be kind, and understand. I have a—a penchant for privacy, based on these years of work alone. Even with you, I cannot share work in progress. Call it superstition if you will, but something will not let me. But if you were sincere about your offer of help with the book manuscript I would be most grateful."

I had very definitely been warned off forbidden ground. Charles's face was smiling, but there was a look in his eyes I did not understand, a look that in anyone else I would almost have called fear. The memory of it lingered in my mind as I turned, in the library put at my disposal, to the *Legends of Glastonbury* galleys.

The spell of Charles's writing enthralled me; I forgot my fears and worked meticulously checking spellings and footnotes and caught several errors that had previously escaped detection. I had learned more skills from my father than I had realized and Charles was delighted. "I cannot express my gratitude! I must confess I find proofreading the most dreadful part of publishing. One tends to see what one knows one wrote, not what is there. I only hope the effort was not too great for your eyes."

"Oh, no! I am so glad I could be of help. And it's such a thrill to read your work in advance of publication!"

"Did you like it?"

"To be able to combine scholarship not only with readability, but with . . . it's sheer poetry. And you know it, Charles Ransome; you are teasing me so you can hear me gush like a dazzled schoolgirl."

"I value your praise because you are not a schoolgirl. May I dedicate it to you? 'To Lydian, who has all gifts but gushing.' How will you like reading *that* in the London bookstalls?"

"I doubt I'll have the chance. I must be back in the States some time before it appears." I smiled brightly, but something had gone from the brightness of the room. We were having tea

45

by the fire, and Lady Meriel had not yet joined us. Then she entered, bringing news of an afternoon spent in the village shops, and Lawrence too appeared, in those puzzling laborer's overalls, and the moment passed.

Lady Meriel returned to Bath after three days, inviting me graciously to visit her home in that Regency city. This time there was no sorrow in my mind when I said civilly that I regretted my visit to England would be too brief. That night, as we talked after dinner, Charles produced the outline of another book to show me.

"The idea came to me out of the conversation we had the other night. A study on women in Celtic legend, raising questions on the implications for twentieth-century life. I've been wanting to discuss it with you when we were alone."

"Lady Meriel would not have been interested?"

"Meriel is passionately interested in everything I do, but not the work itself. Not the way you are."

Is it indecent of me to admit that I rejoiced?

We sat up far too late, excitedly dissecting the projected outline, discussing changes, while Doff glowered in the shadows until he was at last able to persuade Charles to go to bed. When I went to the tower room it was to dream, not sleep . . . and the form and substance of my visions both excited and disturbed me.

I truly intended my visit to Avalon to be a brief one; each day I reminded myself more insistently that this should be so. But the days lengthened and with each one Charles found some new task in which my skills could aid him. For the first time, I experienced the sensation of being known as I truly was by another person.

There was more to life at Avalon than scholastic labor. More, too, I realized gradually, than I was allowed to know. Some work to which I was not made privy was going on; I would occasionally come on Charles and Lawrence Stearns deep in a conference which ceased when I approached. Once I saw Stearns entering the private elevator which led to Charles's apartments on the upper floor, and to my surprise the cage went down, not up. I asked Charles, that evening, where the elevator system led, and he murmured something about cellar storerooms and then began asking me quickly about my day's sightseeing.

It troubled me, knowing Charles thought he could not trust me with his secrets, and then I felt chagrined at the feeling, for he had shared so much. He put chauffeur and car at my disposal, urging excursions through the countryside—to Cheddar Gorge, to Wells cathedral. I spent many hours also in the abbey ruins, writing in my journal in the golden springtime sun. The gift of poetry, so long suppressed, was steadily returning. And at night, Charles and I sat by the firepit, and talked and talked. Those hours were to me what Charles had said that first night was to him: bread and wine.

One night the pattern, to everyone's astonishment, was broken. I returned from an afternoon walk to find the house in bustle, Doff glowering, and Charles sitting among the upheaval like a hurricane's eye. "Lydian! Will it be satisfactory to you if we dine early? Sir Adrian Barker over at Wethersfield House has sent a note round saying there's a chap staying with him who was a member of Schliemann's staff at Troy, and he's having some sort of impromptu reception for him this evening. Would you care to go?"

This time I did gape like an astonished girl. "You're going calling?"

"It's the first time in living memory," Lawrence said bitingly, and Doff added darkly that it could be the last, but Charles just murmured that it was good to break the pattern once in a while to startle the Philistines.

When the time for our expedition came, I could understand why such effort was made so seldom. It took the combined efforts of Doff and Lawrence to lift Charles onto a nest of pillows in the back seat of his motor-car. I sat beside him while Doff drove. Throughout the drive, which was short, Charles was very silent. The night was dark, there was no moon, but I knew without seeing that there was taut pain in Charles's face. Doff may have been right that he ought not to have come, I thought in consternation. I put my hands over his and without a word his fingers tightened on mine as on a lifeline. But when we reached Wethersfield House, where the footman joined with Doff in transferring him to his wheelchair, his bright mask was

47

up, and I do not exaggerate in saying he was the life of the lengthy party.

I ought not to have been surprised when Charles did not appear at lunch the next day. "He asks you to please excuse him," Doff said sullenly, "but he wants to concentrate without interruption on his painting." And then, in a burst, "He *ought* to have finished painting in the morning, and been ready now for rest. But he's killing himself, working on that exhibition, and for what? To impress *you*, nothing more. *He* doesn't need fame! And going out last night in the evening damp, putting up a brave front when we know what it costs him. Before you came, he was content. But he isn't any more. And what's going to happen when you up and leave?"

I turned to Lawrence when Doff had gone, leaving us alone at the luncheon table. Lawrence's eyes, for once, were kind. "Don't pay any attention to Doffman," he said quickly. "Yes, all this is a strain on old Charles. But it could be the best thing that's happened to him. Frankly, I was worried about the way he was slipping into this cloistered life. Doff wants to keep him under wraps, but that is unnatural and debilitating. If you've succeeded in jolting Charles out of that, you've accomplished something."

"What is the nature of Lord Ransome's illness, do you know?"

"No one but Charles and Doff do, fully," Lawrence responded. "Chalk that up to Olympian pride; Charles thinks human frailty ought to be beneath him. They've given up on doctors, and I can't much blame them. The last high-priced quack told Doff in Charles's presence that it would be a blessing if the poor man were mercifully removed. That's what his family's always thought, too, I'm afraid. An eccentric invalid's a continued embarrassment to them, but he's refused to ease their consciences by giving in to death."

"How terrible!"

"Isn't it? Lady Meriel's the only one who stood by him. In the early days, I believe she literally bullied and browbeat him into hanging onto life. Charles had a very bad fall a few years after he came down from Oxford and broke his back. The bones healed improperly, and ever since he's had almost constant pain. And been prey, inevitably, to a host of other consequent ills." Lawrence was silent for a moment. "He was on his first archaeological field expedition when it happened. And his last."

It explained so much.

"He's fortunate," I said at last, "that he has you and Doff."

"More fortunate than he realizes, where the boy's concerned. Barrett's devotion makes him a prickly pear, but he's given his whole future up to Charles, and Charles does take it so for granted."

"Where did he find Doff, anyway?"

"Doff found *him*. The elder Doffman was an obscure clergyman somewhere in the Midlands, and I gather young Barrett was considered rather an exotic plant to spring up in a vicarage garden. He paints, you know. Rather well, I believe, though he'd never condescend to let me see his work. Anyway, when he was sixteen or so, he wrote Charles an extravagant fan letter, begging permission to come meet him. Charles took one of his whims and asked him down. Supposedly he was impressed with Doff's talent; more likely he was warmed by the boy's hero worship and genuine compassion. The upshot was that Charles, learning Doff was an orphan, invited him to move in. If he'd learn enough practical nursing to look after Charles, Charles would put him through Oxford one day and launch his art career. Only, in the five years since, the emphasis has been more on nursing and errand running, and less on art."

I wondered whether Doff was painting at all now, or whether he wanted to . . . but it was to Charles's story, and not Doff's, that my heart went out. That afternoon, as I sat in the peace of the abbey ruins, I took out my journal and tried to write, but could not. Pictures formed in my mind of Charles, that golden youth, younger even than Lawrence Stearns was now, in the high excitement of his first professional excavation. So young, already recognized as a gifted painter, filled with a thirst for experience that had, for the past twenty years, to be filled vicariously through art, books, writing. Like a young knight setting out on the quest for his own grail . . . and doomed instead to grow into an aging Arthur who must sit at home.

Instinctively, I had slipped into Arthurian imagery.

Creating his Avalon out of that fierce pride; working in solitude as the years went by. And inevitably, when he was alone, encountering the ghost of the suffering human I had glimpsed once or twice beneath his public mask. Time was passing, strength and energy were dwindling. If he were ever to realize his dreams it must be soon.

When I went home to tea, still troubled, I found that Lady Meriel had arrived. "Charles says he's in a painting passion, and can't stop. Let us have our tea sent up to my sitting room, shall we? I'm worried about my cousin, and I should like to talk."

I followed her to the apartment she always occupied in the east wing. She caught my eyes traveling over the Georgian furniture, and laughed. "There has to be one place of reality in all fairy-tale castles, and this is mine. Sit down, Miss Wentworth, please, and for the love of heaven tell me what Charles is up to."

She was less overpowering today, or perhaps it was that now she and I were linked by a shared concern. "He's working—too hard, I think," I said. "He's determined to have a comprehensive exhibition ready for the gallery in June, and of course he's completing his book."

"How are the new paintings? Have you seen them?" Lady Meriel asked directly. I shook my head, wondering why the admission gave me a feeling of such desolation. "And with all that, he suddenly decides to emerge on the social scene. Oh, yes, I heard about last night's excursion. Such startling news travels fast within our circle. That's why I drove down." She closed her eyes for a moment and shook her head. "For the past three years, I've been trying to get him to do any one of all these things. Adamant refusal. And now, all at once, everything!"

I had an uneasy feeling Charles might not like my discussing his work with his cousin, however close they were. I made noncommittal comments, and was glad when at last I could leave. I wanted to go to my own room, for I was tired and I had much to think about, but halfway along the corridor, I stopped.

My journal . . . my journal! . . . I had taken it with me to the abbey ruins. Perhaps I had left it in the Hall when Meriel called me. I hoped so, otherwise I would have to run over to the ruins before it grew dark. I prayed that if she or Doff had found it, they had not looked inside.

I ran down the main stairs swiftly, silently and stopped at the foot. The journal was lying on the firepit ledge, untouched. But the Hall was not empty. Charles was there, having a solitary tea. His chair was turned away; I saw only his back and profile, bent as if desperately tired. I took another step, uncertainly, and then he heard me. He turned slightly. A weary smile curved his lips and he held out one hand to me. But not as he had done before. Now it was I who had the strength to give. I went, instinctively; our fingers interlaced, rested upon the firepit ledge. We continued thus for several moments without speaking.

"Lady, lady, lady." Charles drew a deep breath that was meant to be rueful but became a sigh.

"Shall I call Doff? Are you in pain?"

"It's not important." Charles never referred to his physical condition except with a matter-of-fact gallantry that tore my heart. "He cannot help my work. It is the work that dwindles. Day marches on the heels of day, and there is no time. There is never time, and the stench of dying is always stronger at the twilight hour."

I had never seen him in this mood before. It shocked me; it also made him infinitely human. "The paintings?" I asked gently.

"The paintings for the exhibit. The book I started. When I talk with you the thesis is brilliantly clear, but when I work alone, the dream dissolves." He stirred. "I did not tell you; I wrote again making a sizable financial offer for the abbey ruins. And was again refused. One day the fool will plough the whole place under, or put up cheap houses, and a treasure of our nation's heritage will be forever lost. And I shall never, never find Arthur's tomb in time."

"You can. You will. There are months yet, before the symposium. And meanwhile the Glastonbury book comes out, and the exhibition opens. How I wish I could be a witness to your splendid triumph."

"There is no reason on earth why you cannot."

I could not say what more and more I knew: that if I did not

51

make myself leave soon I could not bear to leave at all. So I rose, walked a few steps with my back to Charles, to hide the trembling of my hands. Behind me he said, in a ghost of that magnificent voice which had so first enthralled me, "What have you done? You have indeed the gifts of Guinever. For years I was content, eager, to build an Avalon for myself that none could share. Now you come, and go, and going take with you a radiance that made these cold rooms warm."

He had put in words far more beautiful than mine the very image of my thoughts toward him. He was my light—I turned, I could not help myself, and our eyes met. Whatever possessed me to do as I then did, I shall never know. I swear to God I was not thinking of him as a man, nor of myself as woman—Ason's icy scorn had protected me far too well. I only knew that someone I loved, respected, and deeply pitied was grieving. Knew that I, too, would miss him far beyond what could be expressed in words and time. Self-consciousness dissolved. I bent to him, as naturally and simply as a child. As I moved toward him, his face came to meet mine, I think with as little conscious volition as my own. Our mouths met, and our worlds exploded.

It was the first time, I later learned, a woman had touched him since his accident. It was the first time I had been touched at all.

When I drew back at last, trembling, shaken, he looked at me and all the light of heaven was in his eyes. "Do not go. You belong here. We belong together. The quest for Guinever's gifts is your quest, too. We both have felt it. Stay!"

"How can I?"

"Easily!" His hands caught me, pulling me down near him on the firepit ledge. "Nothing calls you to your old life, you have said that. Everything calls you here. Come into my world—*our* world—and enter into your inheritance!"

It was all happening too fast for my dazed mind to comprehend. "You are asking me to stay as an assistant in your work? As I did with Father? But you have Lawrence, I lack skill and training—"

"I am asking you to stay as Lady Ransome."

"To *marry* you? You want me as a *wife*—is it possible?"

Charles's face was blazing like the sun. "Why ever not? I love you, have loved you since I first saw you. You must know that now. And you love me; you can no more deny it."

I could not. That kiss had come too quickly, told too much.

I drew my hand away, pressed it to my brow. "You take my breath . . . I have never thought that I would wed at all . . ."

"That was Ason's spell upon you. You will be free of that, if you stay here."

". . . and we have known each other such a short time."

"We have known each other since the dawn of time, and we both know it. No, do not speak. Stay. Wait!" He spun his chair round, whipped it across the floor to the great oak chest. I had not known he could travel so fast without Doff to help him. Then he had the key from off its golden chain, had flung the lid back, was tossing brocades, velvets, cloth of gold with reckless purpose.

"Here, dear heart." He had uncovered an intricately carved bronze casket, such as I had never seen before. Now he whirled back to me across the long length of the hall and laid it in my lap. "Open. Look."

Wonderingly, I did so.

"Lord Ransome—Charles—" I felt faint. I touched the exquisite, barbaric jewels with trembling fingers. "These cannot be *real*."

"Quite real, though not authentic. My own imagining of the treasure that I hope to find. That I hope to give you. You see, I have been preparing for my Guinever for many years."

I could not lift them; something held me back. So it was Charles who laid them out upon the velvet cushions. A gold torque necklace, intricately wrought. Gold circle bracelets like slave-cuffs, set with jewels. A pendant brooch, gem-studded and enameled, embodying among Celtic knots the circle and the cross. A thin gold circlet, shining, plain.

"That was the crown of the old chieftains," Charles said, watching me. "The sign of power. Unadorned, for those who wore it were their own adornment. You shall wear it at our wedding, on your unbound shining hair. But for now . . ."

He took my unresisting hand and slid upon my finger an incredible ring. Mythic animals and deep-twisted knots formed the setting for an enormous opal that blazed like fire, and which covered my finger to the knuckle. "Look into it, and you will see yourself. That is your stone, my lady of mists and water. You are one of the Opalescent Ones, lit from within!"

His words, his voice, his touch were as a drug to my senses. I stared into the opal's burning depths and lacked the strength, the will, to draw it off, knew that, now, I never could.

4

Our engagement was announced at the dinner table that same night. Or, rather, verified, for as soon as I appeared with the ring upon my finger the truth was known. I was late coming down that evening. Charles had no lady's maid, of course, to help me, and my fingers were clumsy tonight with hooks and buttons. I searched my wardrobe for my finest gown, but the clothes from my American life were too stiff and tailored; the gowns I had bought in London, by the light of the opal ring, seemed commonplace and too elaborate. Charles was right, my appearance was more suited to the garments of another time. I knew it more than ever as I wound my hair into the requisite fashionable pompadour and donned the plainest of my London dinner gowns, a white silk faille.

They had already gone in to dinner when I came downstairs. Was that by chance, or Charles's deliberate staging? For as I appeared, unsteadily in the doorway, the fireplace flames leaped high, the answering flames from the tall candlesticks upon the table seemed to burn brighter. The room was waiting. At the far end of the table Charles lifted his jeweled goblet high.

"Happily met, my lady and my wife."

A dizziness assailed me. Involuntarily, my hand touched my

temples, and the opal blazed. I heard Lady Meriel's sudden indrawn breath.

"I take it, Charles, this means congratulations are in order." That was Lawrence's voice, perfectly correct. Was it only illusion that made me feel his eyes were boring into me most strangely? I seated myself in the chair the butler held, bowed my head in acknowledgment toward Charles, but could not look up, could not turn my head in Meriel's direction, did not know why, knew only that an energy was coming from her toward me that was no kindly force.

It was an endless dinner. I felt actually ill, and for no reason. It was as if some dark bird were pecking at me, plucking my strength, leaving me stripped and naked, shivering. They did not wish us well; Lady Meriel and Lawrence did not wish us well. I had expected this from Doff, but not from them. I pushed the perfect food around my plate with my bronze fork, and wished they would go, vanish, leave us unsullied in our earlier joy.

It was a vain hope. After dinner there was brandy by the fire. Charles kept us all lingering, talking—or listening, rather, for he was high-keyed, erupting like a Vesuvius with ideas, visions, plans he wanted us all to hear. Gone now was that earlier descent into despair; it was as if the placing of the opal ring upon my finger had kindled in him a flame that could not be quenched. Indeed I feared that this ungovernable exhilaration might place as great a stress on him. And it came to me that these were some of the gifts I had to give; that I could be for Charles not only his listening ear but his hands and feet; not only the spark to warm him, but his serenity; the form that could channel the splendid raging spirit that consumed him.

One thing I knew: whatever the cost to me, I could not, would not allow those around us to pull me down into a fear of inadequacy, into a sense of doubt. Charles needed to believe; he could do all things if there were those to help him and if the flame of purpose he had nurtured through all the empty years did not flicker and die. So I held my head up and answered him dream for dream, holding at bay with the power of a will I had not known was mine those tangible waves of disapproval coming from Lady Meriel and Lawrence. And from Doff.

Lawrence had been right; Doff wanted to keep Charles too

protected. This excitement tonight, like that on the first night of my visit, might be exhausting, but it was the exhaustion of being too much alive. So when Doff began his relentless recital of physical hazards, I countered with the fact that stimulation was good for the creative mind, and creative labor in itself was rest and renewal. "As all artists know." I looked Doff squarely in the eye. Knowing I was throwing down a gantlet; knowing that while Charles looked to Doff to protect his physical well-being, he looked to me for more: for his mind and spirit.

Doff did not reply, but I knew I had made an enemy. That would change, I thought, going wearily at last to bed while Doff rolled Charles off to the private elevator leading to his own apartment. Doff was rough, and in so many ways insensitive, but behind all his actions one thing showed clear: he loved Charles deeply, wanted the best for him. Well, so did I. Surely out of that common goal we could forge a bridge.

I reached my own room and struggled to unhook my gown, remembering Rose at the Savoy Hotel and wishing suddenly that she were here to help. It would have been good, in this moment of my joy, to have a woman near in whom I could confide. I had never known my mother, had no close female friend; and here in Avalon I moved in a world of men.

Except for Lady Meriel. I would have to learn to call her Meriel when she became my cousin, but I could not imagine her as a confidante. Surely, though, as Lady Ransome of Avalon, I would make calls and receive them, become more closely acquainted with the pleasant persons I had met last night at Wethersfield House. And friends would come whom I could share with Charles, opening out his life so that he need no longer be bound by Avalon's walls. The future stretched before me, endlessly glowing.

There was a tap upon my door. Before I could do more than throw a wrap around my shoulders, the door had opened without my bidding. I swung round, clasping the soft robe to me.

Lady Meriel was standing in the doorway.

"May I come in?" But she did not wait for my nod; already she had shut the door behind her. I felt like a butterfly impaled on a pin. Oh, I had been right in what I had already sensed; she and Charles were kin not just in flesh but spirit. That same tremendous energy poured from her, only, unlike Charles's, it drained me. Meriel stood quite still, staring at me.

"Are you merely a hypocrite, or do you also take me for a fool?"

"I— beg your pardon?"

"I thought this afternoon we spoke upon some common ground. Butter would not have melted in your mouth. You seemed quite a nice child, even. And you lied to me."

"I never lied—"

"I asked you what my cousin had been up to, and you said work. *Work.* It never occurred to you, I suppose, to mention *this*?"

She made a savage gesture toward my hand that made the great ring upon it seem somehow obscene. Then my vision cleared.

"Lady Meriel, I am truly sorry. I can understand how you would feel. But when we talked, believe me, none of this had happened. It has all come so quickly—"

"I daresay," Lady Meriel said drily. "I believe it *has* been only a month you've known my cousin? A short space in your young life, but long enough to do irreparable damage." Her eyes flicked over me. "It is cold in here. You had better complete undressing and put that robe on properly."

She was right, of course. But to disrobe, to be naked and defenseless before an enemy, touched something very deep, very primitive. I turned my back and slipped my arms into the robe's loose sleeves, buttoned it tightly to my throat with hands that trembled. My thumb spun the opal ring about my finger, and the look in Charles's eyes as he had placed it there rose before me. I clung to the memory like a talisman as I turned.

"I understand what a shock this must be. You know nothing of me, and you think me young. I am not unaware that I am undertaking a great responsibility in becoming Lady Ransome. But I do promise you, I will be a good wife to him."

"You surely do not mean to carry through with this charade?" She was staring at me with something like incredulity, and to my surprise I saw tears starred her eyes. "Oh, this is too cruel, even for an American fortune hunter, though England has become well accustomed to those in recent years. If you cannot

58

have the decency to think of my poor cousin, think of yourself! How long will you be able to bear it, do you think, and how much will money and title recompense?"

Now it was I who stared, dumb-stricken, as she swept passionately on. "You are young and resilient. You will leave, and you will be none the worse. But it will be the end of everything for him. I beg you, break it off now, kindly. I have connections; I will see that you meet a man of greater wealth and rank who will be able to give you what you can't get here."

Anger turned my voice to ice. "You are under a grave misapprehension. I have no need for money, and care not for title. Do you think I would not be *glad* if he were poor and unknown, so he could be sure it was he alone I love? We *do* love each other; is that so impossible to understand? My goal, my happiness lies in helping him carry out his work . . ."

"It is you who do not understand! You are trying to raise the dead to life, and there is a curse on that, a curse that will lead to your ultimate destruction! And I pray God, not to his as well!"

She was magnificent in her wrath, but I could only stare at her in numb incomprehension, and at last she left. I went to bed, shaking.

I braced myself for a confrontation with Barrett Doffman, and it was not long in coming. The next day was Sunday and as was my custom, I went to the parish church. But I could not properly discipline my mind; it was filled and brimming over with such a strange mixture of apprehension and thanksgiving.

The May morning was vibrant and alive, and I walked home slowly. I must get Charles to spend more time outdoors. The grounds of Avalon could be made even more beautiful with gardens. Perhaps this afternoon we could tour around them, making plans.

I hurried eagerly through the doors of Avalon and was met by Doff. "*He's* in the studio, painting. He won't even take a rest on Sunday now. Why did you have to get him so stirred up?"

I had better establish my position by standing my ground at once, if I were ever to fight for my husband's future. "Lord Ransome," I said coldly, "is more than capable of making his own decisions about exhibitions."

"*Is* he? He never cared tuppence about it before you came.

59

It's for you, you know that, so you can be proud of him. What good will that do him when he's in his grave? Or is that what you really want? The title and all that goes with it, without the man?" He glowered at me from under lowering brows, and I realized with a start that the boy was genuinely anguished. "Why don't you just go, now, before you do any further damage?"

I answered him as gently as I could. "I shall not go. Now, or later, if that is your fear. It is for Lord Ransome, himself, that I want this exhibition—because he wants it, because it is good for him to remain active in his world. You can understand that, can't you?"

"*This* is his world. And he was happy in it, I made him happy. You won't, you can't. You *will* go. But I'll still be here, always, remember that. It's I who'll pick up the broken pieces you leave behind."

Another gantlet thrown.

Charles emerged for luncheon, in a bemused, half-ecstatic agitation. "What? Oh, yes, going well," he murmured in response to our inquiries about the painting. "Almost well. Not at all what it ought to be, but close, so close. If I can just capture . . ." It was the preoccupation of the driven artist, and I was to come to know it well.

I could help him best now by not being a distraction, so after lunch I took the copy of Malory and my journal and went to the abbey. I could well understand, by now, why Charles had said this was undoubtedly a place of worship long preceding the days of Christianity. "One of the sacred places, like Delphi, a navel-stone of the Great Mother." The flat landscape, rimmed with flowering orchards, the cream-gold shells of the ancient buildings did indeed have a potency of peace.

"I thought I'd find you here."

The quiet was shattered by the sound of Lawrence's voice. I started, found him contemplating me grimly with folded arms.

I felt a wave of irrational alarm. "Is Charles all right?"

"Charles is splendid. Radiating light from Mount Olympus. It's you I have my doubts about."

Whatever wary truce we had struck that afternoon in the art

gallery was now gone. There were raw, threatening emotions present here that I could not name. I stood up swiftly, furious to find that I was trembling.

"What in the name of all ancient gods," Lawrence demanded, "do you think you're doing?"

"I scarcely think it is a concern of yours."

"*Isn't* it?"

I must be a peacemaker; Charles needed me for that if I was to help him with his work. His work— I put my hand out quickly. "Surely you can't be concerned that I am trying to intrude in your professional sphere—"

"Oh, I'm not," Lawrence interrupted bluntly. "I'd feel better if that was what it was; I could respect you more for scholarship than sentimentality. Nor do I believe you're a fortune hunter, in case you care. What I do *not* believe is that you are a fool. Good God, woman, you have too much life and sanity, too much potential as a human being, to shut yourself up in this artificial world. Charles is a genius, but he is a monomaniac, and it won't help either of you if you cater to him."

"I thought you believed in Charles's work, liked and respected him!"

"I do. But I also see him as a human being, not a god. There's something in you that needs gods to subordinate yourself to, isn't there, Miss Wentworth? Or are you trying to use devotion to Charles to exorcise your father's ghost? Your father was a brilliant genius too, and Charles adored him. But Charles was also clear-eyed enough to see through him, and to withdraw his financial support from that disastrous expedition. Not because of his own accident alone! Because Ason Wentworth's daemon had exceeded common sense!—Lydian!" His voice changed. "What's the matter? Are you ill? Come sit down."

"I'm all right! Don't touch me." I dropped down on the bench and locked my hands hard around my knee to stop their shaking. "Would you mind," I said carefully, "repeating what it was that you just said?"

"About Charles and your father? I'm sorry if it's painful, but it is the truth. Charles's inheritance made that ill-starred excavation possible, and much as it meant to Charles, he backed off

61

from it as soon as he realized your father's warped judgment doomed it from the start." Lawrence's face altered, warmed. "Lydian! Didn't you know?"

I shook my head, trying to keep my chin and voice quite steady. "I am not surprised, after all, you think me such a fool. There is a great deal, apparently, that I do not know."

"I am sure it was no secret." He seemed to be trying very hard to make amends for the shock he had inflicted. "No doubt it was simply too painful for both men to speak of. They had been friends. And then, of course, there was the damage to Charles's back."

"I understand." I bit my lip hard and strove for an impersonal calm. "You need not worry. I am now quite all right, and I should like to be alone."

He stood for several moments regarding me. At last, still baffled and angry, he turned on his heel. I continued to sit there, silently, among the ruins. But my eyes no longer saw their glory. And when at last I returned to Avalon, I did not say a word to Charles of what had occurred.

Presently I was able to shake off the memory in the excitement of our wedding preparations. Charles said, and I agreed, that the best way to beat down opposition was for it to take place as soon as possible. And despite their personal feelings, once the others recognized they could not alter our determination they caused no further trouble.

We made no public announcement to the papers. What we had not reckoned on was that the press was everywhere. Our banns were posted, as they had to be, in the parish church, and some reporter recognized what after all were famous names. The deluge was loosed; the world was on our trail.

Archaeologist's daughter to wed within months of father's death . . . Union of two noted families in scholarly field . . . Arthur replaces Agamemnon in fair scholar's eyes . . . And, most brutal thrust of all, *Wealthy crippled recluse takes a bride.*

"I knew this would happen," Meriel said, white-faced. "Charles, I beg of you, can you not see? You are turning your precious private world into a circus."

Charles was in one of his mountain-toppling moods. "Let the jackals howl. We'll laugh the world to scorn, will we not, my love? They are jealous, those fools beyond the pale, that it was *I* who recognized you, wooed you, won you."

But he could not but be hurt, I knew, by that vicious headline, and I did all I could to let him know it was not with the world's eyes that I saw him.

That night, as we sat late talking by the fire, Charles turned to me, his face a carved saint's-head in the light of the leaping flames. "Will you go with me? Really go with me, to pursue the dream?"

"You know I will."

"Then shall we make our covenant in secret? No friends, no relatives, no well-meaning, doubting spectators." His mouth twisted. "No reporters. We'll need two witnesses and a clergyman, of course, but that is all. This parish priest's a sympathetic fellow, and I've had a letter from the owner of Glastonbury offering his neighborly felicitations. He will not sell me Glastonbury, but surely he'll not withhold permission for the briefest ceremony there. Can you humor my whims so far as to follow me to a wedding in the abbey shell at dawn?"

I would have followed him to the farthest star.

We determined to be married at the end of May. The few weeks' interval between was busy. Charles threw himself into a frenzy of painting that alarmed me almost as much as it did Doff, but he was determined that the exhibition should open on time and indeed the exertions seemed to be doing him no great harm. He spent hours, also, closeted with Lawrence and began sending him on field research expeditions throughout the whole West Country. When I protested at not being allowed to assist in these labors, Charles only laughed.

"Time enough, my dear, when we are wed! Then I need not be afraid you will abscond with all my secrets."

"Charles!"

He laughed, clasping tight both my hands. "Don't deny me the fun of surprising you, my darling! And I shall be a better companion, I swear to you, once this show has opened. Meanwhile, why do you not run up again to London? You have luggage there that you have not brought down, and I daresay you'd like to purchase trousseau fripperies. And do you not want to hire a lady's maid?"

It was after I was back in my suite at the Savoy that the idea came to me. Rose. Rose, the little maid who had been so kind. I put the suggestion to her, and she was ecstatic. No, she would not at all mind leaving London; I gathered the notion of being employed by "my lady" overbalanced the drawbacks of leaving the sound of Bow bells.

So I again paid a visit to my lawyer, this time in a state of euphoria which even his dubious congratulations could not dim. I made the rounds of the Bond Street emporiums, placing orders, for my wardrobe was in truth not equal to the strain of the life I was about to enter. I bought recklessly, not only tailor-mades and dinner gowns, but French lingerie, hand-embroidered, delicate as cobwebs. My heart pounded as I looked at them. I had never had such things; I had been raised to be so modest, so plain. But I would come now as a bride to a man whom I adored. He must not find me unbeautiful . . . or unwilling . . . or afraid.

At length all purchases were made, all errands done. Charles wrote eagerly, urging my return. He had received the amused permission of the abbey landlord for our nuptials, had charmed the parish priest into agreeing to the hour of dawn. I must come, for all things were ready.

So I went down again to Avalon, with Rose beside me, big-eyed and important, supervising my new matched luggage. Went with a trunkful of bridal clothes and a heart too filled with dreams. And the long-shut gates opened to let us through. There upon the heath, in what had once been the entry arch to the great choir, we pledged our troth to each other for better or worse, in sickness and in health. We exchanged our wreaths of sweet-scented flowers, and the sun broke through a sky of that special Glastonbury blue to gild the great stone monoliths that framed us as we took our vows.

Afterwards—home to an Avalon filled with the light and sounds of spring, for at my orders doors and windows had been thrown open. "You must accustom yourself to being Lady Ransome," he said, and sat watching with delighted amusement as I gave instructions. We breakfasted upon the lawn, lingered so long over excited dreams that at length we discovered lunch was waiting. I told Charles my plans for developing medieval gardens on the west lawns, and he showed me how the new manuscript was progressing.

In the afternoon the footman brought a letter hand-delivered from Wethersfield House. Sir Adrian had heard the glad news of our nuptials, wished to know if he and cousins he had visiting might call to tender their felicitations.

Charles waved an expansive hand. "Bid them all to dine! We'll have a wedding festivity fit for a queen!" So far had he changed already, from the early-old recluse who kept himself from visiting through false pride.

The evening, indeed, was clothed in splendor. A magnificent feast appeared; I will never cease to be amazed at the resources of an English staff. There was champagne; there were favors for all the guests, procured by Charles through some alchemy I did not know. There were bouquets at each place. There were even violins. We dined on salmon and spring lamb, and there was dancing. Charles insisted that I lead off with Sir Adrian, though I was loath myself to leave his side.

"Go! Go!" he urged me, his face alight. "We shall have all the world together, and it pleases me to see you dance!"

In the golden jewelry, the velvet gown, I felt as though I had stepped back through the mists of time. The great sprays of flowers, drooping now, gave forth heady perfume, and candles flickered. At length the last guests left. I saw them to the door, and when I returned Doff was already pushing Charles's chair toward the private elevator to his rooms.

I ascended the great stairs slowly, my own heart pounding. My room, too, was filled with candlelight and flowers. A fire burned on the hearth, and Rose was waiting. She had laid out the nightdress of white French chiffon with the rounded neck that showed the swell of bosom, the peignoir of the same stuff, soft as cobwebs, with its flounces and edgings of rare old lace. She had not turned down the bed; under the circumstances it was I who would go to my husband's side, and we both knew it.

I spoke but little, nor did she, as she helped me out of the velvet gown, the embroidered camisole and petticoat, dropped the thin chiffon down around my bare shoulders and brushed my hair. The sweet scent of the flowers assailed my nostrils, my heart was pounding and there was a ringing in my ears.

"Miss Lydian." Rose's face in the firelight was half-embarrassed, but warm and resolute. "You've no mother here by you, so in case you're scared—oh, miss, if it's your own heart's man, it's ever so lovely. No matter what you've heard, just you remember."

Silently, impulsively, I hugged her. Then picked up my candle, slipped out into the dark coldness of the upper hall. Charles's door was at the far end; I could not see it, but my longing for him drew me like a beacon. I sped in my bare feet over the slate floor with its intervals of oriental carpeting; something possessed me that I made no sound, that I opened the door and entered without knocking.

On the malachite-topped table the tall lamp blazed, sending a stream of gold across the room. The great wheeled chair stood empty. Doff had just lifted Charles to the great bed, was covering him with the red fox spread. The two of them, master and man, were intent on the world of their own actions. Then Charles lifted up his face and saw me. Doff was bending over him, adjusting the coverlet, so it was with Doff's dark figure between us that our eyes met.

"What are you doing here?" The tone, the look upon his face, was of sharp anger. Then as I froze, bewildered, dumb, it changed. "My love, forgive me. I did not want to have you see—"

He hated having me a witness to his helplessness, a grown man needing to be put to bed. I went toward him, my hands outstretched in love and pity. "It doesn't matter. Don't you understand it doesn't matter?"

"I know. That is the greatest gift that you have brought me." He smiled, his face wonderfully illumined. "My lovely Lydian, clothed in light. No, not clothed, for your luminosity comes from within. So you have come, like Aurora, to radiate on me from afar in splendor? Don't come too close; your light can burn."

Some chill, as yet unnamed, pricked at me then. I stared at him, motionless in bewilderment. "But . . . did you not expect me . . . did you not want . . .?"

Doff straightened, momentarily blocking Charles's face from

my sight. I was suddenly conscious of the translucence of the chiffon folds of my gown.

"I'll wait outside," Doff murmured in a quiet voice, and left.

Charles and I were alone together, scarcely breathing, unable to free ourselves from each other's eyes, and the flames of lamp and fire cast flickering shadows across the room.

Charles's face looked suddenly older. "Have you come to torment me? Don't, Lydian. The sight of you like this is more than I can bear."

"I don't understand—I thought you wanted me—"

"Of course I want you! I am yet that much a man! Why must you torture—"

I stared at him, all the daemons of past rejection webbing me with cold. Then suddenly, Charles's face altered terribly. "You do know, don't you?" Bleak. Despairing. "Dear God, don't tell me that you didn't know."

"Know what?"

"That we cannot—*know* each other—in that way." And as I yet stood, numb, bewildered, Charles—brief, taut, explicit— told me, too late, that because of his accident, his paralysis, we could never come together as man and wife.

In shame, compassion, embarrassment—in something more which I was not ready yet to face—the fatal words tore from me. "Why did you not tell me?"

"I thought you knew," he said.

"How could I—after what you asked? And I said then . . . was it possible . . .? And you said why not . . .?"

Charles said bleakly, "I did not know that *this* was what you meant."

Nor had I, then.

"You said"— Charles's arm swept in a savage gesture toward his immobile legs—"all this—my being a shell of what I once was—did not matter. And I believed you. As for . . . conjugal duties, I thought you were perhaps relieved at being spared. Some women are."

But I was not one of them. And I had not recognized, had not known this until this moment, and that was perhaps the greatest shock of all.

"It is not your fault." Charles pushed himself up painfully on

67

his elbows, trying even in his own anguish to minister to my need. "If any woman could dissolve the ice that holds me, it would be you. The torment I am feeling now must prove that to you! God, God, the irony of fate, to take away the power but not the desire. The punishment of Prometheus—" His face twisted. "Oh, Lydian, Lydian, what doom have I brought upon us both?"

I took his hands and held them against me, tightly, as if I could warm them at the fire of my own heart. "It doesn't matter. It will never matter."

"It does. It will. I ought to have foreseen it, but love blurred my vision, inflamed my judgment." Charles's face was like a mask. "It is late now, but with the morning, you must return to London. You can easily arrange for an annulment."

"No!" The word burst from me with no conscious thought. "We are man and wife in mind, in spirit. I will never leave you." Not only because I could not bring that public pain and shame upon him, but because to leave would be the end of all our dreams. Because I loved him; I would always love him.

How long we stayed thus I did not know. The fire was dying and the room grew cold, yet we remained, immobile, he lying beneath his coverlet of fur, I kneeling at his side, his hands imprisoned in mine against my breast, frozen in a spell of love and fear. I was as paralyzed, as powerless as he. And then the burning, betraying tears spilled from my eyes onto our tight-clasped hands, and with a groan he wrenched his hands away.

"Go. Now. Quickly, if there's any mercy in you."

I had become, as he had told me Guinever had been to Arthur, his fair torment. And knowing that therein was torture and no peace, I could not say, as I longed to, Let me stay. Could not say that to lie by the fire with him beneath the warm fur, held tight in the circle of his arms, would be enough.

I rose like a wraith, my whole chilled body aching. Went through the great oak doorway into the cold and silent corridor. Behind me the door closed, shutting out the solitary source of light. Doff had gone in to Charles. Doff, who had been waiting; Doff, who must have known.

They all had known. Meriel. Lawrence. Perhaps even the kindly, troubled priest. That was why they had spoken to me as they did—probing, disbelieving, questioning. They had assumed I knew. They had wondered if I understood the full implications, but had been too discreet to spell them out. I had not known, would not have been aware of the significance if I had.

Ason had not so much protected me from awareness of desire as he had doubted it could ever touch me. It had taken Charles to awaken me from that icy prison; how well he had succeeded neither of us had known until this night. My innocence, my ignorance were gone. I knew, and was known—in one sense—with such devastating totality; in the other sense, not at all, would never be. And for both of us, Charles and me, the world and our self-knowledge was irrevocably changed.

I had not thought to carry away my candle. The corridor was long and black and cold, but not so cold as the ice that was in my bones. Down the vast womblike abyss of nothingness moved the sleepwalking figure that was myself, and the floor that my bare feet trod changed from chill slate to thick velvet and back again to slate. I saw naught; knew naught. Then a wall, thick and hard, loomed up to meet me. I must have given some faint cry. The wall became a door, opening in to warmth and light. Warm hands reached out to me.

"Law, Miss Lydian, you come right in!" Rose's arms went around me, guiding me to the fire. She got me into a chair, wrapped a blanket round me, stood before me like a protective mother. "Lord, dearie, what's that man done to you?"

I shook my head, closing my eyes tight. "It's not that. He can't—"

I could not go on. But Rose, beneath her veneer of proper training, was a girl of the London streets. She drew her breath in, said "Oh," understanding. Said matter-of-factly, "It'll be all right, and who's to say you're not better off? Brandy's what you need now, and I'll find some somewhere. Don't you move."

She vanished, reappeared after an endless space bearing two hot water bottles with her as well. She closed my fingers around the stem of one of my husband's fragile glasses. "You sip that slowly, while I warm the bed. Best thing for you's to get a good long sleep."

"I doubt I can . . . My brain's so tired, but it won't let go, and I can't bear the dark . . ." The brandy was penetrating through my numbness like a pain, and my whole body began to shake. Beyond the bounds of consciousness, irrationally, all my old childhood terrors lurked.

"No need for dark," Rose said staunchly, and tucked me in like a child, and built up the fire. She pulled a chair up to the bed and sat down beside me. It was Rose's hands I clung to through the eternity of that lonely night.

When I awoke from a drugged sleep, the sun was shining. The hands of the ormolu clock at my bedside stood at nine, Rose was moving quietly about the windows. Rose . . . I wondered if she had been to bed at all.

I pushed myself up, and she turned quickly. "Good morning, ma'am." Ma'am—the proper title for a married woman. "I've kept tea warm. If you like, I can fetch breakfast up directly."

Every cowardly instinct, every aching bone conspired to make me bow to her suggestion. I threw the covers back and swung my feet out firmly. "No. Today, most certainly, I shall go down to breakfast."

Rose did not demur, but brought the organdy shirtwaist and pale-blue linen skirt as I directed. Admiration mingled with compassion in her eyes, and I needed that, it helped put starch into my shaky spine. Charles's proud, despairing words rang in my ears: "With the morning, you must return to London." It would take deeds, not words, to answer that. A pattern must be established, now or never. My own pride and a deep pity for my husband demanded that I keep my head high, make all seem well, not let him know what I was only just discovering: how much my belief in Charles's desiring me as a woman had been needed to counteract the self-doubt Ason had implanted in me.

My husband. He was all of that, my heart cried fiercely to the imagined faces of Meriel, Doff, Lawrence with their knowing eyes. If I could not be his wife in body, I truly was in spirit. I could bring him assistance in his research, encouragement in his work, and reassurance that he would be able to realize his goal within his lifetime.

Down the great stairs I went, and across the long hall faster and faster, before my nerve could fail.

Charles was at breakfast in the dining room, with Doff beside him. Doff saw me first; he broke off speaking, and Charles looked up and our eyes interlocked. There was an electric stillness and in it, my knees trembling, I crossed to the head of the table, sat in the chair the footman hastily pulled out, shook out my napkin.

"I had not expected to see you here." Charles's tone was the cool, aloof one with which he would quell strangers. But his eyes were strained.

I willed my voice equable and pleasant. "I am sorry to have kept you waiting. I meant to join you promptly; I will tomorrow. My dear, before you begin painting, may I consult with you awhile? I am wondering what would be the best way to have the rest of my belongings shipped from Massachusetts. And do you think it would be advisable to rent out the house there, rather than have it standing empty? We ought to keep it, don't you think, in case you ever have time for a visit to the States?"

I cannot describe the joy that leaped into my husband's eyes —nor the anger into Doff's. All Charles said was, "I am sorry I did not wait for you, my dear. Try some kippers, they're uncommonly good today," and I replied, "Yes, thank you. Shall I order more coffee?"

The pattern had been formed.

The day passed, so like other days before it; so like, yet so different. Charles worked on his paintings, I on the research he had requested of me. We met at lunch, returned to our separate tasks. And it was I to whom Hodge came, to discuss small household matters and have the menus for the day approved. I assented, with what I hoped was well-hidden diffidence, to all that he suggested; I was not accustomed to the supervision of such a household, and the prospect, now that I confronted it, was daunting. But Hodge's words, as he was about to leave, were reassuring.

"If I may be so bold, my lady, I should like to express on behalf of all the staff our most sincere felicitations to you and to his lordship. We shall endeavor to serve you, as we trust we have his lordship, to full satisfaction."

"Why . . . thank you, Hodge. I am sure I speak for my husband, too, in saying we contemplate no change in the admirable way the household has been managed in your hands."

We parted on a note of mutual esteem. The servants had accepted me, so the incredible must have really happened—I, Lydian Wentworth, was now Lady Ransome.

It was for Lady Ransome that several of the ladies who had attended last evening's impromptu reception left their cards; Lady Ransome to whom bouquets were sent; Lady Ransome who received a gracious letter from Sir Adrian, asking permission to give a dinner party in honor of our nuptials. I put the letter aside to share with Charles, made a note that I must myself order cards engraved with my new name and return the calls.

It was Lady Ransome who poured the tea that afternoon, but it was plain Lydian who blurted out to Charles, "Don't you think we'd better let your cousin know our news? Of what we have done? If the news reaches the papers, as is quite likely, and she sees it, she cannot help but be offended."

Charles laughed ruefully. "You are quite right. Meriel will forgive, but she would not forget." He scribbled a telegram and gave it to a footman, bidding him send it off directly.

"I'm afraid it is I whom Lady Meriel will not forgive." I had not meant to say that, but the words slipped out. Charles only smiled.

"Meriel. You must learn to think of her that way now, as a cousin." He laughed. "When you come to know her better, it will not be hard. Meriel *is* rather like a force of nature, but she's very kind."

"She resents me. I suppose it is only natural that she should." I spoke optimistically, but my heart was not in it, and Charles reached out to put his hands on mine.

"You are right; it is the natural result of our being so close

73

for so long. She was the only one, you know, who cared to make the effort to reach out to me once." He was silent, his own gaze turning inward, and I knew he was thinking back to the dark days when his life had been transformed by that tragic fall. Then he smiled at me again, eyes crinkling. "She has been more like a sister to me than a cousin. We were raised together; we both lost our mothers when we were very young. And, despite her being a good deal younger, she rather does assume the role of older sister. But you are lady of the house now, and she will respect that."

And I knew that, hard as it seemed, for Charles's sake I would have to win Meriel over.

We had our three days alone, for which I was profoundly grateful. I wished, how I wished, that there could have been more time, but there was no thought of a holiday, not only because of Charles's reclusiveness but because the date for the gallery show was fast approaching. Advance copies of Charles's new book arrived, giving me inordinate satisfaction. There were letters or cables daily from publishers or from Mr. Warminster at the gallery. Charles was painting, painting, nearly all day and far into the night. He showed me, at last, what he had been doing, and I gasped.

"You like them?" Charles asked blandly, his blue eyes gleaming.

"*Like* them? They quite take my breath away. The paintings in the gallery here have that same force and boldness, but there's something new now—a freedom, a quality of life."

"The quality of my wife," Charles said, and pulled me down and kissed me. And Lawrence walked in and stood contemplating us with sardonic eyes.

"Congratulations, and many thanks for the wedding invitation I did not receive. The atmosphere of elopement must have been quite romantic, but I must say it was a bit off-putting to have the first news of one's employer's nuptials from a local scandal sheet."

Charles was wickedly unabashed. "Let the press earn their pound of flesh for once, and save us trouble! Knowing you don't care for sentiment, I was sure you would not mind." That was a diabolical thrust, and it hit home. So that is your Achilles heel,

Mr. Stearns, I thought, suddenly enlightened. Like my father, you have carved out a white marble effigy of dispassionate science—and you are much afraid of discovering it is not you.

Lawrence's brown eyes became more opaque, like that concealing glass through which one can see out, not in. He turned to me, bowing slightly. "Since I was not here at the proper moment, allow me to offer my felicitations belatedly, and hope you have all the happiness you deserve from this marriage, Lady Ransome."

I felt as disconcerted as a schoolgirl, which infuriated me. "Please. Lydian. We shall be working together, shall we not? You must not treat me more formally than you do my husband."

"Ah, but Charles and I know each other." He bent, ironically, and kissed my hand, the model of a courtly knight. Charles laughed at the satire, and I was hard put not to snatch my hand away. You will not come near to knowing me, Lawrence Stearns, I thought. Nor I you. I have had enough of Asons in my life.

But we would be colleagues; working on Charles's projects, we would be thrown much together. Very well. I had mastered, long ago, the art of functioning in a professional way with those who did not like me. I have survived my father, I thought ironically; who can hurt me more?

Meriel did not, as I had half-dreaded, come to us, and I must confess that I was grateful. Her acknowledgment of Charles's telegram came in the form of a magnificent Worcester coffee service. "I imagine your bride will appreciate having something in a more contemporary style to alleviate the unrelieved medieval treasures which you possess already. In any event, if you are to take your place at last among the married gentry, you must accustom yourself to demitasse with friends, as well as mead."

We did entertain, at a dinner party, several of the local landed families, and we journeyed again to Wethersfield House for Sir Adrian's entertainment in our honor. But after that I myself said firmly, "No more flights of pleasure until our labors are completed," for I could see without Doff's calling it to my attention that the physical strain of such socializing, coupled with

Charles's pressing concern for the gallery opening, was adding to his burdens.

Other wedding presents poured in. I wrote cards of thanks, paid calls and received them, until Charles said I would need a social secretary to save my own time for more important things.

"What?" I asked, laughing. "I cannot help you with your painting, nor your writing. The research you've had me doing for you is fascinating, but as you've said yourself, the Arthurian trail is thin. Besides the mention in the *Annales Cambriae* and Nennius, there *is* no recorded reference to Arthur till the romances. It's not as if one could get out on a hillside and dig through layers of rock, as at Mycenae."

"Would you enjoy that?"

"I should adore it! But there is no chance, is there, until you can persuade the owner of the abbey grounds to sell?"

My husband became very busy with his manuscript notes. "Tell me," he said, incredibly casually, "if there *were* an opportunity for you to become directly involved—now—in such excavations . . . to look for tangible proof, not literary clues, for presentation at the fall symposium—would it interest you?"

"Charles!"

The look on his face was that of a small boy caught preparing a large surprise. I rounded on him. "What are you keeping from me? After such fine talk of how I am a partner in all your work!"

"May I not prepare a delight for my own wife?" Charles sang out for the footman and instructed him to summon Lawrence from his laboratory office in the front cellar. He appeared in rolled-up sleeves and the laborer's overalls, which had so bewildered me, and he was impatient.

"What is it? Charles! I'm sorry, but you've caught me at a very difficult stage of work, and it's not wise to stop—"

"You always worry about such things, yet you always cope, so it is of no matter." Charles was being his most lord-of-the-manorish, but his excitement was contagious. "Open the vault, and roust out young Doff. I am taking Lydian down."

The very muscles of Lawrence's body became alert, like a crouching puma. "Is that wise? There is much at stake, as you

76

well know. And you know, too, your playing around down there wreaks havoc with your back."

"My bones! I will not be at the mercy of my bones," Charles snapped magnificently. "Nor will I be ruled by my associates, however close. I wish to share my empire with my wife."

"Not quite yours yet, remember. And remember what you risk. This may take years, and women are not the best custodians of secrets."

A duel of wills was being fought by Charles and Lawrence. Suppressing my own outraged response to Stearns's last words, I stepped in quickly. "Perhaps we ought not, if it would be harmful to your health—"

"No, Lydian! I will not be dictated to, nor have you not trusted." I had never seen Charles before in quite this mood; it was the fanatic in him dominating the scientist. Then his tension faded, and he reached for my hand, giving me his irresistible smile. "Dear Lydian, I did not mean to frighten you. But in my work, my dreams, I cannot be held back. And I am determined you shall be a part of all."

And then there was no opportunity for protest or question, for Charles was having his way. Doff came, objecting, glowering; Charles's chair was thrust into the elevator cage, with us squeezed beside him. We were moving down into a part of the house I had never seen. An office, immaculate, white, its dark wood shelves lined like a clean museum with bits of glass, pottery, corroded metal, all neatly labeled. Cupboards filled with artist's tools, chemist's supplies—acid, trays, markers. Reference books and files.

Charles waved a hand. "Lawrence's domain. Artifacts whose proper season for display has not yet come." A locked door led off from it. As Lawrence spun the knob, a curious sensation settled on me, as if I were a character embarking on one of those fictional accounts of visitation to another world.

Another time . . . the door swung onto a narrow corridor, probably part of the original twelfth-century dwelling round which Avalon had been built. We walked past walls of rock, single file; Charles's chair would barely fit, and then only with Doff's most sensitive maneuvering. Even so, the uneven floor caused painful jolts; I saw my husband's eyes shut tightly as I looked back at him. Another door; another set of locks; another room, small, low. "This was originally a storeroom," Lawrence's voice murmured beside me. Evidently he had decided to make the best of my intrusion into what he considered his and Charles's private domain.

Here were not scientist's tools, but laborer's. Picks, shovels, pails, a barrow. I turned to Charles. "What *is* all this—?" But he waved me down.

His face was marked with pain now, but a look of almost mystic dedication filled his eyes. A mixture of emotions welled within me: concern for him, a nameless apprehension, a sense of irrational excitement.

Lawrence picked up a lantern and unbolted another door. We passed into a walkway even lower than the first. I could scarce stand erect, and Lawrence, making his way before me, was obliged to hunch his shoulders so that his silhouette, in the flaring oil-light, cast fantastic flickering shadows on the wall. This route led down, and down; behind me I heard the wheels of my husband's chair scream protestingly over the pitted stones. I dared not now say to him, "Go back!" even though the walls of this corridor gave off a dampness like the grave. There was no way here his chair could be turned round, even if he wished it. And I knew, without having to meet his eyes, that he would not—knew, too, that he needed me to sustain, not contradict, the iron will with which he was surmounting pain.

I felt as if we were traveling back through centuries, to a time even before Arthur's. Then, suddenly, Lawrence stopped, and I was brought up short before a sight so incongruous that I began to laugh helplessly.

It was a bank vault door, mechanically gleaming, such a one as I had seen in London when I had placed my father's important papers in a strongbox. Its great wheel and lever, its shining numbers stared at me like some modern monster. And something in the corner of my mind began to feel afraid.

"What is it? My dear, are you all right? The air is bad here." It was Charles's voice, fighting his own strain to respond to my strange laughter. And I beat down this wave of inappropriate emotion to speak calmly, strongly.

78

"Quite all right. I was merely startled."

"Ah, but wait until you see what lies beyond!" Charles was eager, his enthusiasm as always tapping some subterranean vein of extra strength. Lawrence bent over the safe, whirled the dials, his body shielding the numbers—from me? From Doff? An almost tangible pressure, which my mind told me came from the closeness of the little room, was building.

The vault door opened. Lawrence stepped back, bowing sardonically. I crossed the threshold.

After weeks of living at Avalon, I had thought myself inured to splendor. But I had been wrong. The air was so still it shimmered and everywhere, everywhere, there was the gleam of gold. I had penetrated into a Merlin's cave. Barely head-high, some eight or ten feet wide, this was a corridor like the art gallery far above, but old, so old. The stone blocks seemed to have grown, like fantastic coral, where they stood. Gas torches, as in the gallery, lit the walls. They stretched seemingly to infinity, for at the farther end they made a curve and twisted off at another angle lost in shadows.

Charles was lifting a pair of bracelets with his slender artist's fingers. "See, my dear, this is where the design for your troth gifts came from. One day you shall wear the originals—if the gods smile on us at the symposium this fall."

"Charles, where *are* we? And where did these come from?"

Charles's smile was bland, enigmatic, but intelligence sparkled behind its smooth façade. "Some have been found, some purchased. More things turn up on the world's secret markets than governments dream of."

"And . . . this room?" I demanded.

"May I not dig to clear out debris in my own cellar?" Charles asked innocently. "The original house was constructed in King Edward's time on a site known to have been used far, far earlier. It is common knowledge that many early Christian churches also were thus situated—easier to replace one god with another than to wean the populace away from their sacred places. And the builders of abbeys, like their Druid forebears, knew the advantage in uncertain times of subterranean passages. Folk-myths handed down for years have told of Glastonbury Abbey's being thus linked with neighboring manors. It is our loss that persons like your father were too bullheaded to believe that such country tales could contain a grain of truth."

"You are trying to tunnel through to the abbey ruins?"

"I am doing so," Charles said simply.

"He is indeed," Lawrence corroborated as I turned, dazed. "Totally beyond the boundaries, of course, of all laws but his own. In addition, he's been told not to engage in any such exertions, let alone spend time in a musty climate."

"Doctors!" Charles snorted with contempt. "Young Doff is more in the right where they're concerned than you. Scalawags and charlatans all of them, taking one's money and leaving one worse even than before. When they can raise the dead to life I will listen to them."

And I was reminded of what I had earlier learned, that it was the insensitivity of his physicians as well as helplessness which had plunged Charles not only into paralysis but into almost terminal depression.

"But the doctors are right about one thing," I said aloud. "Surely the dampness here is harmful to you." I found Doff actually looking upon me with approval, and I went on. "If you are . . . digging down here, surely Lawrence can supervise the labors for you, and you can hire workers. There is no need to submit your body to the ordeal of coming here yourself."

"He's caught between two evils," Lawrence said, ironically. "The physical strain of being here, or the strain of knowing what he's missing when he's not. And as for laborers, no chance. He will trust no hired help except yours truly in this endeavor. Which, considering its dubious legality, is no doubt wise."

"I wish you would not discuss me as if I were not present," Charles said with dignity. His eyes gleamed. "In any event, I now have *two* persons I can trust with my life's labor, do I not? You ought to be enormously grateful, my dear boy, that I have wed—and wed such a lady. Now, if you will kindly take my wife on a tour of your current efforts, Doff shall return me to where, as you insist on pointing out, I properly belong."

Doff swung the chair round. He and my husband disappeared into the shadows of the outer corridor, leaving Lawrence and me alone together.

80

We eyed each other warily. "He is right, you know," Lawrence said. "You can be useful. If you can be trusted."

"A chance which you are not inclined to take."

"Oh, I trust you with keeping Charles's little secret," he said bluntly. "You don't want to see him fail. You're as obsessed with his dream as he is, otherwise you never could have married him."

I sheered off that subject by attacking. "You aid and abet him in this bending of the law, yet you're not obsessed?"

"Oh, I have my obsessions, too. But at least they're rational. I expect to prove the existence of a pre-Saxon leader. But Charles is staking all his future on discovering not *an* Arthur, but *the* Arthur, England's pride incarnate. And frankly, I'm afraid of what will happen if he fails."

"You mean there could be serious consequences to his making these excavations?"

Lawrence shrugged this off impatiently. "He's tried to buy the place legally; the owner won't sell, mainly because he regards all this investigation as stuff and nonsense. Once a find is made and the news out, Charles will be able to square things with him easily. No, I mean the effect on Charles of making a fool of himself before the archaeological community, if his hunch *is* false. It will be the end, not just of a scientific inquiry, but of a holy quest. It could be the end of him, too, literally. You must realize he's drawing on reserves of energy and health that he can ill afford."

There was no answer I could make but a quiet, "What can I do?"

"Learn to help me," Lawrence said. "By which I mean properly, not with amateur enthusiasm. An archaeological dig is one part excitement and ninety-nine parts tedium. Sifting everything, sorting everything, taking nothing for granted, being conscious every moment where one is walking. Do you have the patience for that, or does it somehow lack in glamour for Lady Ransome?"

"You forget that I have been associated for many years with Ason Wentworth."

Lawrence looked at me, and rubbed his jaw. "Forgive me. I sound harsh. But Doff was all athunder once to try assisting, and instead of using proper care and caution he plunged in helter-skelter. He broke an important fragment of early pottery through carelessness, and Charles fairly skinned him. He's not allowed down here without Charles, now."

"I'm not Barrett Doffman."

"You're Charles's wife. Dash all, Charles is a lunatic, but an inspired one, and in spite of everything I don't want to see him hurt."

"Don't you think," I said coolly, "that you ought to show me what you are working on currently, as my husband said?"

So it began, those hours of work with Lawrence Stearns in that timeless subterranean world. Lawrence showed me where he had cleared a Bronze Age passage which had been later utilized by Norman monks. He was following the path of the breastwork which formed the right-hand wall, removing shovelful by shovelful the debris and mud that had built up across the centuries until, presumably after the abbey fell, the passage became a dumping ground and clogged from use. Each shovelful had to be sifted through a screen, its remnants dusted with an artist's brush. The slightest fragment could prove precious. And so it was that my fingers, once employed in the watercolors and fine needlework that Ason scorned, learned to work delicately, painting corroded metal with an acid that would reveal its secrets, cleaning the hardened dust of centuries from pottery inscriptions with a needle-sharp tool.

Time passed as in a dream, down in this tunnel. My fingers grew cramped and my shoulders stiff; I missed the hours of contemplation in the abbey ruins, but there was satisfaction in the knowledge that I was growing every day more skilled. There was even a curious pleasure in the technical talk Lawrence and I occasionally exchanged, like a proof that despite our antagonism we were gradually learning to work together. We spoke seldom, but we fell into a kind of silent rhythm; I felt more comfortable in his presence, though an underlying anxiety I could not explain remained.

There was, above all else, supreme delight in emerging from that secret world in time for tea, in stretching at last, removing the linen smock I had learned to wear, and running across the lawn into my husband's arms.

We had tea in the side garden most days now. I had had rose bushes laid out, violets and columbine, in duplication of a medieval pleasure garden pictured in one of the Great Hall tapestries. By the time I arrived Charles, elegant in a Byronic shirt and pale linen suit, would have stopped his painting, been wheeled out by Doff. We would sip orange honey tea and eat West Country scones, and share our day, I to display the discoveries of my tunnel labors, Charles his painting. The gallery show was now ten days away.

"They want me to come up to London for it," Charles said. "They seem quite set on it, in fact. What do you think?"

"You should, of course," I said promptly. "Lawrence can drive you. Or if the auto trip's too strenuous, we could go in style—a couch in a hired ambulance, like Arthur himself riding out on progress in a litter. Doff can come, and Rose, no doubt she'd like to see her family again. Your book comes out, too. Isn't there some sort of reception planned for that, as well?"

"The press will be agog."

"Would it not be better to beard them in their own jungle and face them down?"

"By Jove we shall!" Charles caught my hands. "I shall take my bride to London Town, and none shall say me nay. And so you shall have a honeymoon after all, my love."

Charles broke the news of our impending journey at the dinner table that night. With reservations about the strain of travel on Charles, Lawrence was approving. Doff was livid. "You know you oughtn't. It will be the death of you. When will you learn your limits?"

Charles's nostrils flared. "When will my subordinates learn the limits of their *own* authority? Your mind is too much on your wretched painting, not my needs! You will either make it possible for me to travel in relative safety up to London, or I will find someone who can."

Doff's eyes flashed with such frustrated anguish that even I thought Charles had gone too far.

That was Wednesday. On Thursday Charles was seized with inspiration for one final painting, the composition of which demanded background detailing he did not have on hand. Lawrence was despatched with a camera, ordered to photograph the desired locale and return posthaste to develop and print his finds.

"You'll be traveling toward London. You can run on in, take this new series to the gallery for me." Charles was pleased with this arrangement, but Lawrence was not.

"You wanted me to concentrate on the archaeological work, remember? And you've no business commencing another major painting now, with the show nine days off and your energies to be husbanded."

"Lydian shall continue with the other work in your absence," Charles said grandly. "And I shall continue painting. It restores me, it does not exhaust me. I will hear no more of that from any of you; I am determined."

Indeed, he was sparkling these days like a Roman candle, and my heart rejoiced. Perhaps this London journey would be a turning point, a recognition on his part at last that he need hide no longer. So I said, "Of course I shall carry on; the work goes well," and saw Lawrence off shortly thereafter, as my husband bid.

When I went back into the house, Charles had already vanished, his attention all consumed with his projected painting. I was starting for the elevator to the cellar when Doff cut me off.

"Come inside." Before I knew what he was about, he had actually seized my arm and was propelling me into the dining room, where he shut the door.

"How dare you—"

"Oh, I dare," Doff retorted, leaning against the door and watching me as I rubbed my wrist. There was no other exit from this room; my heart was pounding but I willed myself quite calm. I must not, could not let him know I was afraid. Charles was in his studio, barricaded behind thick stone walls beyond the reach of sound. All the servants at this hour were free. I forced myself to speak as Lady Ransome.

"If there is some trouble with my husband, certainly you could find some more civilized fashion to ask for an interview."

"There's trouble," Doff said. "I wonder if you know just how much trouble. Has he told you anything at all of his condition?"

"I know his accident, and its result."

"But do you know what it still does to him? Why travel's bad, and all this fool exertion?" From my silence, he could discern the answer, and his face changed slightly. "I thought as much. I made him promise he would tell you, but he was afraid. Sit down, Lady Ransome, because it's time you knew."

I obeyed, silently.

"Are you aware he's endangering his life every time he becomes wrought up? Excitement's as bad for him as depression. He tries, God help him, to become active."

"I should think that would be good for him."

"It's murder. He collapses, or nearly so, after every extra effort. He'd do anything, of course, to keep you from knowing. But it's killing him."

"But the accident was years ago. It's paralysis he suffers from, not progressive illness—"

"It's what that paralysis caused I'm talking about. He *is* alive, you know, and he still can suffer. Can't you imagine what it would be like, frozen the way he is, all those endless hours? Any jostling or pressure, any damp or cold affects him seriously. Sitting or lying endlessly in one position, when one can't move, does that, you know. His skin's like paper; a bump or a push can tear it. He's always in danger of blood poisoning, even, eventually, of gangrene. And that," Doff said brutally, "is what's going to kill him. Sooner or later."

His voice went mercilessly on. You could stick a knife in Charles's legs and he wouldn't know. A too-hot water bottle could burn the skin off his legs. The weight of too-heavy books resting on his knees could cause bad bruises that eventually would abscess. Charles was never, never going to get well. He was never going to finish his lifework, and before I came, Doff had been on the way to making him accept that. But I had brought belief, brought inspiration, kindled in Charles the fire that was driving him to what he could not finish and which would burn him out too soon.

"You made him hope, and now that hope can kill him. If you've got any pity, let alone the love you claim, make him slow down."

"How can I? His work is all his life."

"That's your problem," Doff said bluntly. "You brought it

85

on. All I can tell you is he won't have any life at all if he drives himself much harder."

He left me then, turning on his heel. I went alone, shaken, down to the tunnel. But I did not work long. I kept seeing the dark visions evoked by Doff's words. Kept hearing, too, Lawrence's terse stricture for carefulness, and knew that at this moment I dared not trust Charles's precious artifacts to my trembling hands.

I spoke of none of this to Charles at supper. I walked a tightrope, trying to be sensitive to his mood, trying to adapt to his conflicting needs to have me first gay, then soothing. He was frenetic, keyed to a high pitch of both excitement and apprehension. The sense of time passing, time running out, rang in the background like a tolling bell. The London exhibition in a few more days; the symposium in September; so much not done.

I quieted myself that night by writing for long hours in my journal, and in the morning I had Rose bring me tea at an early hour. I would work in the tunnel while the house was still, make up for time lost yesterday, take advantage of transient serenity. And perhaps then I would not feel guilty about stealing away to the abbey ruins in the afternoon for my own soul's restoring. I had much need of nature and of summer air.

The atmosphere in the tunnel was thick, like a close, damp blanket. There was ventilation of some sort, so Lawrence said, but nonetheless I felt a lead weight on my chest, making it hard to breathe. I had noticed this before, but never so strongly. Or perhaps it was simply that I had never been alone down here before. Walking through the anterooms, I had such a strange sensation, a precognition that I could not articulate but which was related to the panic I had experienced in the gallery upstairs.

I have been reading too many books, I thought; too many accounts of subterranean burials and trances and escapes from danger. Nonetheless my feet moved faster through the storeroom, to the great vault door which Charles had bid Lawrence instruct me how to open.

I wished Lawrence were here now, and that in itself was strange, for normally his presence evoked in me a guarded tension, a defense, against what I did not know. Now, the closeness

86

of a human being—any human being—would have been relief.

I must not think so stupidly. I was allowing the press of time to conjure up fantasy. We were engaged in scientific work—calm, reassuring, rational fact—and so long as one worked within that structure, all would be well. It would not mean the collapse of our dreams if Charles did not complete this latest painting for the exhibition, if we did not, by autumn, find the proof we sought within this tunnel. There would be other seminars, there would be more time. I would *see* that Charles had more time . . . and hope . . . and strength. Now that Doff had revealed to me what to guard against, I would somehow find the means to create a balance for my husband between debilitating effort and equally debilitating despair. It would not be easy. But I would learn how, because I loved him so.

I was beginning to sound, to my own mind, like a sentimental novel. Like Tennyson, creating a rhapsody of marital love in "The Idylls of the King." The earlier myth writers had been at once more ruthless and more profound.

I was not down here to contemplate myth and its meaning, but to complete a certain amount of a set task, so that I might then feel free for a few precious hours. I knelt on the kneeboard in the rock-sharp tunnel, sifting the fine debris mechanically through my fingers, and thought longingly of the abbey ruins. The abbey in June sunlight, pale filtered gold; white candytuft growing round the edges of the crumbled steps. An ordered tranquility, serenity and peace—so different from the intensity of Avalon.

If I worked steadily, did not pause for luncheon, I could stop at two without feeling like a schoolgirl creeping away from important work. I could take bread and cheese with me, a ploughman's lunch, and picnic on the grass. And dream . . . and write . . .

I felt hazy, dreamy, which was unlike me. My own instincts, as well as Lawrence's warning, schooled me in clinical concentration on the task at hand. There was an almost rhythmic concentration in the scoop, sift, sort, lay aside, scoop again . . . this must be rather like the altered consciousness in meditation that the mystics felt. But this now was different; now, rather than soothing rhythm, there were dreams, fragmented images that drifted through my brain as I started, shuddered, forced my wavering eyes to focus on my hands.

They came . . . went . . . distorted, disturbing, oddly threatening visions from myth, from old nightmares, from my past. It was all I could do to will my dull vision clear, to force myself forward with my allotted task. Three more square yards of sifting . . . two . . . then I would stop.

I must stop now; for some reason I could barely breathe. I pulled myself up heavily, stumbled toward the far vault door, which wavered and receded. I was ill; I could scarcely move. I must rest a moment . . . I leaned my head against the wall of rock in an odd passive inertia as the terror I could no more hold at bay closed in about me. The corridor grew bright, grew dark . . . I was paralyzed like a pinioned victim at the edge of some high cliff, and below me in the vast grayness a nameless chaos swirled. And then I was falling . . . falling . . . sucked down and down into an endless, clamoring dark.

It was dark, and cold, and lonely. I was in the land of my old nightmares, being carried helplessly along on a crashing wave of inner pain. A voice was screaming, crying out my name. It was an angry voice, and the grip that held me, shaking me, forcing me back to consciousness was angry too.

"Lydian! Wake up! *Hear* me, damn you!" Something hard and sharp struck my face . . . a human hand. There must have been a ring upon it. My head bobbled like a buoy drifting on an ocean; dropped back, as I was lifted by the shoulders. The grasp was brutal. It was the anger that finally reached me, like the great arm of God stretching down into the swirling waters to force me to respond.

My heavy eyelids struggled up. Fresh air and sunlight smote me. A face loomed, fiercely . . . Lawrence's face . . . very close to mine. It was Lawrence's hands which were brutalizing my bruised flesh, and something very deep and primitive, beyond the range of conscious will, caused my lungs to gulp in the saving air, my arms to struggle.

"Thank God." Lawrence's tone changed from rage to a kind of incredulous relief. "Don't thrash around. Save your energy for breathing, slowly—"

I was lying on the lawn of my own cloistered garden, not far from the side door. My organdy shirtwaist had been ripped open at the throat, as if in urgent haste. I could not speak, my lungs and throat felt as though seared with fire. But Lawrence was bending over me, and my eyes implored him.

"I found you in the tunnel, overcome by gas. And it's a damn good thing I got back here earlier than expected," Lawrence added grimly. "Another half hour and you would have been forever with Charles's precious immortals. Whatever possessed you to stay down there alone?"

"Had to . . . promised . . ."

"There are too many fool vows made in ignorance around this place. No, don't sit up . . . If you're so determined to, hang your head over, or you're going to be very sick indeed, and you won't like it."

He was right. It was humiliating to be seen, thus defenseless, at his mercy. In his debt . . . I shook my head, pressed my hand hard against my throbbing brow. "What . . . happened?"

"I don't know. I was hoping you could tell me." The anger was back in Lawrence's voice again. "There was a gas leak. For God's sake, woman, couldn't you even smell it?"

I struggled to remember. "There was something strange. I thought it was just my imagination . . ."

"It was somebody's criminal negligence. Or worse. Charles had me check those gas valves only two weeks ago. He wanted to be sure nothing like this could happen." He answered my unspoken question. "The gas flames went out, then the gas came on again and overcame you. And you can thank your stars for that scary blackness; if there had been flame while that gas was escaping, there'd have been an explosion that would have blown you into kingdom come."

"But how—"

"That is what I am going to find out. I *know* I checked everything." Lawrence was speaking to himself in a kind of impotent fury. "Either I missed something or—"

He stopped abruptly, but my eyes had widened. "You don't think it could have been deliberate? But *why?*"

His face changed, with effort, into reassurance. "Why indeed? Don't let yourself think of such ridiculous things. But I want you to promise me you will never go down in the tunnel again unless I am there."

I forced myself upright, stared at him levelly. "Not unless you tell me what you are thinking. I am not a child; this is my home and I have a right to know."

His eyes returned my stare, measuringly, and then all at once something changed. It was as if the wall of wary distance so long between us had dissolved, and we were reaching each other at last as human beings. "Very well. I did not want to alarm you. But are right. Beyond a certain point, solicitude can be demeaning. And noninvolvement a kind of cowardice—" He went on quietly. "There have been other . . . incidents. Not sabotage, but attempts at breaking in. That is why Charles has made the place into such an embattled fortress. You must have realized the value of Charles's buried treasures here. Not only the artifacts, but his secret paintings. The existence, although not the nature, of these things is well known in the criminal world. There are many collectors, you know, who fancy a treasure even more if it's obtained by stealth."

I knew. I had learned much from Ason of the private code of ethics of fanatical collectors.

"Personally," Lawrence added, "I should not be at all surprised if that trove of objects Charles keeps hidden in the cellar came from just such means. Illicitly, not by violence; he would draw the line at that, I think. But others might not."

My brain felt as if it must still be gas-befogged. "You are not trying to say someone deliberately tried to kill me to get that treasure."

"Not kill. Send you into a deep temporary sleep. Just long enough for lorries to pick up—" Lawrence rose swiftly to his feet. "My God! I went straight to the tunnel, and then dragged you here—I never thought to check if Charles—!" He was off at marathon speed toward the house before I could try to struggle after him. I dragged myself upright, swayed queasily, sank down on a stone bench and waited.

Lawrence returned, looking grim but much relieved. "It's all right. The servants are all in hall, Doff's been off somewhere with the car for hours, so they say. And Charles is incarcerated in his studio; he spoke loud and clear when I hammered on the door, so there's no gas in there. Now we had better organize our thoughts. You must recall everything that happened, as accurately as possible, so we can report this properly to Charles."

My hand flew out. "Lawrence, no!"

"Lydian, he has to know. He has a right to. And if there has been a criminal attempt here, he must take precautions."

"But not now, please!" My words tumbled over each other in their haste. "He has so much on his mind, all the pressure of the show—I'm so worried for him! You *said* it could be an accident. Please, tell him that. Do your own checking—we can be careful, but don't give him more to worry about till the opening's over. His life is more important than all that treasure!"

"You really do love the old boy, don't you? All right, you need not glare at me like that. I shall not say anything but 'accident,' not until I have made the most careful examination, but Charles must be told that much. And *you* must promise not to go down there without me."

I nodded, lacking the strength to fight. I did feel ill; my knees were behaving shamefully, and I was obliged to lean on Lawrence's arm to make my way inside. He turned me over to Rose's anxious ministrations, and as she led me slowly up the stairs, I heard him pounding peremptorily on Charles's locked studio door.

Rose put me to bed and brought me chicken sandwiches and tea. "Make an effort," she said firmly, when I murmured that I could not eat. "You must try, ma'am dear. The way you've all been carrying on, meals at all hours, up half the night—gallery opening or no, it's plain crazy. There's much that's crazy hereabouts, and that's the truth."

Something in her tone made me look at her sharply. "What do you mean by that? Rose!"

Rose flushed. "That Mr. Doffman and his pinching fingers. I'm a good girl, I am, as he'll learn to his sorrow if he takes more such liberties."

I had an uneasy feeling that this was not all that had been on her mind. Before I could probe further, my bedroom door flew open, and Charles was there. Charles in his wheelchair, self-propelled, his face taut and strained. He sped straight to my side and took my hands in his.

"Lydian, my dear love! Lawrence just told me—such an

appalling experience for you, and inexcusable that he should have been so careless! I told him he must make certain the gas installation was absolutely safe. I ought never to have exposed you to such risk."

I sat up hastily. "You must not blame Lawrence, or yourself. It was an accident, Charles; things like that can happen."

"Nonetheless, you must not go down there again."

"Certainly I shall. When we know it's safe. I *want* to go on with the work. Charles, you must not worry, I will not have you worry."

"You might have died," was all my husband said.

"But I did not. Nor am I likely to. It was a freak accident. What are the odds of anything like that happening again?"

Did a current like cold air change within the room, or was it only Rose by the window adjusting the striped silk draperies?

"She ought to see a doctor," Lawrence's voice said from the doorway. "Yes, I know your opinion of physicians, but Lydian ought not be penalized because of it."

"Yes, of course. Send for him at once," Charles said tersely. Lawrence vanished, but my husband stayed, his face etched with concern. He looked old; he looked burdened with some anxiety that I could not know. To reassure him, I dutifully choked down food that gagged me, sipped the tea. I felt faint, and drowsy; I fell asleep still holding onto Charles's hands.

"He wouldn't leave, not till he was growing ever so stiff, and then Mr. Doff made him," Rose reported when I woke at last hours later.

"Doff is back?"

"Yes, with a whole load of gewgaws Lord Ransome had sent him to buy in Bath. *She's* here, too, that Lady Meriel; she drove down with him. The doctor came, but he said he'd not disturb you, only you're not to stir from that bed for two whole days."

Was it cowardly of me that with Lady Meriel in residence, I was only too grateful to remain in my own apartments?

I dined in luxurious privacy, with Rose attending, and in the early evening Lady Meriel appeared.

"My dear child, what a dreadful experience for you. Charles

has told me." She threw a cool glance in Rose's direction, and Rose obediently vanished. I felt defenseless, there in my nightdress beneath my cousin-in-law's speculative gaze.

"It was really not serious. An accident. Please do not let Charles worry."

"You have backbone, don't you? I should have thought that narrow escape would have driven you straight to the safe modernity of London."

"Would it you?" I asked evenly.

She inclined her head with grudging respect; a point made. Then, unexpectedly, she smiled, her face becoming suddenly warm and human. "May I sit down? It was a draining dinner, since, as you have correctly guessed, my cousin needed to be constantly admonished not to work himself into a state."

"Please do." She seated herself on the satin slipper-chair, a superb figure in black point lace with a demi-train, and I pushed myself up against the embroidered pillows. "Lady Meriel—"

"Meriel. Please."

"Meriel, do make Charles understand I am feeling quite myself. He must not be alarmed; he is under intense strain already with the gallery show, and the new picture."

"Charles loves intensity; you must know that. His spirit thrives on it, though his health pays. No one has ever succeeded in teaching him moderation."

"You do, somewhat. Charles is more open to reason when you're here." I leaned forward and surprised myself. "Meriel, could you possibly stay down here until we leave for London for the show? He's so looking forward to it, and he *must* be rested for the trip."

"If you would like. I must not tire you now; I shall go down and attempt to make Charles listen to reason and give up his plan to paint all night." She rose, crossed to the door, then paused. "I want to tell you something. I was wrong about you. You *are* good for Charles; I can see that now. That is all that matters to me, you know—his welfare. Otherwise I should never have spoken to you as I once did. I am very glad, now, that you are here. Only I warn you, Lydian, you must never hurt him. If you ever do, I swear I will destroy you."

She smiled as she spoke, a singularly attractive smile that explained the charm she had for Charles, but I knew she meant it.

It was not until late that night, lying in the moonlight-silvered dark, that a strange thought flashed across my drowsing mind. Suppose what happened had been no accident? Suppose it had been deliberately caused, and not by Lawrence's suggested thieves. The fantastic dream-visions of my half-conscious state, the sense of panic, had been of a threat—not to Charles's treasures, but to *me*.

I laughed at the notion in the bright light of the following day. But still it lingered, that remembered sensation of private danger.

Dutifully, I stayed in bed as bidden, taking the opportunity to catch up on much reading. But my mind kept wandering, wondering what was happening downstairs. Rose brought bulletins. "His lordship's barricaded in that workroom painting, and says he'll not be interrupted for lunch nor dinner. If you ask me, he's overdoing it, ma'am dear. And that Mr. Doff's not half angry! Mr. Stearns, too. You ought to've seen him, coming up to luncheon looking like a chimney sweep from scratching round below stairs. What's he up to down there, anyway?"

That was what I would have liked to know.

Although I had not realized until now how very tired I had become from my recent labors, yet I chafed at this enforced confinement. Next day, putting on a sturdy waist and skirt that would survive hard use, I went down to the tunnel and insisted that Lawrence let me in. Rose was right, he was both work-worn and irritable. He had been working, not on the excavation, but on the gas lines—and he had found nothing wrong.

"Then it was *not* an accident."

We looked at one another, and as the full weight of this implication settled on me, I felt a chill along my spine.

"I shall have to tell Charles now," Lawrence said. His tone was surly; he expected fight from me, and he received it.

"Not until after the gallery opening! I will not have it! He is operating under too much pressure now. If you add this knowledge, how can you answer for the consequences?"

Lawrence threw the wrench he was holding to the floor with a clatter. "I can't, and there's the danger. When do you go to London? Friday? With Doff and Rose attending. So I will have a week alone here. You may be sure I shall turn this whole place inside out as thoroughly as if I were Mr. Sherlock Holmes."

"You will not speak to Charles."

"When he gets back," Lawrence said inexorably.

On Thursday, the day before we were to begin our journey, Charles had still not completed the new painting, and the atmosphere was fraught with tension. Making matters worse, a journalist and photographer from London appeared in midafternoon, seeking a story that would be run coincidentally with the Saturday opening.

"His lordship does not grant interviews," I heard Hodge saying frigidly in the entrance hall.

"Oh, I think he had better, don't you know?" The intruder lounged with easy insolence against the doorjamb, flicking ashes from his cigar on the entranceway's slate floor. "The story will run anyway, you see, and wouldn't it be better for it to come from the horse's mouth than other sources? Is the old boy really going up to London? Rumor has it he's so deformed he daren't show himself. And what about the wife? American fortune-hunter, eh?"

My blood boiled. I rang the bell-pull grimly and told Hodge, "Inform the persons that *Lady* Ransome will grant them a brief interview in fifteen minutes. You can show them into the entrance hall."

Let them wait, I thought. If they wanted to find out about Lady Ransome, it was Lady Ransome that they would see. I ran upstairs, yanked the bell for Rose, rummaged furiously in the armoire till she appeared, breathlessly wondering if anything was wrong.

"A great deal, but I am shortly going to set it right. Do something with my hair, please, Rose, and hook me up!"

It was a proper lady that swept downstairs again with her head held high. Rose had made rapid magic with pins and combs, and I knew that my Parisian white embroidered muslin bore the unmistakable mark of quality. My opal ring shot fire. I felt like an actress about to go onstage to play a role; my nostrils flared, and not with terror. I had survived Ason Wentworth—what was there left to fear?

The two men jumped up belatedly when I entered. I glanced pointedly at the smoker, and he reddened, and stamped out the cigar.

"Your ladyship, we're from the *Express*," the photographer began. I interrupted with a cool nod, as I had once seen Charles do to an intruder.

"Certainly. You want information about the events of Saturday, of course. His lordship's new book, *Legends of Glastonbury*, will be released by the publishers at a luncheon in his honor. Following that, there will be tea at the gallery by invitation only. Mr. Warminster of the gallery will naturally supply you with a list of the exhibits. You will want to know, of course, the most significant works to be displayed. There is a large canvas depicting the knighting of Lancelot, which marks a turning point in his lordship's style, an employment of a brighter palette and much use of knife instead of brush." I was beginning to enjoy myself as I saw the reporter's pencil racing over paper. I had not sat down, therefore obliging him to stand, an arrogance I would not have indulged in if it hadn't been for his cavalier rudeness with the cigar. Charles should have been watching; I could fairly see his eyes twinkling with amusement as I heaped esoteric technical detail upon detail, which they did not understand but were obliged to write down nonetheless.

The photographer had been fumbling with his equipment. "If we might have a picture, perhaps in his workroom—"

"No one is admitted there. If we step out onto the lawn, you will find the light quite bright enough." They had to follow as I led the way and posed collectedly, head high, my hands clasped lightly where the opal ring would catch the camera's lens. According to etiquette no gentlewoman permitted her photograph to appear in the public press, but times were changing. The photographs of many titled British ladies were available in shops for an admiring populace to buy. And in any event, it was better far for a picture of the real Lady Ransome to appear than to have a distorted word-portrait in its place.

"And now if we might have some personal details. Human,

you know, the public likes that. When you were married—"

"I think not, gentlemen. It is my husband's work that matters, after all, and you have information enough now for quite a good story." I bowed, impersonally gracious, and swept back to the house in the best copy I could make of Meriel's manner. Hodge shut and locked the door behind me firmly.

I felt exhausted; I did not know whether to dissolve in shakes or laughter. Hodge, for the first time since I had known him, unbent with a look almost human in his eyes. "Your ladyship, I regret deeply that you were thus troubled. If I may say so, my lady, your ladyship has an excellent grasp on the necessities of the situation. Tea is in the Great Hall, your ladyship, and his lordship is waiting."

My heart lifted; I fairly ran inside. "Charles, darling! What a good thing you did not emerge five minutes earlier! Can you stop for tea, truly? Is the picture done?"

"Done, complete, finished! Turn and behold!"

I spun round, encountered an easel standing in a shaft of sunlight. *"Oh, Charles!"*

He had painted a portrait of me as I had looked upon my wedding day, in the abbey ruins at dawn.

Charles's face was radiant. "Do you like it?"

"But you have made me beautiful."

"You are. If I have done anything, it only was release your inner light." He caught me close as I turned back to kiss him. "Sit! Have tea! By all the gods, I have missed this hour with you, my lady, while I was at work."

When he held me I could feel what his dazzling enthusiasm had hidden—he was trembling with tension, and desperately tired. His eyes looked strained, and irritation made a vein throb in his temple. One word of misplaced solicitude from the hovering Doff and it could precipitate a scene, the very thing it was so necessary to avoid.

I smiled at Charles and smoothed his hair. "Have you waited tea? Let me pour, and then— Oh, dearest, if the picture's done, can we take time to read aloud? I've found such a fascinating Arthurian poem by William Blake!"

I fetched the small volume from my bedside table, and as I read the measured stanzas I was glad to see the lines begin to soften on my husband's brow. I wished I could suggest we not go in to formal dinner, but I dared not; Charles wanted celebration.

"No peacock pie? No larks in pastry shells?" Lawrence asked wickedly when he saw the menu.

The wine flowed, an excellent vintage, and champagne. There were toasts. Charles was indulging himself far too well, and none of us had the heart to stop him, except Doff, whose remonstrations Charles resolutely would not hear.

Charles and I sat late that night, the two of us alone beside the fire. It was a magic time, a serene and glorious moment in which we could share together all the anxiety, effort and fruition of these past months' work. We had never been so close, so truly wed.

The next morning, when Rose brought in my early tea, she was distraught. "Oh, ma'am dear, you'd best go straight inside! Something's dreadful wrong, everyone's in a dither about his lordship, and Mr. Doffman refuses to tell me anything."

Charles was having one of his worst attacks.

I stood by the door of his room, and I could not go in. Lawrence would not let me. "He does not want you to see him in extremity; give him that much. Doff is coping; he knows what to do." He took me by the shoulders and sat me down on a straight chair in the corridor, not unkindly. "It's the fever, of course, and muscle spasms. Doff will get the fever under control in a few hours. But it's good-bye to the London opening, I'm afraid."

"Oh, Lawrence, no!"

Lawrence shrugged grimly. "We all knew he was building toward this, but what could we do? Charles is a law unto himself, and now he pays the price."

The sun was bright before Doff appeared beside me to announce grudgingly, "*He* wants to see you. It's not pretty. I told you that you'd be the death of him."

I ignored him and went straight to my husband's side. Doff was right, this was mortality, stark and ugly, and I steeled myself not to let Charles see the horror that I felt. His face was puffy, bloated, but his eyes burned with their unquenchable fire.

"Oh, my darling, I am so sorry. I wanted to give you splendors, but you must go up to London and claim them on your own."

"No. I will not leave you."

Charles's hands tightened on mine. "There is a train in an hour and you must be on it, you and Rose. I *want* you there in London. You must speak for me. If I am cut off again from triumph, then I must see it through your eyes."

I could not refuse, though everything in me cried out against it.

Rose already had my bags packed, and we boarded the train at the last moment, she proud in the glory of a new tailor-made and the custody of the monogrammed jewel-case Charles had had made for me as a surprise. I wore the cloth suit of pale opal-green Charles had selected for my traveling; he had weeks ago deliberated, with an artist's eye, on my costume for each planned public appearance. But then I had expected only to be a bystander; now, I was on my own.

"You'll do splendid," Rose said loyally, and giggled. "Ever so good, isn't it, you've had practice already in being interviewed?" Apparently the tale of my encounter with the press had traveled round the servants' hall.

We arrived in London and took a cab to the Savoy, where I was welcomed with cordial deference. I spent the afternoon engaged in business, acquainting the gallery and the publisher with the fact that it was Lady Ransome who must be guest of honor at the planned fetes. I was able at last to take a stroll in St. James Park, and watching the comical ducklings, feeding the sparrows that clustered on my hand was soul-restoring. But I was very glad to dine alone in my suite that evening, and I insisted, over Rose's protests, that she take her own meal at her "Mum's," in the East End of London, as she had planned.

"Spend the night there, too," I told her firmly. "I shall not need you until it is time to dress for luncheon."

In truth I was glad to be alone, to compose my thoughts and prepare intelligent remarks to make when speaking at the planned affairs. I had available the speech that Charles had long since written, but I could not speak in my husband's style. It was fortunate I had this task to discipline my mind, for I was torn with anxiety over Charles's condition.

In the morning Rose arrived early, bearing copies of all the London papers. "You've a lovely press. And oh, ma'am dear, look here!" The enterprising interlopers who had interviewed me had succeeded somehow in obtaining a photograph of Charles's portrait of me and here it was, next to the picture they themselves had taken of me on the lawn. "First public appearance of new peeress . . . America's latest lovely export," blazed the headlines. I closed my eyes and muttered a swift silent prayer.

Rose did my hair up in a becoming modern style. "You can't go today looking like one of those old queens to please his lordship," she said, and I quite agreed. But the sea-green crepe de Chine gown, with its soft embroidery and pointed sleeves, had an indefinable suggestion of medieval line.

I felt not unlike the old woman in the nursery rhyme when at length, hatted, gloved, and parasoled, I embarked in a hired carriage for the luncheon. *O lack a day, O lack a day, this never can be I.* This was some stranger, elegant and gracious, smoothly playing the role of titled lady, of archaeologist, while the real Lydian, Ason's daughter, hovered around, apprehensive and invisible. But my host the publisher, the gentlemen and ladies brought up to be presented, seemed to find nothing wrong.

I glowed at all the splendid comments made over Charles's work; colored with a more personal emotion when I was presented with an enormous bouquet of roses from the publisher, and a spray of delicate tiny green orchids—Charles's telegraphed order; in all he must be going through of mind and body, he had thought of that.

The luncheon was a repast of seven courses, ranging from oysters through croquettes to sweetbreads and petits fours. I made my speech; I shook innumerable hands; I signed copies of Charles's book. I went back to the Savoy and allowed Rose to redo my hair, to array me in delicate ice-blue chiffon and point lace for tea. At the gallery there were more roses, there were knowledgeable associates eager to escort me personally through the exhibition in advance of the opening time. Charles's work looked splendid, but I mourned the loss of that special ambiance lent it by the gallery at Avalon. I made small talk, congratulated Mr. Warminster on his perspicacity. The hour of the opening arrived. I shook more hands, met several duchesses and numerous other personages famous to me by name; was presented to a member of the Royal Family who made me think of the Red Queen. I felt indeed like Alice in Wonderland.

I was served tea, delicate and fragrant, and watercress and smoked salmon sandwiches; I was by this time very grateful for the opportunity of sitting down. But this was only temporary respite. Too soon, Mr. Warminster, like a genial Pickwick, was clapping plump hands together and announcing from the platform that her ladyship, the wife, nay, colleague, of this distinguished artist, had graciously consented to speak about her husband's work.

Her ladyship's knees were knocking beneath the blue chiffon. Then, as I turned toward the sea of faces, it was one visage only that I saw in my mind's eye. Charles. Charles, so eager and excited, so anxious to have me participate in his triumph. I would not let him down.

"Dear friends," I began, and then, as before, that curious dichotomy of personality occurred. Lady Ransome the public figure had taken over and was doing very well.

Ason would have been both startled and disconcerted; my husband would be proud. I realized something else as well, and the effect of it was heady: these people were favorably responding, not only to Charles's work, not only to my knowledge, but to *me*.

I concluded my remarks amid a little rustle of pleasurable approbation. There was an initial question from the rear, a query regarding archaeological technique that I could easily answer. I looked over at the questioner, and my eyes traveled beyond his shoulder to the far wall, and I froze. I was Cinderella at the ball, and the clock had just struck twelve. Despite the reality of opal ring and blue chiffon, I felt exposed. I was again the inadequate Lydian Wentworth; Lady Ransome was gone. But it was no ghost of my father who stood there watching me. It was Lawrence Stearns.

He stood against the wall, just inside the door, his arms

crossed, regarding me with those dark and opaque eyes. For a moment, I almost hated him. I tried to speak, faltered, and was still. My throat burned.

And then a voice said easily, courteously, "Perhaps I may speak in answer to that question," and it was Lawrence's voice. Lawrence was coming forward to stand beside me, saying, "I am Lawrence Stearns, Lord and Lady Ransome's archaeological assistant. As you may know, while Lady Ransome is active with her husband in all his endeavors, her own considerable scholarship is particularly exercised in her special interest, myth and literature. She has already spoken to you at length about this, and must be fatigued, so if she will permit me, I will answer for her the questions on the technical aspects of Lord Ransome's work."

Easily, effortlessly, the burden was lifted from me. Lawrence's eyes remained opaque, but nonetheless there was something in them that surprised me. Something which, in any other man, I would have called respect.

I was weary and very grateful to sit down. Someone brought me tea. The formal speaking dissolved into little knots of conversation. Several persons pressed forward, so kindly, to comment on Charles's work and mine, to express the hope that we might meet again, for luncheon . . . for tea . . . for dinner. It was over, and I had been a success. Except for that one misstep, which Lawrence, of all persons, had covered for me.

Lawrence was before me, saying quietly, "I have a cab waiting, if your ladyship will permit me to escort her back to her hotel."

I nodded, took his proffered arm. Not until we were in the cab, with the door closed upon us, did I speak. "Thank you— for rescuing me just now."

"You could have answered that question in the middle of the night while reciting the multiplication table backward," Charles said calmly. "You were just bone tired, and no wonder."

I pulled myself together with an effort. "What are you doing here?"

Lawrence grimaced. "Charles was having a great and glorious orgy of self-pity, and knew it. Knew it was justified, which only made matters worse. He threw us out, all of us but Doff.

Lady Meriel's gone back to Bath, and I was sent on a wild-goose research chase which is going to involve at least two additional sojourns anyway. So I bethought myself to come to London and tell you Charles really is recovering quite well."

"Oh, I am so glad!" I exclaimed fervently. I was astonished to discover that my hands were trembling. I had not allowed myself to realize, until now, just how desperately worried over his condition I had been.

"Charles has nine lives," Lawrence said, "and he's only on about the fourth one now. But what of you, Lydian? You've been burning your candle at both ends, too. You must rest."

"Don't worry. I've a lovely day planned for tomorrow. Late breakfast, then church service at Westminster Abbey, and then I think I shall go out to Kew and contemplate the flowers."

"It sounds exactly what the doctor ordered. Fresh air and sunshine, and no worries." He looked at me. "What about to-night? It would not do to take you to a restaurant, I suppose, but may I have the pleasure of your company in the dining room of your hotel?"

Lawrence called at eight, with my permission. By then I had bathed and rested, and Rose had hooked me into a princess gown, quite plain, of heavy Irish lace. I wore Charles's wedding jewels, as I knew he would want me to, and the gold torque gleamed, throwing up light against my face.

Lawrence looked at me and nodded. "I see what Charles means, about the opalescent quality of the Sidh."

Unaccountably I felt myself flushing. "It's the gold collar."

"Not entirely."

Lawrence himself, faintly to my surprise, was correct and darkly handsome in formal evening clothes. When we entered the great restaurant together, the waiters hurried to do our bidding.

Lawrence ordered champagne. "It's *de rigueur*, after all, for a celebration."

"We celebrated on Thursday night. And look what happened."

"That celebration was for Charles's triumphs," Lawrence said calmly. "This one's for yours."

I did not know what was happening to us. Perhaps it was the

cumulative excitement, or the weariness, or the headiness of the champagne that loosed our tongues. All that sense of wariness was gone. We were, incredibly, able to say anything to one another. "It wasn't easy for you, was it," Lawrence asked, "carrying through with this today?" And I found myself telling him about my early experiences with Ason. The barriers all were down.

It was, in a way, what I had experienced that first night at Avalon—but with a difference. For one thing, I had fallen head over heels in love with Charles, and of course with Lawrence I did no such thing. And Charles had had magic, charisma; Lawrence was simply human, with even his detached cynicism for once safely tucked away. But there was another difference, too, which I only gradually began to realize. I felt young, alive; I was having a joyously good time with someone my own age who spoke my special language, something I had never before experienced.

We dined, we danced, we lingered over coffee and talked and talked. Over and over again, continually, like swirling loops curving back to one sure center, our conversation kept turning to Charles. His gifts, his daemonic energy and suffering, his genius.

Lawrence swirled his brandy glass, looking down into its amber depths. "Tell me something. When you married Charles, did you know the truth?"

I knew exactly what it was to which he was referring. It was a question no gentleman ought ask, nor any lady answer. And yet . . . "No," I said simply, and Lawrence nodded.

"I thought as much. Or, rather, was afraid. I couldn't warn you. I did ask Charles if you understood, and he swore you did. But he was so afraid of losing you."

"He never shall."

"Yes, I can see that." He looked at me directly. "I am beginning to understand why he was concerned. You are a very comfortable person to talk with, Lydian Ransome."

I could have, unbelievably, said the same of him. Something had happened tonight; a circle of companionship had been formed. Not like the spell of magic that united Charles and me—an intensity like an all-consuming fire. This was quiet warmth, a liberating serenity. Charles was my destiny, my deep love. But now at long last, and in Lawrence Stearns, of all unlikely persons, I had found a friend.

I smiled, irrelevantly, and he smiled back, and then we both were laughing. He rose, and held out his hands to pull me to my feet. Then my laughter ceased, cut off as by a closing door. I felt a chill, although there was no draft here. For my eyes had traveled beyond my companion to a table at the far side of the room.

It was like a recurring dread, this inevitability of discovering myself, at unguarded moments, being watched. Across the length of the Savoy restaurant, all crystal and silver, Meriel was regarding us both with dark, unfathomable eyes.

7

I half expected Lawrence to appear at the Savoy again next day, but when I returned from morning worship at Westminster, I found instead a note saying he had gone about the business Charles had assigned him. I was quite surprisingly disappointed, but I spent a most pleasant day, making the excursion to Kew Gardens as I had planned. An invitation arrived by messenger inviting me to dine with one of the titled families I had met while at the gallery tea, and through the following week other invitations—to luncheons, concerts, theater—poured in.

I felt a bit guilty having such a splendid time while Charles missed all the glitter, the triumphs, the admiration of his work that went so gratifyingly beyond mere flattery. How wonderful it would have been to share these moments with him—but as I could not, I stored up treasures to take back to him in my memory and in my journal.

Lawrence telegraphed, saying he would return from his research by way of London and drive me home, an offer I most gratefully accepted. He arrived on Saturday in midmorning, to find me surrounded not just by luggage but by bouquets, purchases, mementos I was taking home to Charles.

Lawrence laughed. "Are you surfeited with society as yet, or am I rescuing you from incipient addiction?"

I shook my head. "It has been glorious, but I'm looking forward to getting back to reality, and work."

"Then we'd best be off. It looks as though there are showers brewing, and I'd like to cover as many miles as possible before they break." Lawrence loaded articles into the tonneau, seated Rose beside them and me by him, and we set off through a London already feeling a faint gray dampness in the atmosphere.

"How did your research fare?"

"Equivocally. In this business, one so often seems to be playing fox and hounds."

"Charles's proof exists," I said. "It must; there is that record of the twelfth-century discovery and the reinterment of Arthur's coffin."

"There is a record that a monk of that period *said* it happened. But did it really? Or more accurately, *was* the body Arthur's? That tomb-cover, you know, which was sketched in the monk's record, was definitely in the style of the eighth century, not the fifth."

"Charles says it was placed there then by the abbey builders, either to replace an earlier one or to record what hitherto had been of common knowledge."

"Charles has a habit of believing whatever he wants terribly to be true. He's an artist, not a scientist. We'd better stop and put the curtains up. That rainstorm's going to hit."

Within minutes the heavens opened. Sheets of water battered at the canvas roof. The road was deserted, save for an occasional farm wagon, its driver hunched inside cap and mackintosh. I had never been in an automobile during a storm before. The miles fell behind us, the celluloid windows in the side curtains became opaque and dripping, but the car itself was dry. Damp drafts touched my face and throat with clammy fingers.

"There's a lap rug in the back if you can reach it." Lawrence's voice was muffled by the slapping rain. I dragged at the plaid throw and wrapped it round me, grateful for the comfort of the Scottish mohair. The English climate, in this summer downpour, made it feel like March.

We stopped outside Woking for bread and cheese; stopped again near Warminster for a cottage tea. We had expected to reach Avalon long since, but our progress was slowed by poor visibility and the condition of the flooded roads. We scarcely spoke, which might seem odd after the way words had flowed between us that night at the Savoy. But today we were wrapped in the companionable stillness of separate solitude. In the back seat Rose was quiet, drowsing. My mind wandered over the events of the past week, and I thought of Charles.

We reached Avalon in a preternaturally early twilight. "I hope Charles has a fire going," Lawrence said. But he did not. The Great Hall, its gas jets yet unlit, was like an echoing cave. Charles had given up waiting tea for us, Hodge said; he was engaged in important work, and would see us at the dinner table. I went straight to my room, where Rose soon was bustling round, ordering tea, and a fire on my bedroom hearth; drawing my bath.

"Like to give them a piece of my mind, I would, ma'am dear." Rose tossed her head. "Not a fitting reception for the lady of the house, it isn't."

I laughed. "They're still not accustomed to there being a lady of the house, that's all." I soaked luxuriously in the scented tub, sipped my tea, sorted eagerly over the hoard of news and memories I had brought back for Charles, wondering which ones first to share. He would be as eager to hear them all as I was to tell them.

Rose laced me into the aquamarine silk gown I had worn to the Duchess of Manchester's dinner; Charles, I knew, would want to see me in it. The color picked up magnificently the depths of the flashing opal, and as I fastened golden earbobs in my ears I could feel my heart rising in excitement. London had been splendid, but it was here in Avalon that I would be reunited with my love. It seemed inconceivable to me, now, that I had stayed away from Charles a whole week long.

I ran down the stairs, my skirts rustling over their lining of taffeta petticoat. The firepit blazed, the gas jets flamed, and there in the midst of the medieval aura, Charles was waiting. I ran into his arms.

"Lydian, my dear!" He held me tightly, so tightly that I almost could not breathe. "You were much delayed. I expected you hours earlier."

"Lawrence drove me down, and we got caught in a rainstorm."

"Yes, so I understand. It must have been difficult, too, for you to tear yourself away from the gaieties of the London season."

I looked at him, bewildered. "Charles! I was in London only because you wished me there!"

His face underwent one of those now-familiar transformations. "Love, forgive me. It has been hell on earth without you, do you know that?"

He was very tense; with my arms around him I could feel that, and a flicker of fear ran through me. I had not realized until this moment how much I had taken for granted that once the gallery show had opened, once the book was published with all the attendant furor and recognition, the stress and pressure I had been so conscious of in Avalon this past month would be gone. But I knew, even as I held my husband close—was carried along on his surge of excitement to a festival dinner on the dais—that it had been false hope. The atmosphere in walled Avalon was the same.

No, not the same. Something had subtly altered, emphasis shifted. Afterwards, try as I might, I could not quite put my finger on what specifically occurred. Yet, as in a dream only gradually remembered, individual moments, significant in retrospect, became sharply clear.

We had champagne. "To your triumphs," Lawrence said, lifting his glass toward Charles. But Charles cut in sharply, almost brushing him away. "No, no—that is finished; we must look ahead! To life! *Quondam et futurus!*"

"Tell me what happened in London!" Charles demanded. Lawrence and I both began to talk at once. Looked at each other; laughed.

"You first," Lawrence said, eyes twinkling.

I drew a deep breath. "I don't know where to start, there was so much— Oh, Charles, you would have been so proud! Everyone at the luncheon was so disappointed that you could not come. There were such splendid comments on your book. The Duchess of Manchester said you shamed them all into recognition of their blindness to the national treasure Glastonbury represented. And the *Times*—"

"Yes, of course. They always drivel and slaver in ignorance, but it is of no real account. A prophet is never truly honored in his own country. I have been down in the tunnel; you have not progressed nearly as rapidly as I had expected. You must not stop to sort so carefully, that can come later. Concentrate upon the excavation! Time is running out. We must find that passage to Glastonbury soon!"

We never got a chance, either of us, to speak one more word of all that we had seen and heard in London.

Charles had the stage. I was accustomed to that and usually loved it, for his excited words fired my imagination and summoned his fascinating visions for my sharing. Tonight it was I who had so much to share with him, and he would not listen. Something that had been waiting within me, trembling on the brink of life, remained stillborn.

I asked Charles how the manuscript on women in Celtic myth was coming, and he gazed at me blankly for a moment, then launched into a convoluted dissertation on a totally different book idea. "Lydian, if we commence on it directly tomorrow morning, I should be able to complete it in time for distribution at the symposium in September. I shall have to pressure the publishers to rush it into print. They will say it is impossible, but they shall have to understand."

"I thought publishers preferred a greater time lapse between author's books," Lawrence said drily, and Charles looked affronted.

"It is not their preference which is the issue here. Do you realize, nothing significant has been published for the scholarly community on the link between the historic Arthur, the Arthur of the romances and the much earlier Celtic myths which are embodied in them both? There is importance in the fact that accretion progresses backwards as well as forwards. A whole new path of exploration has opened to me, like a flash of light. Stearns, you understand now it is absolutely imperative that we discover the coffin of King Arthur in time for me to disclose my revelations in the fall."

"The tomb of the man who may have been an Arthur figure," Lawrence corrected temperately.

Charles's eyes flashed. "The tomb of Arthur! I have had done with the chains of skepticism. 'A firm persuasion that a thing is so, makes it so . . . all poets believe that, and in ages of imagination this firm persuasion removed mountains.' Lydian, my dear, I am much indebted to you for discovering Blake! I have neglected him, but in your absence I have read your volume through, and he speaks much matter."

Lawrence's brow lifted. "Wasn't Blake that painter who had such mystic visions he was frequently considered to be insane?"

Charles was impatient. "He lived in altered reality, yes. But is not altered reality precisely what we are seeking when we prove a link between King Arthur and the Sidh? There are more things on heaven and earth than this world dreams of, as Shakespeare says, and you need not always be so devilishly scientific."

"But the September meeting is a scientific symposium." The words slipped from me involuntarily. I realized too late that Charles was truly angry.

"I should have thought you of all persons would understand, with your combined heritage of poetry and classics! Did you not know there were trade routes in the Bronze Age between the West of England and your father's own Mycenae? Has it never occurred to you to wonder whence came those elements in the Greek pantheon that dealt with the supplanted Titans, the parents of the race? Cronus; Atlas, incarcerated in a primordial Atlantic world—in a deathless sleep, reincarnated in the fifth century as Arthur, who will in time be reincarnated again!"

Lawrence, unfortunately, laughed. "There you are hoist on the petard of two conflicting myths. If Arthur sleeps forever and will one day again emerge, how then could his quite-dead corpse have been buried at Glastonbury, and how can we find it?"

"You scientists persist in examining everything with narrow minds! Those conflicts only developed in the Middle Ages, precisely when a rigid scholasticism refused to accept non-rational proofs. Why is the reappearance of an Arthur dependent on the preservation of his *physical* body? The most respected intellectuals of the ancient East believed in the possibility of spiritual reincarnation!"

Lawrence's eyes met mine across the table.

Charles went on and on, quaffing champagne, sending Doff to his room to fetch the volume of Blake's poetry, reading whole sections of the work aloud, his voice echoing magnificently through the Great Hall. It was a spellbinding, bravura performance, but Charles was vibrating like a violin string; and I sensed that something had gone askew, like the Glastonbury landscape that at first glance was so serenely ordered, but which time revealed to contain subtle, almost metaphysical distortion. In the week that I had been away, the thrust of Charles's obsession had shifted from proving that a literal Arthur once existed, to an area far beyond. I did not understand what was happening, only that there was an element now in Avalon which was disturbing.

Both Lawrence and I ceased trying to participate in the conversation—because there was no chance, because we could tell our efforts in that direction were displeasing. Charles wanted an audience, not collaborators. By the time we left the table I felt drained.

I went to kiss my husband good night, but he would not let me go. "The night is young; I could not possibly sleep! You did not used to steal away so early!" So we sat very late beside the firepit. Lawrence was allowed to leave presently, but I was not. Doff hovered intermittently in the shadows as Charles held my hands and expanded in poetic flights on his new reincarnation vision. He thought that he was making himself clearer; I could not tell him he was growing ever more obscure.

I did not like to tell him, either, that he was drinking too much brandy. But Doff finally did, and Charles actually struck him across the cheek. "How dare you take it upon yourself to dictate to me? Am I the master here, or you? Do not presume to consider yourself my keeper, or you will find your services no more required!"

It was brandy and tension saying that, I knew, not Charles. Doff knew it too, but for a moment a look of such naked rejected love crossed his face that my heart ached for him.

When at last I went to bed, contrary to my expectation, I fell

113

asleep at once. My brain was filled with vague disturbing dreams but I remembered none when I awoke to a gray morning and Rose hovering with a tray of tea.

"Good morning, Rose. Another rainy day, I see."

"The rose garden's fair drowned. How is his lordship feeling?"

Non sequiturs were not Rose's usual conversational style. I looked at her sharply, my memories of last night all returning. "Why do you ask? Rose, if there is something that I ought to know, you had better tell me."

Rose's words came in a rush. "Mr. Hodge says I mustn't repeat what's said below stairs, but you've a right to— Oh, ma'am dear, his lordship had a dreadful turn while you were gone, and he's given orders that we're not to tell you."

I sat up quickly. "I knew I ought not to have gone to London. He had worked too hard—"

Rose shook her head. "It weren't the usual, that's what was said. There was a fair—over in Street—and his lordship gave everyone leave to go, including Mr. Doffman. And while he was out, his lordship—I don't understand it quite, but he was in the cellars all by himself, and he was taken all queer, the same as you. It was only Mr. Doffman, coming back unexpected and working over him for hours, that saved him."

"Rose!"

She nodded slowly. "And after that he had an awful spell, thrashing and fever—they could hear him through the night, they said, and it was bad enough Mr. Doff actually sent for a doctor."

That distressed me, knowing Doff and my husband's sentiments about the medical profession.

"All's well now," Rose said hastily, as she saw my face. "The doctor got the fever down, and he's given his lordship some draught to calm his nerves."

I wondered if the medicine could have accounted last night for Charles's overexhilarated condition. But the thought was driven out by another memory, tolling insistently and with foreboding. Lawrence's voice, saying there was nothing wrong with the gas system in the cellars—either before my accident or now. Lawrence's voice, suggesting deliberate tampering.

I had been wrong. Charles ought to have been told at once that there was danger. In my urge to protect him I had exposed him to a greater harm. Who would have thought, I tried to tell myself, that *Charles* would attempt to go into that tunnel all alone? But I ought to have remembered that to Charles nothing he wanted was impossible.

I went down to breakfast, hoping I would get a chance to speak to Lawrence privately, but he did not appear. I was just finishing my second cup of coffee when I heard voices, raised and heated, emanating from the chamber next door which Charles used as an office.

Charles was ripping Lawrence to shreds for criminal incompetence in the matter of the gas lines. I ran over and, contrary to my usual respect for Charles's privacy, did not pause to knock. So heated was their argument that they did not even hear me.

"—assured me it was absolutely safe! If you have no regard for your own safety in the tunnel, you might have thought about my wife's! Or mine! I gave instructions that attending to that leak was of primary importance, and you told me you had done so!"

"I told you," Lawrence said evenly, "that you ought to get proper workmen down there. Not that they would have made any difference. I'll stake my life on it there was nothing faulty in that system—either before Lydian's accident, or now!"

"Then how do you account for the two of us being almost fatally overcome?"

"Tell him," I said steadily.

Lawrence looked at me, and Charles's eyes flashed from one of us to the other. "Tell me what?"

"Charles, I am sorry. Lydian was loath to have you troubled when you were working so hard on the exhibition, and I agreed. What happened to her that day in the tunnel was no accident."

"What did you say?"

"I'm saying the gas flame could not have gone out, the gas then begin leaking, of its own accord. Someone arranged that when work was going on in the tunnel—the only time the vault door would be unlocked—whoever was in there would be . . . temporarily overcome. Just long enough, I should imagine, for the artifacts to be removed to a waiting van. Each time, apparently, the conspirators were frightened off by a rescuer's unexpected appearance."

If we had hoped to divert Charles from his harangue about Lawrence's carelessness, we had succeeded. Charles's face went a mottled gray, and when he spoke, quietly, it was mostly to himself. "I was right, then. It is not—chance fate that is unrolling, but a definite pattern. Only how—we have been so careful, taken all precautions so that no one knew of the treasures that were here."

Lawrence pulled a newspaper from his pocket, flung it on the table. "Have either of you seen Tuesday's *Express*? No more had I, until late last night when I tried to catch up with the accumulated post."

The article, splashed across two pages and illustrated with imaginative art, purported to be an exposé of the fabulous treasure hoard secreted by the mysterious Lord Charles Ransome in his West Country hideout. There were references to the fact that Lady Ransome and the archaeologist Lawrence Stearns were up in London, leaving Lord Charles alone with his treasure and a skeletal staff. There was mention of the fact that "according to his American wife, many of the priceless artifacts which figure in Lord Charles's Arthurian cycle paintings are pieces from his personal collection."

"Oh, no," I said slowly. "Oh, Charles, I'm sorry. I did not realize that to have this known would cause you danger."

Charles's face was rigid with a kind of bleak despair. "It has come at last. I have known for years the Fates were pursuing me, and the net now tightens."

"Lawrence said there had been earlier robbery attempts. Oh, darling, I know how you feel about your privacy, but you must see we need to call in the police!"

He looked at me then as if suddenly remembering my existence. "No. I will deal with this myself. We have had enough publicity. I need time. If I can just hold them off until after the symposium—"

He was speaking quite calmly, but I saw a shudder run through him, and he closed his eyes.

"Charles," I said carefully, "if you do know who is responsible, will you not at least tell me?"

"Especially not you. I will not have you placed in further danger." He smiled, and took my hand, but his grip betrayed the tension he did not wish to have me know. "You must not worry. I am accustomed to facing the consequences of my own actions." His voice obeyed his will to charm, but his eyes were bleak, and a sigh escaped him. "Three months to the symposium. If I can just succeed by then, I will not even care."

Care about what, I wanted to cry out, but Lawrence's face signaled me to silence. Charles, with an abrupt effort, made a switch of subject. We had no time to lose. Lawrence must proceed at once on the tunnel excavation, pressing on toward the abbey grounds, which they calculated were now not many yards away. I was to begin immediately helping Charles organize the outline for the book he had just formulated. He had made notes; put markers in reference books. That driven intensity began to spiral in him again, and I dared not oppose it.

I sat dutifully at my husband's side all that gray day, listening, refraining from comments he obviously did not want to hear. And as I listened, my apprehension grew. What has happened here? my heart demanded. That dazzling feat of scholarship, that paradoxical union of poetry and science I had so admired in Charles, was gone. I listened with Ason's ears, and was appalled. Charles's mind was leaping from peak to peak, making dizzying metaphysical conclusions, skirting rational fallacies with Olympian unconcern. Once I attempted, tactfully, to suggest that some of his theses needed more buttressing of fact, and he brushed my interruption aside as my father would have. I was ignorant of the esoteric disciplines he now pursued; I ought not to argue until I had more comprehension.

Charles was building up a book of what he meant to be hard fact, exactly as if he were creating a work of fiction.

I longed to talk to Lawrence, but I got no chance, either that endless day or in the days that followed. Lawrence was working steadily in the tunnel. Charles kept me constantly by his side. He wanted me always handy with a note pad; he would be seized with inspirations for convoluted passages at any moment.

He wanted me, not as colleague, but as sounding-board and mirror, reflecting back magnified images of his own ideas and voice. I was useful to him as a hand to hold, a presence to assure him, and I was glad I could give that much relief from the dogged drive that consumed him. But I might, I thought, have been just anyone. The person that was Lydian Ransome was not wanted there at all.

So the week passed. Doff hovered blackly, showing he held me responsible for Charles's excitation. If Charles was driving Lawrence and me to the edges of our strength, he drove himself even harder, racing as against some unidentifiable doom. He seemed ever brighter, imbued with a frantic energy, and it was only on rare instances that he allowed his guard to slip and I could see visible signs of his desperate tiredness. Nonetheless, he would lock himself into his studio and paint until far into the night. Whenever he emerged—at ten, or twelve, or two—he would expect to find me waiting by the fire.

"Why must you paint now?" I could not help asking. "The show has opened, to a great success. After you work so hard on the book all day, why do you not rest?"

"Painting is my rest. That, and you now. But if I came straight from book to here, my brain would still be racing in tangled circles."

Charles's hand shook as he reached for the brandy he had bid me pour, and my heart ached.

"Ought you drink that? If you have been taking medicine—"

"I am quite capable of judging for myself what is proper for me to consume! Are you my wife, or do you too aspire to be my keeper?"

After that I held my tongue. In his present state, there seemed but two ways I could help him—following dutifully where he led in research and book discussion, and trying to make for him a circle of quiet by the fire. It was exhausting, it was draining, it demanded all my powers of concentration and suspended judgment.

More and more, Charles was becoming obsessed by metaphysical theories linking Glastonbury and King Arthur to legends of an earlier, superhuman culture in some remote golden age. He spoke of the Sidh as though they were real. He was even dipping into astrology and the occult, playing with old notions that all the primordial "sacred places" were linked by some obscure line not only of geography but of psychic energy. Charles was convinced he could find significant geologic evidence to back up these claims, and began sending Lawrence all over the West Country, under strict oaths of secrecy, with surveyor's instruments and microscopes.

Despite his avoidance of the police, the matter of the attempted robberies—if that was what in truth they were—was much on his mind. He began making vague references to an unnamed person, enemy or rival, who was determined not to allow his quest for Arthur to succeed. These allusions, coming as they did out of the blue while Charles was dictating, startled and alarmed me. Charles sounded more like the beleaguered King Arthur in his later days than like a scholar preparing to propound a scientific theory, and I was frightened that the pressure and the pain were becoming too much for him to bear.

"Declare a holiday for the weekend, can't you, please?" I begged him. "The summer is so wonderful, and you've seen none of it. We could pack a picnic, and motor to the sea."

Charles shook his head. "There is no time to lose. If I drive myself, I can complete this manuscript in a few more weeks. By then, if that tunnel passage does lead to Glastonbury, we should know it. August then can be spent correlating arguments for the symposium. If I am not prevented from that labor."

"What could prevent it? Charles, do you believe those—accidents were a deliberate attempt to hinder you?" I leaned forward. "Dear, I implore you, go to the police! At least they could tell you whether there are grounds for your suspicions, and protect you!"

And if that worry was lifted from his mind, I thought, he might be able to approach his work more rationally. But I could not say that, and Charles shook his head.

"There are some things against which there is no protection. And private matters which I cannot trust to His Majesty's public servants' bovine efforts. 'If it be not now, yet it will come; the readiness is all.' " After a moment he dragged himself away from his inner vision and gave me a parody of his old smile. "My lovely Lydian. You must not worry. For you, at least, all will be well. I at least have this: the surety of your carrying on my work."

And I ached that he no longer could draw from me the bright optimism which had illumined him before.

So it went, those periods of driven, feverish intensity punctuated with what was even worse for him, those moments in a cold hell of bleak despair. We were all of us—Charles, myself, Lawrence, even Doff—swept along like a motor-car careening barely within control on the brink of an unguarded precipice.

On Saturday night, at dinner, Charles appeared almost brittle with excitement. He had spent the afternoon poring over photographs of Tintagel with a magnifying glass and was persuaded that the patterning of stonework showed Cretan influence, thus linking Arthur's legendary birthplace with the Minoan culture via the Mycenaeans.

"If we can verify this, we then have proof of cross-cultural influences which would account for the classical Titan, the ultimate Celtic hero-god and the Dark Ages British king being one and the same." This would indeed have been a significant scholarly contribution to the history of myth, if Charles had only stopped there. But he went far beyond. "I am convinced there is some abstruse linkage of unseen psychic power in the way sites of ancient importance all align. Early man was aware of this power; harnessed it by erecting his temples at significant points. That is, of course, the secret of Glastonbury's magic, and if it proves possible to demonstrate such intersection of all the places sacred to the ancient Arthur— Lawrence, you must motor to Tintagel, make photographs and careful measurements."

Lawrence was as disturbed as I at the way Charles's current research kept veering off onto so many different tracks. "You said you wanted me to concentrate on clearing the tunnel as rapidly as possible."

"I want both; can you not understand? Why must you work so slowly!" Charles's temper flared. "Surely you can motor to Tintagel, complete your task there in a single day. It is not so far!"

Tintagel, Ygraine's fortress-castle by the sea . . . a more alluring prospect, this hot July day, than the thought of endless hours shut in with papers or tunneling underground. Lawrence must have seen the involuntary longing in my face. "I will tell you what. Lydian can come with me; she can look for your cross-cultural verification and make notes while I survey and photograph. That will complete the job in half the time."

I was unprepared for the violence of Charles's reaction. "Why would you take her from my side? Can you not understand my own work suffers if she is not here? I will not have her going to Tintagel!"

He had gone incredibly white and rigid, and the pulse was throbbing dangerously at the corner of his eye. I put my hand over his quickly. "Darling, do not take on! I'm sure Lawrence only thought that I could be of help—"

"You are not thinking of helping *me* or you would not defend his thoughtlessness! You have lied to me; you are not truly dedicated to my work at all. You care only for yourselves, and I have the added burden of the lonely quest. I had thought there was an end to loneliness, but I was wrong—everyone is against me, even you— Oh, God, God, God—"

The pain was hitting; Charles stiffened against it, his face contorted. Doff, screaming at us that the damage was done and we must go. Lawrence, gripping my arms to hold me back. "You must not allow yourself to listen! Do you understand? Let Doff handle it; I'll see that he's all right. Sit and finish dinner."

"I could not—"

"Then go up to your room. Read. Write. But you must not let yourself be infected by this subtle poison. Charles will regret it when he feels well. Go upstairs; I'll tell Hodge to send you up some coffee."

He left me, then, and I obeyed. But far into that disquieting night, as I sat writing at my window table, I could see light flowing through the skylight in Charles's studio. That meant the pain was gone, and he was painting. Or he was painting all the same, to surmount pain, even as I wrote to drain out my disturbing thoughts. Either way, the cost upon him was too great.

I awoke next morning early and, on impulse, dressed and went to early communion at the village church. The air was fresh, with only a faint hint of the heat to come. Gardens were alive with flowers, and birds were singing. I walked, after service, past the great closed gates of the abbey ruins, remembering our wedding dawn, wondering what had happened to all our hopeful joy. I loved as deeply now as I had then; I knew, without need for question, that for Charles it was the same. But something was happening, like blight upon apple trees which in their springtime flowering had shone so fair. I am failing Charles, I thought. Whatever daemons drive him to this self-consuming passion for work or to this malady of despair, he had married me to save him from them. And now, however great our love, it seemed the more I tried to give, the less I was useful.

I went home, almost dreading the silent tension of the shadowy house, and found the windows thrown wide and sunlight streaming in. Charles was at the breakfast table, in his summer suit of pale cream linen, his gold hair gleaming, turning to my apprehensive gaze a quiet smile.

"My dear, I owe you a most profound apology." His face was haggard but composed, and his eyes were again the eyes of my dear love. I went toward him as he held out his hands and took mine in them. "My behavior last night, I understand, was inexcusable. I can only hope that in your great mercy you will recognize it was the illness speaking, and not I. Of course you must go to Tintagel; it is far and away the most sensible arrangement."

"I would not think of it. You need me here."

Charles lifted my fingers to his lips, but his eyes were firm. "No. My mind is set now. You are to go to Tintagel."

It almost seemed as if he was compelled to it by some threatening fate.

So we went to Tintagel, Lawrence and I, riding out from the battlements of Avalon into the loveliness of the English summer. The sky was of that limitless blue one finds in Italian paintings, and the sun glowed golden. The canvas roof and curtains that had enclosed us on our journey home from London were down, and the air trailed caressingly against my skin.

Part of me wished with such passion that Charles could have been here to experience this healing joy. Part of me, God help me, was glad I had this momentary escape from the tension. I loved Charles so much, but I needed, right now, to be separate, to re-establish my perspective.

As the town fell behind us, I felt as though a heavy cloak were dropping from my shoulders. I was in sunlight, free from pressing responsibilities, and the memory of the conversation Lawrence and I had had at the Savoy was like champagne within me.

I leaned back in the seat and took a deep breath; Lawrence grinned.

"You're happy, aren't you?"

"Yes!" I laughed aloud, startled at the pure astonishment of my own words. Lawrence started to say something, looked at me, and did not speak. Instead, unexpectedly, he tilted his head back and began to sing.

> "*Alas, my liege, you do me wrong*
> *To cast me off discourteously . . .*"

He had a magnificent baritone voice. Also surprisingly, he began to improvise mischievously with the tune. I forbore heroically for the length of the first verse, then found myself joining in the chorus:

> "*Greensleeves is all my joy,*
> *Greensleeves is my delight . . .*"

"An appropriate theme song for you, that one," Lawrence said. "Makes me think of that velvet confection you trail about in on some evenings."

"Don't speak of that. Please. Do you know this madrigal?" I took up what I could remember and he followed, our voices interweaving a pattern of melody as we left Somerset and penetrated deep into the Dorset moors.

"Where are we?" I said suddenly.

"On the main moor road, heading down toward Bodmin. I thought since you're here we'd make a proper exploration, and you can have a look at Dozmary Pool and Camelford."

"Ah, yes. The possible Camelot."

"Highly unlikely, if you ask my opinion. If Arthur *was* a *dux bellorum*, a leader of combined British troops against the Saxons, his battles were more likely fought close to the Somerset area than on the southwest peninsula. You're familiar with John Leland's account of 1542, of course? 'At South Cadbyri standith Camallate, sumtyme a famous toun or castelle. The people can tell nothing but that they have hard say that Arture much resorted to Camallate.' "

His dropping into the old country speech made me dissolve again in laughter.

"You should laugh more often. It becomes you. At any rate, Camelford is a pleasant enough place to see, and near Tintagel."

"And Dozmary?"

"Leading contender for the dwelling place of Scott's Lady of the Lake, who received the sword Excalibur from Sir Bedivere's hands at the request of the dying Arthur. Dozmary was considered bottomless until it confounded the natives by drying up completely in 1859."

"And no sword found therein," I added drily.

"No sword found. Not that that would discourage determined believers of your husband's ilk. There's also Loe Pool, of course, which has supporters. The description given in Tennyson's 'Morte d'Arthur' fits Loe exactly. But Dozmary seems likely, and has much magic."

"That's a remark more poetic than scientific."

"There's poetry to science, for those who have the wits to see. Science, too, is in the business of making form from chaos. We're into Dartmoor now. Do you remember the Hound of the Baskervilles?"

Three times within the hour we had trespassed onto the edge of private hauntings, and had shied away. It was as if we had made a mutual convenant of silence.

I had heard the phrase "automobile elation," but had never experienced it, having had so little resort to motorcars. Now, however, I found myself responding to the blowing air, the smooth and steady motion, much as my body had responded to a similar rhythm on the deck of the transatlantic liner. But how different now, I thought, for then Ason had been there, exercising upon me, even though I had not recognized it, an omnipresent chill. Here in the auto, in the summer sun, my hair pulling loose beneath the veil-tied Panama, my bare arm beneath its somewhat daring elbow-sleeve occasionally being brushed by Lawrence's, I felt another emotion altogether.

Now it was I who began to sing, and he responded. We ran through the repertoire of my schoolgirl music training. The road spun out before us like a shining ribbon, punctuated here and there by wild ponies, blinking at us unafraid. On either side rolled the moorlands, down into valleys, up over quiet hills.

"This is so unlike what I expected," I exclaimed spontaneously.

"In what way?"

I gestured, incoherent. "No terror, no grayness, no wild winds or fog."

"You should see it in the winter. There are legends enough and to spare of houses appearing and disappearing, of persons long dead who've been seen to walk. No Dorset man, however stalwart, would cross these moors alone at night."

"But it's so serene." I contemplated with quiet pleasure the patchwork greens, fringed occasionally with bands of trees; the stone cottages hidden in the folds of hills; the grazing sheep, the luminous golds and purples of gorse and heather. I heard myself saying, somewhat to my own surprise, "It makes me think of home."

Lawrence did not question, only gave me an intelligent, sympathetic glance.

"There is a road like this, along the crest of a ridge that runs down Cape Cod. No tin-mine hills nor peat bogs, but there are sand dunes higher than one's head. And beach plums, and wild grapes, and cranberry bogs. It has this same ambiance, a wild, sweet peace . . . Once, when I was young, we went there. Whatever possessed my father, I do not know, but I still remember it as a good time. I think he almost liked me, then."

I had not meant to say that; I was very grateful Lawrence did not reply. I stared off across the emerald landscape and thought back. I had been eleven that summer; it had been the year before I had found my mother's book and picture, and the dreams began.

Why was I thinking of that now? Ason was gone, and I a woman grown. And wed; and doing important work; the old insecurities were forever put to rest.

Charles had sounded much like Ason the other night when he had lashed out so irrationally. It had been his illness speaking; he himself had said so. There was no reason for me to feel this sudden chill. Nonetheless a cloud had passed across the sun.

"I think," Lawrence said, his voice carefully commonplace, "it would be wise to stop soon for lunch. Are you New Woman enough to dine with me in a tavern, or must we observe proprieties?"

"I'm child enough to think it would be more fun to picnic. Don't laugh; I'm perishing to go for a run across those fields!"

Lawrence did laugh, though, and I with him. "Very well. There's an old coaching inn near Bolventor where we can buy bread and cheese, and then we can pull off and let you run back through time to your lost youth. You'll have to be careful, though; there are quicksands in those moors."

"I don't think I ever had a youth."

It was happening again; the guard had fallen from my tongue and I was speaking naturally, things I normally would never say, would scarcely even think.

The sun was high. Far off on either side, beyond the shimmering sheets of golden gorse, loomed the raw hills—Brown Gelly, Kilmar Tor, Brown Willy. Here and there on the rolling moorland rose green, tree-circled mounds and rings of stones. Now and again, by the side of the road, had been raised a rock mound or a Celtic cross.

We soon came to a gray inn, long and bleak. Lawrence said, "This was supposed to have been a stopping-place for highwaymen in the old days, but we'll see if we can't get some bread and cheese here."

He went inside and soon emerged with bread, cheese and a jug of cider. "Do you want to stay here or shall we go into the moors? There's a path across the road leading toward Brown Willy, and perhaps we can find a patch of shade."

"The moors, by all means."

He offered me his arm and I took it gladly, for the ground beneath our feet was treacherous with pit holes and boggy patches. We found a table rock surrounded by cushioning heather, and spread out our lunch. I opened my parasol; took off my hat to smooth the hair that had fallen, damp with heat. The boned collar of my tucked lawn shirtwaist was like armor round my throat, and I longed for the flowing comfort of the medieval robes I was becoming accustomed to wearing at Avalon.

Avalon.

A stillness had fallen upon me that I could not shake off.

"It's time, isn't it?" Lawrence said. "We have to talk. It's been behind our songs all day. Shall you go first, or I?"

"Lawrence, what's happening to him?" Despite the heat, there was a shivering along my spine. And my words made

Charles an invisible presence at our *fête champêtre.* "Ever since I came home from London—his ideas, his whole personality have changed so. I don't *know* him."

"We have to face the fact that organic changes are an inevitable part of his condition."

"I thought his condition, aside from those attacks when he overworks, was stable!"

"*He's* not stable," Lawrence retorted bluntly. "Oh, I don't mean he's unbalanced. But a placid, uneventful life—the kind Doff keeps trying to push on him—is a living death to Charles. He has to live on the edge of chaos, that's what feeds his soul. *And* destroys his body. It brings on the fever; all the moving round he insists on causes more bruises and *that* means more gangrene. There's always the danger that one day it cannot be controlled. I wish to God he'd get over this imbecilic aversion to doctors and go up to a London hospital for a thorough checkup. The medical profession has to have made some progress in twenty years. Then at least one would know—"

"Know what? What do you think is happening to him? Lawrence!"

When he answered me, it was indirectly. "There are any number of hidden pitfalls for someone with Charles's combination of disabilities and temperament. Doff's quite right in saying he drives himself too hard, that these peaks and valleys of emotion are a danger for him. He could die at any time, and knows it. That's why he's so determined on this symposium in the fall; determined to carve out his niche of immortality before it's too late. But what happens if he drives himself for nothing?"

That was the very thought which had been haunting me.

I said abruptly, "I have such a strange feeling . . . it's as if he's driving himself to his own defeat. All these occult theories —they're *not* calculated to gain him respect in the scientific community, and we all know it. Yet he persists. It's as if he's forgotten the historical, the real Arthur who lived and died. He's really looking for the immortal who sleeps until the future golden age."

Lawrence was cutting cheese and did not look up as he spoke. "Has it occurred to you he's trying to ensure the immortality, not of the once and future Arthur, but of the once and future Charles?"

A chill ran through me.

"He's had a few bad scares. Your coming gave Charles both a will to live and an awareness of impending death. I don't think he can bear the thought of separation from you, so he drives himself."

"And this new change—"

"I think now it is more important to him that his soul lives on; he cares less about the future of his work."

"I'm all in a muddle . . . I don't know how to act toward him; I don't know what he needs." I caught, with something like relief, at the one thing that was hard fact. "This business of the gas being tampered with—"

"That should and can be handled. It's ridiculous, considering the worth of Avalon's treasures, that there are no guards. I'll confront him with it, and if he balks I'll see to it myself without his knowing."

"Can you?" I asked, and he nodded.

"I have *carte blanche* for any expenditures necessitated by research, and Charles rarely checks the books. I can easily conceal the salaries under some other heading."

"Lawrence, why is he so against the whole idea of guards?"

When Lawrence answered, I had a feeling he was choosing his words carefully. "Perhaps he fears that they would see too much. Or perhaps he already knows from what source the danger comes. He does make references to enemies, you know."

"But you surely don't believe—" I stopped. It felt disloyal to say, as I'd been about to, that this had seemed to me but part and parcel of Charles's imagination.

Imagination. Delusions. Irrationality. Those thoughts had been ever-present in my brain these past weeks, even though I had not spoken of them. My mind sheered away from the precipice toward which they led me.

"Haven't you noticed," Lawrence said, watching me, "that for all his talking, there are whole chapters in Charles's life which he never opens? I'd give a deal to know what history lurks within them. There could be flesh-and-blood enemies, not phantasmagoria. Have you never asked yourself why he's shut himself into a walled fortress all these years?"

"His accident."

"Or just how and where he's gotten all those hidden artifacts whose acquisition he dazzlingly glosses over?" Lawrence hesitated, then went on firmly. "Lydian, I have no proof; I simply know that, under our current laws, there is no way Charles could have legitimately purchased some of those objects on the open market."

"You mean he *stole* them?"

"Let's say he let it be known he would not be averse to acquiring them even if they should be stolen. Or entered into the transaction after the fact, but knowing full well he had no clear title. Do you think, if there's something else he has his eye on, he'd hesitate applying some sort of pressure? I strongly suspect that in Charles's mind, where artifacts are concerned, the end can frequently justify the means."

Something in me needed to deny this fiercely. "Charles wouldn't. For one thing, 'might making right' is totally contrary to the Arthurian Code."

"To the Code of the Round Table, perhaps, but not to the archetypal Celtic figure whose identity Charles now pursues."

"You mean, 'assumes,' " I said. And then there was a silence, while the implications of the word sank in. Assume—to take as being true without proof; assume—to take upon oneself. Charles Ransome believes in Arthur, *Rex Quondam, Rex Futurus*. Charles Ransome = *Rex Quondam, Rex Futurus*.

I began to shake.

"There is that other thing, isn't there?" Lawrence said. "One of the results of Charles's accident was a degenerative muscle failure. The other is those raging fevers caused by gangrene. We have to face the fact that either of those conditions can affect the brain."

Bees were buzzing in the heather; the gorse was very bright; yet for a moment something passed before my eyes that blotted out the sun. My voice, coming from me at last, was like a child's, still and high. "One of the things I so loved in Charles was his ability to make magic and yet be so sane."

"That's what we have to help him to hold on to. One way or

other. But you have got to recognize, Lydian, that you are married to a human being. Not—no matter how much you or he may want it that way—to a heroic idol."

"You did not have to say that!"

"Didn't I?" Lawrence gave me a long look. "Are you sure when you married him you weren't looking for such an idyllic king?"

Or the perfect, all-supportive father I had never had?

"It's not for myself," I said when I could speak. "Not just for myself. Charles's dreams are what he lives for; my belief in them—in him—is the one thing I had to give him, the one thing he needed. When a dream dies, and there is nothing left . . ."

"My father was a dreamer," Lawrence said slowly. "A visionary, one might say, like the besotted Blake. Hallucinatory would be more like it. He saw so clearly his great scheme for universal brotherhood and peace, all mixed up with revelations of God and the perfectibility of man. He got mixed up when he was young with the Owens group and other utopian communities, and felt it incumbent on him to sell his small holdings and travel round to preach this gospel. My mother sank gratefully into her grave after a few years, but he still dragged me with him. Reading schoolbooks in the back of a jolting wagon, living on handouts . . . but he always told me I didn't have to worry; I would have Oxford; he had the means for it safely locked away in that old chest he'd never let me touch." He laughed shortly. "He died when I was sixteen, and there was nothing in the trunk but reams of notes for the magnum opus of philosophy he'd meant to write. Oh, I got to Oxford anyway, under my own power, but I learned then to have no more faith in a golden tongue, nor in anything I could not study under a microscope or hold in my own two hands. I know what it's like when one's illusions die."

He turned round then, deliberately smiling. "You're not planning to eat any more, are you? Dozmary's a few miles off, and then we must double back toward Tintagel. Would you like to drive?"

"What did you say?"

"I suggested that you take this opportunity to learn to operate Charles's infernal machine. Come along; it's not hard, and it would be a great advantage to you." And he caught my hand,

and ran with me back along the stepping-places of the moors to where the motor-car waited in the sun of early afternoon.

Whether it had been his deliberate intent or not, Lawrence's treatment of the melancholy that had fallen over us was therapeutic. There was no chance for thinking of lost dreams while concentrating on the mechanism of engine turnover and steering bar. The dusty ribbon of road was deserted; I had not replaced my hat, and the breeze tugged at my hair and loosed it behind me. "Turn off here," Lawrence directed presently. "Easily, slowly. Mind the hedgerows; this lane is wide enough to accommodate us, but you must not swerve." And then, "Look, now."

Before us broke the blue and brown-gray of Dozmary Pool. Lawrence was right, it was magic. So shallow was it round the edges that strands of reeds and watergrasses grew among the rocks; so clear and still that the very grains of sand upon its bottom sparkled through the depths. Far to the other side, green-gold of swampgrass rippled like a shining sea; the horizon was infinite; it almost seemed as if one could reach up overhead and touch the sky.

Involuntarily I heard myself murmuring the lines from that childhood-remembered poem.

> "... *the great brand*
> *Made lightnings in the splendour of the moon,*
> *And flashing round and round, and whirl'd in an arch,*
> *Shot like a streamer of the northern morn ...*
> *So flash'd and fell the brand Excalibur."*

" 'The old order changeth,' " Lawrence said behind me, in the same tone. And I knew that of all the revelations of this enchanted day, one of the surest was this which he would not allow himself to know: he might have made science his god, but the mark of the visionary was still upon him too.

We reached Tintagel in midafternoon, driving through towering hedgerows toward the sea. The scent of wildflowers and grasses mingled with the scent of salt, and there was a mysterious, vaguely alarming sense of otherworldliness about these closed-in lanes. But the sun glowed, and we drove on and on, as through a sea of grass, and then came out onto an open road along the seacliffs which turned inward, spiraled down into a sleeping town.

"We can have a cream tea at a cottage," Lawrence said. "You cannot visit Cornwall without sampling clotted cream." So we approached one of the small stone houses with its inevitable hand-lettered sign advertising tea, and a fresh-faced matron served us in the garden. The tea was strong, invigorating in its thick cups, and the scones with cream and jam were like ambrosia. We ate in quiet companionship, seldom speaking.

"And now," Lawrence said firmly, pulling me up at last, "we must get working. If we don't accomplish everything on that list Charles gave you, he will be most unnerved."

"We can manage, with two of us. Just tell me what to do."

We ran, somewhat breathless, down the twisting street, onto the narrow path straddling the causeway. The ruins of Tintagel —the twelfth-century castle and the much earlier monastery— crowned the sheer rocks which thrust like an island into the blue Atlantic. So high they rose, so bleak beneath the sun, so close to the endless sky that they reminded me disturbingly of photographs of Mycenae. Mycenae, where my father died.

"Come," Lawrence said, as though he read my mind, and taking my hand he led me at a quick pace up the narrow rocky steps.

"You know what Charles wants, don't you? Make as accurate notes as possible, especially of any traces of a culture earlier than the fifth century. He's a bee in his bonnet that there's a relationship to Mycenae here, and now that I look at it closer, I'm blessed if I don't believe him."

"I see it, too."

"Then be off with you. I'm going on with Charles's precious surveying, blast his eyes. I'll come up here and take photographs of your observations later."

Left alone, I wandered quietly, feeling the spell of the place envelop me. Golden sunlight sparkled on a sapphire sea. The water was as green as emeralds among the boulders, and the rock cliffs rising beside me were a strange mixture—black slate, stratified into sharp thin layers, above pale granite coppered with minerals and carpeted with velvet moss. Heather and

133

golden gorse mingled with brown grass on the sheer outcroppings, and narrow stone steps were cut into the cliff edge, leading to nowhere.

Up I went, looking and searching, making my careful notes. I was falling into the rhythm of the work, as I had in the tunnel excavation. Far way, on the opposite outcropping, I could see Lawrence bent over his surveying gear. I waved, and he straightened, waving in return.

The hills of Tintagel were crisscrossed by paths new and old, crisscrossed by rock carved by man and nature. From a distance the patches of drying heather made splotches of dark brown like dried blood. Far to my right, one rock outcropping loomed like a gargoyle's profile out of a high plateau, pointing toward the sea. Like a ship's figurehead; like a figurehead of death.

Why was I thinking like that so suddenly?

I walked on, and I realized gradually that a strange thing was happening. My eyes kept being pulled from my work to gaze over the precipice toward the waves crashing far below. I was having difficulty breathing, and I realized that this was ridiculous; I could not blame a shortage of oxygen, the condition that had caused these symptoms in the art gallery and tunnel at Avalon. I had to confess to myself I was afraid; unnecessarily, irrationally afraid. It was all I could do not to call out to Lawrence to come join me.

He would not hear me anyway; he was working too far away, wrapped in his calculations. He would laugh, and rightly so. I sat down on a ledge of rock, turned to a blank page in the back of my record book, and jotted down some thoughts to be transferred to my journal to calm my nerves. A cool breeze made a dark undercurrent beneath the sunlight that wrapped me in a veil of loneliness and nameless yearning; wrapped me in a somehow macabre sense of peace.

It was absurd, yet fear kept burgeoning like some monstrous growth within me, a terror greater than any I had known before. I opened my mouth to cry out, and no sound came.

How long I sat there, thus paralyzed, I do not know. The wind rose, suddenly; the gold glow vanished. I was shaking with a genuine chill.

Lawrence appeared, running up the ancient steps. "It's getting late; there's a chance of rain, and I've not finished. Did you get over to the promontory with the gargoyle's head? Charles wanted me to inspect that, specially."

"I . . . no."

"Are you all right?" Lawrence looked at me closely. "Why don't you run back to the car?"

I wet my lips. "I'll stay." Not for the world could I confess, even to myself, that I was afraid now to cross that narrow causeway on my own. Something I could not explain exerted a dark, irresistible pull toward the edge of rocks. "Give me something to do, and we will finish sooner."

"Then come!" Lawrence grabbed my hand and pulled me after him. "That's Merlin's Cave, so-called," he flung back across his shoulder, pointing down to the yawning opening at the water's edge. "Look, you go on up to the gargoyle, will you? There are supposed to be some rock markers on the flat plateau that have megalithic symbols on them, possibly Minoan. I'm going to attempt some pictures of the cave entrance before the light fails completely."

I went doggedly, grateful for a concrete task that would discipline my mind. I could control my footsteps, but not the wracking shivers that shook my body. The path was steep and difficult to climb, and the strong wind buffeted me. I kept going, kept making the requisite notes as rapidly as I could, kept telling myself that this rising panic must be fought, that if I once surrendered to it I was lost.

But my heart was making a great hammering within me. The outline of the castle ruins on the neighboring promontory was thrown into sharp relief. The gulls cried, and the waves crashed, and the fragments of long-submerged memory came together. Suddenly, in the gathering twilight, I knew, I knew.

This was why the recurring sensations of danger and of fear as I climbed, drawn in a terror I did not understand, toward the jagged beckoning rocks in the treacherous sea. I had seen it all before, in Charles's painting and in my own nightmarish dreams. I knew, and I could have taken a blood oath upon it, that I had stood here long ago—in another time, another life— stood on the cliff-edge, paralyzed just as now, with death beside me.

"Lydian!" Lawrence's voice called sharply. And my legs could move again, and I ran . . . ran . . . as if all the hounds of hell were at my heels. I tripped on a rock; my ankle gave way beneath me and I pitched forward down the sheer side of the hill.

Strong arms held me. I clung to Lawrence, and he held me tightly, silently. Held me until my shuddering and sobbing ceased, and even longer, closer, until I could feel his own heart pounding against my bosom. I could have stayed forever thus, and that was the second truth Tintagel had revealed—a truth pointing not into a dream-shrouded past but more alarmingly, disturbingly into the future.

My eyes had been opened, and oh, his as well—we would be forced, now, to recognize what both of us had hitherto avoided. We were not only friends, and scientific colleagues; we were man and woman.

g

We drove home from Tintagel through dusk and rain, wrapped in the auto rugs. Wrapped also in our own thoughts.

"What so upset you?" Lawrence asked, when I could speak again. And I said, "Falling. It frightened me, and I was hurt and—shaken." Although I was sure he saw beyond my evasion, he said only, "Oh, I see," and for that I was grateful. I desperately needed to talk with Lawrence, but not yet. My perception of myself and of my world had been profoundly troubled, and I had to sort the pieces out before they could be shared.

We went back to Avalon, changed to dry clothes, and sat down to a very late dinner exactly as if nothing at all had happened. Nothing had changed, yet everything had changed. Or perhaps it was only that I was seeing us all with different eyes.

"Did you find what I sent you seeking?" Charles demanded, and then at once embarked on his own soliloquy, as though, again, he did not really wish to hear what we had to say. He had been working hard; there was pain in his eyes, though he strove to conceal it, and my heart ached at the gallantry of his efforts.

"Were you able to do much writing, my dear?" I asked.

"Some. My thoughts come too fast. They explode one on top of another like comets in my brain, vanishing before I can set

137

them down. If I could only find the pattern! It is there some-where, just beyond sound and sight, and I cannot grasp it." Charles looked at me and frowned. "Why are you not wearing one of your lovely flowing gowns?"

I glanced at my dinner frock, a tan lawn trimmed with em-broidered bands of golden brown. "This is part of the Bond Street trousseau you wanted me to order. A Paris model in the latest mode." In truth, having been away from Avalon today had given me something of an aversion to appearing in semi-medieval style, an uneasy sensation of having been indulging in a masquerade.

"But I like to see you robed in splendor." Charles stirred uncomfortably, then reached for my hand, pain fading to ten-derness in his eyes. "My Guinever. I long for the day you shall be that regal queen incarnate, in her own dower gifts. We must find them. We must find them soon." His tone altered, sharp-ened. "Lydian, what is the matter?"

"Charles, my dear, you must prepare for the eventuality that they may not be found."

"They *shall* be found! I have always known it, despite every-thing my enemies have done and said— Lydian, *you* can't have lost faith, have turned against me . . . not you. Not you!"

Charles was right about one thing; it was necessary for the existence of both tomb and treasure to be proved or disproved soon. How much more of tension and torture could this man take?

"No one's turned against you," Lawrence interposed with more calmness than I was capable of summoning. "We're sim-ply begging you, for your own sake, to be realistic."

"Don't speak to me of realism! That is the voice of rejected faith! If you really cared as much as you have claimed to, you would both try harder."

"Very well then," Lawrence said evenly. "Let me get more workers, trained, trusted men. And guards, if you'll not permit the police, so you need not have to deal also with the threat of danger. In a few weeks' time, you'd have your answer."

Charles's fist came down on the tabletop so hard that his glass tipped over and the dregs of wine spilled like blood. "No! No other persons! If you truly understood what I am struggling against, you would not suggest it."

"What danger?" I cried out involuntarily. "Oh, my darling, why can you not tell us? Then we would know how to help—"

But Charles's face had become closed and shuttered. "I do not wish to speak of it. I have said too much. The best way you can help is to carry on with the work, and to believe in it."

Why was that suddenly becoming so hard to do? I needed to talk to Lawrence; we had to determine how best to deal with the situation. As it was, no matter what we did—encouraged Charles in his driven pursuit of visions or warned of possible failure—we only hurt him more. I felt as if I were looking down from the balcony above, seeing us all in miniature like chess-board figures—king, queen, knight, even Doff the pawn hovering in protective animosity at Charles's back.

We were all pawns in some game we did not understand.

Why had that thought come to me from nowhere? Oh, I knew what Charles meant about images intruding like comets in one's brain, exploding and vanishing. It was happening to me more and more often lately.

We rose from the table. Lawrence excused himself, saying he wished to record his Tintagel findings properly while they were still fresh in his mind. I made to follow him into the office, but Charles caught at my hand.

"Stay with me! My love, I missed you so today. I want to read you what I've written, and you must give your judgment. But first we shall have brandy." He drew me down to my old place on the firepit ledge, and scanned my face. "You look like a weary child."

"I'm rather tired."

"You should not have gone today. It is wrong of me to let you work so hard."

"I want to help you." He looked so worn; instinctively I brushed my hand across his hair and down his cheek. "Charles, you must know that."

"I want to believe it." He caught my fingers to his lips. "How was Tintagel?"

"Very beautiful." His eyes, dark with compassion, searched

me, and suddenly I so longed to throw myself into his arms and find safe harbor; to tell him, as I had not told Lawrence, of the terror of that attack of panic and the blinding, illogical truth of having lived through it all before. He would understand; he could give me absolution. But I could not. His mind was already overburdened, and I would not add to it.

So we sat, and I strove to put all memory of Tintagel from me. I listened to Charles read what he had written, listened as he expounded on theories growing more and more occult; held back from saying, as I ached to do, that he should return to the earlier, simpler plan for his book and symposium lecture.

Stay with the historic Arthur, I longed to say. Prove there was a *dux bellorum*, a warrior leader of the fifth century buried here, and you will have done as much as Schliemann did at Mycenae and Troy. Use your gift for brilliant insight and for poetry to show that the myths need not be literally true to teach us. Let that be enough!

But I could not say it. And this was what troubled me as, hours after midnight, I dragged myself to my solitary bed: Was it truly concern for my husband's precarious balance that held me back? Or was it something more, something threatening to my own self—that sense, when I had stood at the cliff-edge, staring down as if magnetized toward the jagged rocks, of having stood thus before, in another age and time? A sense that there was in these primeval places a savage, reincarnated power beyond the ability of my rational mind to comprehend?

I finally fell asleep. Fell as it were through layers of mist, endlessly swirling. Blue-gray, blue-purple, black . . . the ceaseless, seething shadows of an Otherworld. This was what Hell was, no place of burning torment, but of coldness. Emptiness. Solitude. I wandered hopelessly, like a child lost in a loveless dark.

Then the mists separated, shaped themselves into relentless forms. I was running—not away, but toward them, drawn by a terrible, an inexorable need to know. Everything screamed at me to flee, but I was caught, held, looking on through measureless depths of space, so that I was at once both bystander and participant. A pawn, as in that waking vision I had had earlier . . . a tiny, tiny Lydian, a Guinever, a Sidh, a woman whom I both knew and did not know, moving by some unseen power across the chessboard rock plateau of Tintagel's cliffs. The stormclouds thundered, and the seagulls cried; the spray leaped high, and terror like icy fingers clutched my skull. Still I could not flee . . . Figures, other figures, lunged straight at each other, like warriors in a Dark Ages' battle. A knife flashed, arms interlocked, struggled. There was a cry. The woman that was and was not I rushed forward, and now there were three locked together as in a ritual, sacrificial dance. And the darkness hid their faces, there was a rushing wind, and then one, one only silhouetted against a purpling sky. Then nothing but the knife-sharp rocks calling and the seagulls' cry.

A voice cried out, and it was my own. I was sitting bolt upright in my bed, my body damp with fear. The curtains stirred, although there was no breeze. And there was a presence in the room. I knew it, although there was nothing to see. I wanted to cry out, *Who's there?* but my parched mouth would not obey. Trembling, I groped for the matches on my bedside table, knocked them over; the silver candle-holder crashed to the floor. Something instinctive, deep and primitive, screamed that I must get out of this room.

My faint, lingering grasp on reason told me that I was being absurd, but my heart was hammering. Like quicksilver, impelled by what power I could not say, I was at the door, my fingers fumbling with the latch. I was out in the blackness of the upper gallery, the door behind me slammed to hold back the bedroom's terrors. The Great Hall below was a yawning cavern pulling at me like the cliffs beside the sea, and panic washed over me like a cresting wave.

In that abysmal emptiness one beacon glowed, one memory, one sanctuary where I had found safe harbor. The depths of my soul flung back at me the vision of that first night at Avalon, and I plummeted toward my husband's room.

I did not even knock, just threw myself in, and shut and barred the door, sagged against it. Someone was gasping in shuddering sobs, and I did not even know at first that it was I. Then there was Charles's voice, filled with concern. "Lydian, what is it?"

"I'm afraid . . . I'm so afraid . . ."

"Come here," Charles ordered, and I flung myself down on the great bed beside him. He pulled the brocade coverlet over me and held me, like a child, so that all the terrors of the night were kept at bay.

"What was it?" Charles asked me when we waked at dawn. I wanted to pour it all out and have him soothe my fears away. But my instinct told me not to burden him with that imagined presence by my tower bed.

"The old nightmare . . . I told you once." I frowned, striving to remember.

"The same?"

"There was something more . . ." I started to tell him that the nightmare place now had a name: Tintagel; to say I knew now this was not dream only, but memory from some earlier time. But I could not.

"Best not to think of it. It will just upset you." Charles was saying exactly what I wished to hear, but a voice in my brain said no, said there was some truth which must be faced and wrestled with behind this veil of dreams. I turned my mind resolutely from that voice.

I bid Charles good morning and slipped out into the upper gallery. Morning light, filtering through the stained-glass windows high above, cast luminous jeweled colors on the parquet, and I thought how foolish had been my fantasies of the night before. Yet even as my mind laughed, a remembered chill lingered in my heart. My room was quiet and waiting, pearl-colored in the early light. Yet there was an uneasiness in the atmosphere.

I crossed to the window, stood for several moments looking out. It was possible, it would be just possible, for a person to make his way along the wall outside. The stone ledge beneath the window's edge circled the house and connected with the carved pillars that framed the entry door. It was about the width of a human foot. How easy to maintain one's balance by holding to the great branches of ivy that covered the wall . . .

I leaned out, looking left and right, and my throat tightened. There beside the window, a great vine of ivy, tree-branch thick, was loosened. Its leaves torn, crumpled as though they had borne a human weight. Charles's talk of enemies . . . I stared toward the abbey ruins, and the broken monoliths that had once been arches bore silent witness that nothing was absurd, nothing impossible; man was capable of all, even irrational violence.

The door opened; Rose entered bringing early tea. Set down the tray; sniffed, frowning; crossed to the gas fixtures on the mantel wall. "Ma'am dear, did you mean to light these during the night? Why didn't you ring?"

I gazed at her blankly. "But I didn't . . . Rose, what's wrong?"

"The handle's not tight off. Like someone started to turn on the gas and forgot to strike the match. It's just a blessing it's not open enough for much gas to come through."

"I must not have turned the gas completely out last night. It was an accident," I heard my own lips say automatically.

The broken ivy; the sense of a presence in my room. Someone could have been there, bent on mischief, and my stirring frightened him away.

"Too many accidents hereabouts, to my mind," Rose said grimly. "Isn't healthy. You ought to go back to London where there's safety, is what *I* think."

"Certainly not."

"Then I ought to sleep on the sofa in your dressing room, I ought. It's not right and proper you've no one to look after you, all alone in one wing of this big house, with none nearer than a long corridor away, and he—" She stopped abruptly. *And he a cripple*, she had been about to say.

I touched her gently. "Rose, dear, you're kind, but there's no reason for *me* to be in danger. It was only by chance I was working in the cellar that other day. There's always the possibility, of course, of robbery in any great house where there's much of value. But precautions shall be taken, and in any event such attempts would be on objects of value, not on persons."

"Then why is it it's you and his lordship that's been touched and none of that folderol downstairs?" Rose demanded stubbornly, and I could not answer.

Had something been stolen, and we had not noticed? Did Charles even have an accurate record of all that he possessed? I must find out at once, and if not, make a proper inventory. Then, at least, when the police should be called in, we would know—

When the police were called in. I had made the transition in my mind already from *if* to *when*, as though something in me knew this was not the end of trouble, but the beginning.

Rose had been right in saying life would be safer up in London. A town house there, sane, sensible, with no nooks and crannies . . . but Charles would not hear of it; he adored his Arthurian Avalon with its fabled splendors.

But Arthur had not lived at Avalon. His court was at Camelot. Avalon had been . . . my mind leaped backward through the dim pages of the myth; stopped abruptly. Why had it never struck me before? Avalon was the name of the misty isle to which the mortally wounded Arthur had gone to die. To die, or lie in suspended life until a future time . . .

I felt, as I had in my nightmare, that I stood on the brink of something of profound significance which I did not yet understand.

I must ask Lawrence, I thought. Lawrence had known Charles longer than I. Lawrence had the scientist's detachment and also the poet's grasp of the irrational. He would not admit to that paradox, yet after yesterday I knew I could trust it.

The breakfast gong rang. I dressed swiftly and hurried downstairs. Charles and Lawrence were already in the small dining room, deep in talk. Charles looked up at me with a singularly tender smile. "Good morning, my dear."

"Good morning, darling. Lawrence—"

"Good morning, Lydian," Lawrence said briefly, scarcely glancing in my direction, and turned back to Charles, resuming a technical discussion as though I were not even in the room.

I felt as if something had struck me across the face. I sat down numbly, accepted coffee, ate mechanically, waiting for a chance to speak. But no chance came. Lawrence finished eating, rose, said to Charles, "I shall have those specifications completed for you by this afternoon," nodded to me impersonally and left.

What has happened, I thought stupidly. Have I offended him in some way? Was he disgusted, that I should have been so human, so vulnerable, as to weep in terror on Tintagel's cliffs? To cling to him— My face colored in shame, but something in me cried out with the memory of his holding me until my panic ceased, holding me so long the rain soaked us through. Held me as Charles had done, that night of nightmare. But that had been different; oh, it had been so different. It was Lawrence who had understood the strain of trying to cope with Charles's moods. Lawrence who had let down the barriers of his own childhood, Lawrence who had led me into sharing more of myself than I had ever done before, even with Charles.

And it was Lawrence, now, who very definitely had shut that briefly opened door.

"Come, Lydian!" Charles said, already preoccupied with his own racing thoughts. "You said you would help me organize the data for that fourth chapter. I had it so clearly in my mind when we talked last night, and now it's escaping."

"Yes . . . of course. Where were we?"

"The proof of the astral theories," Charles said impatiently. "I told you . . . They are getting too tangled together; I wish I had not already embarked upon that second book. And there is the new data to be worked into the notes for the symposium, as well. The Board of Governors is anxious to know the exact thrust of my message. I cannot understand why Stearns has not been able to produce the necessary archaeological proof by now."

Because you have not allowed him to concentrate, I felt like saying. Because you will not allow him to hire proper help. You try too much, hold in too much, are endangered by your own self that drives you like a demon.

"Come," I said aloud. "It is beautiful in the garden. Let us take the manuscript and work among the roses."

It was not until we were seated in that peaceful setting that I recognized what I also had been thinking: here in open air, space, daylight, surely we could see if danger threatened. I progressed so fast: I was anticipating a danger whose name I did not even know.

We worked steadily for several hours, and at length Charles's chaotic material started to take on coherent form. Its thrust disturbed me, and I wondered what the reaction of the Board of Governors would be. The emphasis had veered decisively from the original concentration on a historic Arthur to an insistence on supernatural metaphysics.

145

"Are you certain," I asked carefully, "that this is the wisest direction to pursue?"

"It pursues *me*. Insights keep surfacing, and they must be spoken or they tear one's brain to shreds. If there were just more time! If only so many visions did not come at once." Charles slashed at his manuscript with such pressure that the pencil snapped. "Paintings, the excavations, the symposium, lecture notes, two books—the other book goes nowhere, it keeps doubling back upon itself and will not find a form."

"Would you want me to take your notes and see if I can develop them into a pattern?"

"If you like." Charles put his hand up to his eyes. "God, God, I am so very tired."

It was the first admitted crack in his armor of invulnerability.

I took all Charles's notes on women in Celtic myths to my room that night, and weary as I was, I was glad to have them. Charles had kept me working with him all day. Lawrence had not joined us for tea, and had sent word he would be dining out. Charles raised his eyebrows, and I felt a sick coldness that was at variance with the summer heat. Lawrence was avoiding us; avoiding me. I did not understand, but I knew one thing for sure: he had opened himself to me—at Tintagel, at the Savoy—in a way he now regretted.

And I had responded. Oh, I had; I could no more deny it. But it had not been entirely of my own doing. I had been taught by a master not to give myself where I did not know in advance that I was wanted, had been told endlessly—do not believe in being valued, being respected, being cared for as a woman. To trust is to be betrayed. You have no gifts that would make you wanted. That was not true; Charles said I had all the gifts; Charles valued me not only for what I could do and give but for what I was. But Lawrence . . .

It was ridiculous to feel so hurt, so betrayed and used. It was absurd that so new a friendship could have become so deep that aloofness seared like acid on an open wound. Irrational and undisciplined of me to let it matter. I, Lydian Ransome, with all my blessings—work that engrossed me, a husband I adored—was acting not like a married woman slighted by a friend, but like an unschooled girl in the throes of a tumultuous love.

Like a girl in love.

Dear God, what was happening to me?

It was two in the morning, for after the day's intense concentration on the manuscript, Charles had been too keyed up for sleep, and I had sat with him in the moonlit garden until he had relaxed enough to let Doff take him to bed. Now it was I who could not rest. I spread the bulky pile of notes out on the window table and tried to concentrate upon them, but the words all conjured up visions behind my eyes.

The ideal woman of the Celts was a total person, a crucible uniting flesh, mind and spirit. In this she partook of the mystical, divine quality of the Sidh, who were simultaneously a part of the world present and the world beyond. Charles, on that first night, saying it was my mother who had showed him the truth of this. Naming me one as well, and myself feeling as though carried along on a rushing wind. *The woman was wholly free, wholly conscious and responsible for all her gifts.* My mother's book, inscribed "To Virgilia, who has all the Gifts." Inscribed by Charles. Charles telling me those gifts were my inheritance, to claim whenever I would.

Guinever, Iseult, Grainne, all the great Celtic heroines, are prototypes of the Immortal Goddess, she who unites within herself the whole spectrum of man's experience—mother, maiden, mistress, wife; birth, knowledge, death. Charles saying rational man found this myth-truth threatening; that was why, in so many of the legends, the maiden won, having become the nurturing mother, was denigrated then to the adultress, consumed by lust—as if this defiling, this naming, could curb her awesome power.

Charles, his defenses down, whispering, "What have you done? You have the gifts of Guinever. For years I was content, and now you come—"

I applied myself doggedly to the mass of papers, and there was much here that was new. Charles had been working through the night hours; his handwriting showed weariness and strain. There were scattered references to mythic patterns, some unknown to me. And then I came upon a great batch of notes clipped together, labeled "Guinever—the Quest for the Grail." Charles's writing was no longer regular but jagged and broken,

147

as though something had driven his hand across the paper. "Quest for Grail inextricable from quest for woman. Woman the unknowable, unpossessable—quest is the *geis*, the fate of pursuing what can never be obtained, only freely given. Guinever's dower gifts, symbolic union of sacred and profane. Guinever. Guinever. *Guinever*." Then bits, pieces of plot, unidentified quotations. All the tragic sweep of the Arthurian saga, related to Arthur's queen. Her coming in the spring of innocence; her loving; wedding. The Queen of Love and Beauty; the Round Table, the perfect kingdom. The arrival of Lancelot, the ideal knight. Arthur and Lancelot, king/vassal, mentor/disciple, father/son. Lancelot, to whom the Queen Guinever drank from her chalice-cup; who wore Guinever's favor on his lance. Years going by; the shadow falling. Two men, one woman, bound by love, desire, compassion, pity, guilt.

My head was throbbing. I did not even hear the door open, but Rose was there, saying, "I thought you promised me you'd keep that bolted. I've brought you up some tea; I saw your light."

That was not all she'd brought; her arms were full of sheets and pillows. "I'm sleeping in the dressing room. I've told you before, you're too alone and cut off here at night. Anything could happen, and us not know."

"I told you there's no need."

"Discharge me," Rose said flatly, and went to make up her couch. She reappeared to shepherd me to bed, and I began to appreciate Charles's impatience with Doff. When she began to tidy the table where I had been working, I stopped her quickly. "Do not disarrange those. They are quite important."

Rose sniffed. "Slaving away like that, you'll be old before your time, and to what purpose?"

"A very important purpose. That is going to be a significant and worthwhile book." Yet when I closed my eyes against the pillows, my head was churning. Charles's frustration had entered into me—there were flashes of great insight in those notes, and an aching passion. But no form, no pattern. Or—the thought drifted into my mind just before I fell asleep—was it that I was unwilling to perceive, not a *literary* pattern, but a too painful personal one?

10

That night I dreamt my dream again. Panic, and mists, and the pull of Tintagel's cliffs, and running, running. Only all was subtly different. It was not I who ran, but Guinever. The men on the rocks who struggled were Lancelot and Arthur, transformed into antagonists, love turned to hate. Guinever pulled toward them by equal love and anguish, driven away by an equally powerful need to flee. To sanctuary? Safety? Innocence? Her fate flashed before her eyes and then she fell and was lost from sight.

I was sitting up, wide awake and trembling. But this awakening too was different. The first pre-dawn light paled the sky outside my window, and from the dressing room I heard the comforting sound of Rose's breathing. And my mind was occupied, not with terror, but with Guinever. In a flash as the dream ended I had seen whole and complete the outline for the book on Celtic women—on the nature of women, once and future—as personified in the pattern of Guinever's own myth.

The experience was so intense I found myself breathing hard as though I had been running. I had a subjective, fleeting sense of the absolute rightness of the whole scheme. Before the remembered awareness could escape me I had thrown back the sheet and was searching feverishly for clean paper and a pen.

By the time the clock struck eight and Rose was behind me, scolding, I had covered many pages with close writing, had developed the book's whole outline, chapters and sub-chapters, had even written opening and closing arguments and a whole section explicating the significance of Guinever as the embodiment of all major aspects of woman's gifts and life.

"No use trying to slow you down, is there?" Rose said grumpily. "As bad as his lordship, lost in your own world, forgetting all about ordinary life. He's changing you into his image, that's what he's doing."

I laughed; I felt astonishingly exhilarated. "Help me dress, Rose! I want to see my husband quickly."

Charles was alone at the breakfast table, gazing out the window toward my cloistered garden. For a moment, standing watching him, I again experienced that sense of detachment, of seeing him with my eyes unclouded by his charisma or by my own love. What I saw caught at my heart, made my eyes sting. Mortality is the only word that would describe it. How glad I was that I could run to him with the gift of my own insight into the book he had begun. The book which, though it disturbed me deeply, had within it the seed of Glastonbury's own strong magic. How willing I was, then, to put from me all thought of my own uneasiness, in the knowledge that I could use my gifts to lighten the heavy burden of his work.

"Charles!" And for the first time in weeks, I think, the lilt of my voice echoed against the walls of Avalon. "Oh, darling, wait until I show you! I have done so much—"

"Ah, Lydian." He turned and smiled, and there was a troubled look about him. "My dear, I am glad you are down early. I have reconsidered; I do not want you saddling yourself with that manuscript. We will put it by until some future time." He saw my face then, and his expression altered, became almost wary. "What is it, dear?"

"Oh, Charles, you must not put it by. This is going to be the best work you have ever done. And look, I believe I have found the connecting link that you were seeking."

I spread my pages out on the table and he read them, slowly. Looked up, and now his face had become masklike. Only the eyes were alive, with some pain I did not understand. "You are right. This is of profound significance, and must be written. But by you, not me. It has become your book, Lydian."

"Oh, Charles, no."

"Yes. I want it so." He put his hand over mine, and the band of my ring pressed into my finger. "Your father would be proud. *I* am proud; I say that with all humility. You have learned how to give felicitous form to a rare gift—a synthesis of scholarship and real poetry."

"If I have, I learned the way of it from you."

"Perhaps." He moved restlessly, passing his hand across his brow. "You must work on this, Lydian. No matter what else you have to put aside. I have that much of the scholar and artist in me yet, to know this must not be suppressed."

"I want to work with *you*. To give you help."

"I daresay you do. And who can say, perhaps this may be the best way you can do it." Charles straightened in his chair, a trace of the old regalness returning. "We will accomplish most if we deploy our strengths. I shall concentrate on the lecture preparation and the accompanying book. It is imperative that Lawrence complete the tunnel excavation. And you, my dear, must write." He gazed out the window again at the fading roses. "August now. The symposium will fall in mid-September. Autumn; that is the real death of the fruitful year. I shall have a birthday, did you know that, in another week?"

"Then we must celebrate! Can we not ask Meriel to come down? I shall order a feast for you, and a special cake." I was speaking gaily, glad for this propitious means to lift his mood. "Do you know, I do not even know how many candles to put upon it!"

"I shall be fifty years old. Does that appall you?"

"Certainly not. It is the prime of life."

"Arthur, if he lived that long, would have been thought old. The ideal then was to die at the height of one's powers, in pursuit of glory, surrounded by friends, poets and dead enemies. Of such stuff the myths are made."

"You are not Arthur. You are Charles Ransome, whose life began again when he married Lydian, and who is just entering

151

into a splendid renaissance!" I kissed him, and went up to my room to work.

I had not understood what Charles had told me earlier, that writing, painting, any creative act could, like birth itself, be both ecstasy and pain. That book, if book it should become, was written out of my own blood and bone, and every word set down became a mirror to my soul. Guinever, Charles's archetypal woman, maid, wife, mistress, mother-figure. Arthur and Lancelot loved each other, loved Guinever, who loved them both. Innocence, knowledge; trust, betrayal; power, fear. And Ason had called this an inferior myth that had no meaning!

Ason would have felt threatened by such a woman, Charles had said.

What sort of woman had my mother been? Charles, though not Ason, had told me I was much like her.

If Charles had known my mother, he must then have been about the same age Lawrence Stearns was now.

Was Lawrence really still avoiding me, or was it just that he was much occupied in the tunnel digging? He scarcely ever joined us now for meals, and when he did his talk was all with Charles. I still longed to speak with him, open my heart to him, yet the thought made me feel vaguely guilty, ashamed. I had let him know me, and he had walked away.

Why? Because of what he had not seen, or because of what he had? In himself—or me? And why could I not control this longing in myself? Why should I, who prided myself on my self-discipline, feel so anxious and threatened whenever he was near, feel again like that lost child I once had been, hovering on the fringes of approval?

There was a picture I had seen in the Tate Gallery in London by Wright of Derby, portraying just this admixture of rationality and emotion. An experiment with an airpump—a family gathered round to watch a cockatoo die in a bell-jar as the oxygen was slowly pumped away. It seemed to me, at times, as if we here in Avalon were living in just that sort of environment, an artificial world imprisoned under glass. But here, no outside power was depriving us of the means of life; it was something within ourselves that kept us here, while the same air, circulating over and over in our lungs, became ever more enervating and more stale.

Could such air eventually become poisonous? Lawrence would know.

I was thinking of Lawrence once again.

I was plagued with headaches all that week but I still worked, wrote to Meriel to invite her down for Charles's birthday and gave orders for a sumptuous meal. Charles would not want to interrupt his own concentration for a party, but I could at least provide a brief period of renewal. I sent instructions to a London tailor for a magnificent purple cloak, fur-lined, the latest gentleman's style but reminiscent in a way of Arthur's splendor. Charles could wear it if, as I hoped, I was able to persuade him to spend the winter in town.

Rose fussed over me constantly, which annoyed me when I noticed. For the most part, I was scarcely conscious of anything but the tasks at hand. Increasingly, my labors on the book possessed me. I was becoming conscious of how much I did not know, but also of the fact that within me *was* both a poet's emotion and a scholar's brain. At last, in late afternoon, I would put down the manuscript and, to keep Rose from nagging me, walk in the abbey or the garden, my brain still lost in work. Practicing driving the motor-car in quiet lanes—that did distract me, forcing me to concentrate on the empty road. I would go home to tea, briefly refreshed. Then would come the evening's task of trying to keep Charles from becoming either over-elated or too depressed. He needed me for listening, comfort, encouragement. And he was no fool; he would know if the slightest word or look was insincere. By the time he would release me, very late at night, I would be completely drained, would go to my room with my brain still throbbing from my day's labors. Often I would go to bed only to rise again and write—by candlelight, so as not to disturb Rose's slumbers—for several more hours, and would fall asleep at last only to sink into the mists and terrors of my dreams.

Those dreams and the book I was writing possessed me. There was some link between them that I did not yet understand. Perhaps I would find the answer as I followed the trail of

Guinever. She had already become for me so much more than the seduced wife of Tennyson's saga, and I was beginning to understand why she fascinated Charles.

In my reading I came upon references to magical objects, platters, bowls and cups. But these are exactly like the articles in the tunnel room, I thought, astonished. Even the jewelry Charles had designed for me . . . no wonder the quest for the real Guinever's dower gifts exerted such a hypnotic spell. I was about to succumb to it myself.

How many readers, though, never having had access to such treasure, would be able to evoke an image of these things in their minds? Could Charles be persuaded to permit reproductions of his Arthurian paintings in the book? I could include word-pictures from our collection, I thought, and I might as well embark on that at once. It was tedious going back to fill in blank spaces in manuscript at a later time, and I had been bent over my writing-table all this hot August day. My neck ached, and physical activity might bring relief. Even if Lawrence was working in the tunnel I could disregard him.

He was not there. The vault door was shut tight, and I felt again that prickling of my skin that always accompanied my visits underground. I'm being weak, I told myself sternly; there have been no further—accidents.

I spun the knobs of the vault door, and they responded easily to my touch. The tunnel yawned before me. A wave of nausea overcame me as I looked into its depths. Stupid, I thought. I could examine the objects in the storeroom, make my notes, be back upstairs again in such a short space of time. I turned on the gas, making quite sure it burned with a steady flame, and hurried in.

The room that had contained the trove of golden objects was completely empty.

For a second my senses reeled, then my first thought was that I must run for help. But to whom? If Lawrence was on the premises, he would be here. I dared not break such terrible news to Charles, not until I first was sure of all my facts.

If there had been robbery, obviously the thieves were long since gone. The vault door had been properly locked, and the tunnel was dark and quiet. There were no signs of a break-in.

Perhaps Lawrence had moved the objects somewhere for safe-keeping, as he had once spoken of doing, and my brain leaped swiftly at the memory. What I ought now to do was make a careful inspection of the tunnel, lock it up, then report to Lawrence whenever he appeared.

I willed the observing, scholarly side of myself to take command. This first passage was empty, otherwise undisturbed. Beyond the turn, Lawrence's excavations had been going forward at a rapid rate. No more careful sifting of all fragments; his objective, at Charles's insistence, had been to clear the ancient passage to its farthest end. Rocks and rock dust were everywhere. I stumbled, and almost fell; picked myself up, gritted my teeth and kept on going.

The tunnel came, as before, to a blind stop. To my left was an opening in the rock wall, scarcely big enough for me to squeeze through. But the gas fixture on the wall beside— Lawrence must have been extending the main steadily with each yard he worked—threw fingers of light onto a narrow way already cleared.

I picked up my skirt and squeezed myself through the aperture.

If there was a warning, the rumbling of shifting rock, my ears heard it only a split second before the pain shot through my shoulder, before I was knocked sideways onto the jagged pile of stones, was pinned there, helpless, by the great weight of rock which had fallen off the ledge above.

It was the culmination of all my falling nightmares.

And then there were footsteps, pounding ever nearer as I tried frantically, unsuccessfully to pull free. My arm and shoulder ached with intolerable pain. A figure loomed in the opening, and the gaslight glanced coldly off dark metal.

Lawrence, with a gun.

"Lydian? Good God, what now?" Distorted reality came crazily back into focus. Lawrence was wedging his way in to kneel beside me. "I told you to stay away from where you don't belong. What are you doing here?"

"I could ask you the same thing," I retorted acidly. "I came down to examine one of the gold platters, found it gone and began to search."

"I took them out of here so they'd be safe. No, Charles doesn't know, and I don't intend he should find out."

"I thought you were going to hire guards."

"I have; they start tomorrow. Disguised as yard men. If anything happens from now on, at least we'll know—"

He stopped.

"Know what?"

"That it's not outsiders. Have you been prowling around down here before?"

"I've not been down here, if that is what you mean." Why was he so angry? I longed to know. And why was it so impossible to be civil? The pendulum had swung, from the intimacy of more than friends, not to mere acquaintanceship or strangeness but almost to enmity. I forced my voice to stay cool. "If you could find a way of releasing me—and would you mind putting away that gun?"

He thrust it in his pocket. "I thought I'd found evidence of prowlers, so I set a trap. No, not that block of stone; I let it be known I'd be away this afternoon, then lurked around. And found—you, risking your neck where you already knew it might not be safe." The disgust in his tone was evident.

"If you will get me loose, I will be only too happy to withdraw." I rubbed my aching shoulder gingerly. Lawrence was looking, not at me, but at the block of stone.

"This is a fine piece, a keystone; I must have been working carelessly or it would never have come loose. I'm sorry, but it's too valuable for me to take a pickaxe to. We'll have to tear your skirt free, and I'll knock out some stones in the wall behind you so you can squeeze past."

Thank you so much, I felt like saying tartly, but I held my tongue as he fetched his tools and started, in a taut silence, to loosen the wall. Stone chips flew, and I turned my face away.

"You can get past now, if you'll make an effort." He did not even bother to offer me his hand. I ripped my skirt free, grimly, and pulled myself up, trying not to jostle my bruised shoulder.

"Thank you," I said stiffly, half turning round. And then my eyes widened, and I reached involuntarily for his arm. "Lawrence, look!"

The rocks he had knocked loose had opened a small aperture, and in the hollow beyond something gleamed in the faint light.

It was Lawrence who reached for it and held it in his palm so that it caught and reflected back the gaslight. A knife, a ceremonial dagger, its blade intricately scrolled in the Celtic pattern, its hilt adorned with glowing jewels.

"It's old, isn't it?" I whispered, and Lawrence murmured, almost matter-of-factly, "Old. You see the pattern?"

If he could find just one object, Charles had said, to prove there were fifth-century remains under Glastonbury Abbey—

With one thought in mind, we raced through the tunnel, Lawrence carrying the knife, I clutching my arm in a vain effort to ward off pain. We scarcely remembered to slam the vault door behind us, then we were running for the elevator, ascending, hurrying across the Great Hall out into the garden where Charles was waiting.

"Darling, look!" I cried out, and Lawrence laid the dagger in Charles's lap.

Never will I forget that moment of reaction. Of non-reaction. Charles merely glanced at the object, then his eyes swept over us. Cold, austere, a ruler displeased with the performance of his servants. "I was under the impression you planned to work straight through till dinner time," he said to Lawrence, dismissingly. And to me, "My dear, I have been waiting for some time. I was beginning to believe your writing was more engrossing than my company."

A muscle flickered in Lawrence's cheek, and without a word he turned and went. Tears stung my eyes. Charles was looking at me, evenly. I ought to sit down, find out what was troubling him, pour tea. But I could not do it. "I am sorry. I am not feeling very well," I said, and fled.

Rose brought me tea in my room and bound up my shoulder, giving me a lecture about seeing a doctor, which I did not heed.

"It's only a bad bruise, so there's no real harm done, I'm quite sure."

"No harm!" Rose snorted. "What does it take to convince some people there's things going on around here that aren't natural?"

"You certainly can't construe this to have been anything but an accident."

"I may not have your fancy words, ma'am dear," Rose retorted, "but when there's a bad smell I can tell sure enough there's something rotten near."

"Anyway, you need not worry. After tomorrow there will be guards on the premises. But you are not to tell that to anyone, not even his lordship, do you understand?"

"There's none here but you, making no exceptions, I'd trust with *anything*," Rose said huffily.

My arm and shoulder became more painful as time passed, but nonetheless I went down to dinner, grateful now for the flowing looseness of Charles's favorite gowns. Lawrence was not there; Charles and I spoke but little, and after our meal he said formally, "My dear, if you will excuse me, I believe that I will work on my manuscript tonight." Doff, looking triumphant, wheeled him off to his study, and I was left alone.

The Great Hall was filled with the curious poignance summer evenings sometimes have. It was not yet near dark; the long English twilight filled the luminous sky. I had a need for air; I went out the front door across the lawns and then, without conscious volition, found myself turning toward the abbey ruins.

It was some time since I had come here, and I was struck anew by the healing sense of peace. The ruins gave me perspective. I should do as I had done in spring, make myself a daily hour of retreat and write my journal. But with the development of my book, public and private writing had become inextricably intertwined.

I sat on the stone foundations of the chapel and thought about Guinever and her gifts. The gift for enabling, for passing on strength and power, via love; the gift for becoming not what men wanted, but what they needed; the dubious blessing of being all women in one. It was at once Guinever's talent and her fate. Charles had been right in saying once that gifts were inexorable; they were ours, whether we would or not; our choice was only our willingness to use them.

I had read somewhere that the true mark of grace was one's

"obedience to the unenforceable." It was that which I felt pulling on me now. Something in me longed to flee, almost as if my body was fighting for its life in an alien atmosphere. Something longed to rebel—as Guinever and the flower-daughter in the myths rebelled—against the high-handed treatment of a husband-father. But as twilight faded I rose, and turned toward Avalon. I loved and was loved, and had thus voluntarily assumed bonds I could not ignore.

Charles was nowhere in sight when I entered, and the house was still. I was grateful; I was not strong enough for one of those long, difficult conversations. I went upstairs slowly, into my own room. Candles burned on the window table, their flames glancing off a cross-shaped object of shining gold.

The ceremonial dagger was impaled, upright, in the smooth surface of the dark oak table. A note lay pinioned by it, in the jagged writing I knew so well.

My dearest love—forgive. Not finding it myself was more than I could bear.

For a second a picture rose before my eyes—Lawrence and I, young, excited, running forward with the discovery that had been the answer to one of Charles's dearest hopes. Envy might not be a pretty emotion, but it was deeply human; I, of all persons, ought to understand Charles's feelings.

I sat on the edge of my bed, gazing toward the windows beyond which the broken arches of Glastonbury loomed. Broken arches, broken covenants. The dagger gleamed, its rays piercing the closed corridors of my mind, and I faced at last the truth I had been avoiding all these past days. I loved Charles deeply; he was child, husband, father, mentor. But I loved Lawrence too. It was the old Arthurian triangle come to life.

"Glastonbury is strong magic," Charles had told me, "and not dead." In creating on Glastonbury land his own Avalon, in throwing himself—and us with him—so totally into the quest, he had unleashed that power, and it was controlling us, moving us inexorably toward a predestined fate.

I shuddered, gazing at the dagger, trying to draw serenity from the cross-shaped hilt. Slowly, a strange thing began to happen. My pulse slowed, my heart ceased to pound. I was filled with a curious, fatalistic tranquility, so that I could barely move. The outline of the golden object shimmered, wavered; my eyes grew heavy, the room seemed dark and far away. Tiny at first, growing gradually clearer, visions were taking form before my dazzled eyes. Lawrence and I, together—in the tunnel, in London, in the garden. Myself at Tintagel, struck by panic, running. Myself that first day in the gallery, overcome by suffocating fear. My early nightmares, re-created, growing monstrous . . .

I was awake, yet it was as though I were asleep. I was both a part of those visions and separate. They shimmered and dissolved and formed again . . . into the same scene of terror that had driven me into Charles's paternal arms. The struggle on the looming cliffs, myself watching; figures, at once alien and familiar, their faces hidden. And as I watched, the mist that veiled them began to lighten and dissolve; the figures turned; the features began to grow clear . . .

"Ma'am! Ma'am dear!" Rose's voice, sharp and insistent, came to my ears as over a vast distance. With great effort I dragged my eyes away from the dagger.

Rose was standing by my side. "Ma'am dear, what is it? You gave me such a turn, you looked so queer!"

"I'm all right, I was—daydreaming. Yes, you may turn down the bed. I think that I shall make this an early night."

But I read, and wrote in my journal for several hours, and I was reluctant to turn out my lamp and fall asleep.

Was I glad, or sorry, that Rose had entered when she did? Strangely, I did not know. I had been much alarmed. Yet something in me confirmed a conviction that had been growing stronger with each terrorizing dream.

My early nightmares, this sense of foreboding, the disturbing ambiance of Avalon in some unknown way were all connected. I had been on the brink of discovery, in that waking sleep. And I knew too that, somehow, *I* was the link, the catalyst that had set all these separate, slumbering patterns into fateful motion.

I fell asleep at last, and for once I did not dream.

More and more I was recognizing the change taking place in my husband's personality—or had I heretofore been too blinded by love and admiration to see it? He no longer wanted me to bring the outside world for him to share; he was living what amounted to a denial that any era but that of Arthur existed. There was no other truth, no other value; the discovery of the tombs and the dowry treasure they allegedly contained had become for him not merely a significant archaeological discovery, but a validation of his life. And in an odd sort of way I served that purpose for him, too.

Lawrence, somewhat to my surprise, sought me out to inquire about my injuries. It was not at all a comfortable interview. There was tension in the air, and now that I had recognized what was for me the cause, I could scarcely look at him for fear he should guess it too. I asked if the guards he had engaged were now on duty, and he replied they were, adding tersely, "They cannot, of course, patrol the tunnel, so I hope from now on you will have the good sense not to venture there."

"You certainly do not think what happened the other day was deliberately engineered?"

"If it was not, it was due to your carelessness or mine, and personally I should prefer not to have further accidents to account for. I have enough to do without effecting unnecessary rescues."

"I assure you I don't care for them any more than you! And if it will ease your conscience, I can promise you I will not go wandering about down there again. Not even with the lure of fifth-century daggers to draw me. I have enough to contend with." In spite of everything, the urge to talk to him was strong in me again. My voice wavered slightly. "The book I'm engaged in is a world in itself. Not to mention editing Charles's material when he wishes, and making preparations for his birthday celebration."

"You're not planning to make a party of that, are you?"

"I wish I could. We could all benefit from some outside air. Even I am beginning to see things now."

"What do you mean?"

Lawrence's tone came so crisp and sharp that I answered more than I'd intended. "I was staring at that knife the other night, and found myself seeing visions. Undoubtedly because I was overtired."

The expression on Lawrence's face changed to something like

relief. "Oh. That was scrying. You knew about that, didn't you? It's a form of self-hypnotism, still used I believe in various witchcraft rites. Visions project themselves from one's unconscious; to the oversensitive they may actually seem real. Possibly it was staring at the vessels of the Mass while praying that seduced the knights of the Round Table into believing they had seen the Holy Grail. So you've had an experience of that sort, have you?"

Lawrence left then, before I could say more. This short exchange drained me; my whole body hurt, and my bruised arm made writing difficult. I would go to the library, blot out with research the turbulent questions that kept surging round my brain. But there was no surcease from thought; each page I looked at was like a scrying-surface, opening disturbing vistas to my eyes.

Scrying. Lawrence had said this phenomenon was related to the legends of the Grail. The quest for the Grail was inseparable from the quest for Guinever. Guinever, and the immortal triangle that for fourteen centuries had exercised its hypnotic spell. Hypnotism; scrying; why had I been afraid last night to pursue that vision to its end? For I knew the worst already—the parallel of Lawrence, Charles, Lydian.

Charles must not know what I was feeling. I could not, would not have him hurt. If we could just keep going until the symposium was over; if I could get Charles up to London, away from Avalon. Away from Lawrence. As long as I did not keep encountering him this hunger in me would surely die.

I scanned the shelves for books on the Grail legends; took one down and began to read. Here was scrying, an explanation of its role in the Grail visions. Here—and this was new to me, this was fascinating—the suggestion that the dissolution of the Round Table community was brought about not by the introduction of sin, adultery, temptation, but by what the appearance of the Grail evoked: the pursuit by separate individuals of their personal visions. This was happening to us, to Lawrence, Charles and me, originally united in a common search, now becoming more and more swallowed up by our separate dreams.

I read, and as I read the intensity of the light around me seemed to change. A deep conviction blazed in my brain that I was eating of the fruit of the tree of knowledge and there would be no going back. By an act of will, my vision cleared. I was staring at an account of the myth of the Fisher King.

A pre-Christian source of the Grail quest legend, the page read. Recurring most popularly in the Arthur-Lancelot-Guinever triangle, it was an interesting Western European appearance of the universal fertility-death-resurrection myth of the king who must die. The Fisher King was an impotent ruler who had lost his power through a wound received in a mysterious amorous adventure; he ruled over a kingdom of wasteland, where all life hung in a state of suspended animation. Among the inhabitants was a queen who grieved alone, infertile, in the depths of her hidden castle while the land was cursed. The only man who could restore the blighted kingdom was the seeker who could pass through the dangerous seas, penetrate the surrounding water to the almost invisible castle and recognize the Fisher King behind his many guises. If he then saw truth as it truly was, if he asked the right questions, he would receive from the woman the Grail and drink of the power and sovereignty it contained. The wasteland would again be green, the youth and maiden would form the ideal, perfect union, and replace the burnt-out, impotent Fisher King.

Time passed, and I was still standing there trembling, gazing at the terrible, prophetic page, and I knew this was why Charles had wanted to snatch back from me the manuscript material on Celtic woman: why, when it had been too late, he had surrendered.

The myths had that terrible faculty of being mirrors. Here were all the familiar elements: male-female talismans, circle, fire, water, blood, vengeance, impotence, sacrifice, heroic tasks. The king whose power had failed, the son-figure who replaced him, the nurturing woman. Here were Guinever's dower gifts, the circlet collar and the chalice, symbolizing the joining in her of the sacred and profane. In the strictest sense, a woman's dowry had never become the possession of her husband; he shared its benefits, through her grace, but it belonged to her alone. That was why, in so many of the old tales, woman was both attracting and threatening; men preferred to be the owners and the givers. Just as Charles, grateful for my help, still resented having to accept it.

Just as Ason had resented the very skills and intelligence with which he had endowed me. He had been threatened by them, I could see that now. What had he done to my mother and her gift of magic, and why had I never wondered about it before? What was Charles doing to me? And was I now beginning to understand why Guinever, for all her love of Arthur, had been irresistibly drawn to Lancelot as well?

The old myth had been right. The key to making the wasteland fertile lay in asking the right questions.

But I would not ask them. I slammed the book shut and put it back on the shelf, my hands trembling. I must break the pattern; the inevitable unwinding of the tangled Arthur-Lancelot-Guinever skein would not happen here at Avalon.

11

Meriel came down to stay with us over Charles's birthday. I am not sure precisely why I asked her—a wish to give Charles a festival day; a hope that her presence might ease some present tension; a need to have *someone* who also cared for Charles sharing the burden of keeping him in a balanced state of mind. But I knew almost at once that I had only succeeded in introducing another disturbing element into our tight circle.

Looking back afterward on that first teatime after Meriel's arrival, I could not put my finger on anything concretely wrong. There was only an uneasiness within me telling me that in some way the pressure had been increased. Charles was brilliant, summoning up reserves of strength, sweeping us with him on a wave of excitement over his latest plans. They all seemed so right, so possible, so sane; it was not till I was away from his dynamic presence that I realized all his visions were as yet all based on clouds.

Meriel stopped in the upper hall as I was going down to dinner. "What is the matter with you?" she demanded without preamble. "Don't look bewildered; you are not a fool. He's living on nerve and impossible illusions, and you must know it. Why don't you stop him?"

"I wish to God I could. I'm so afraid of what will happen to him if he is not able to complete his work in time."

"Have you thought of the consequences if he *does* complete it, only to have it regarded as a madman's fantasy?"

"Yes, I have. But if one suggests moderation he flies into a rage." I put out my hand impulsively. "Meriel—help me. Please! I am at my wits' end. He's making himself ill, and I don't know how to help him."

Meriel looked at me. She was standing by the railing over-looking the Great Hall below; a shaft of late light arrowing through the stained glass high above haloed her with a pale-blue light. Her skin, against the midnight color of her gown, was luminous, and her eyes were searching. After a moment, she nodded gravely. "Oddly enough, I like you, Lydian. You *have* been too heady a dose of life for Charles; I was afraid of that, but I grant you full marks for good intentions. Yes, I will try. Charles needs careful handling when he's in these ecstatic fits, as I've cause to know."

She moved, slightly, so that she could look me directly in the eyes. "Charles's welfare is all I care about. To protect that, I will let nothing—personal considerations, concern for others stand in the way."

Side by side, we descended the staircase to where Charles was waiting.

Charles's birthday still was three days off, and in those three days I grew nearly frantic, for despite Meriel's attempt to intro-duce serenity the atmosphere grew steadily more intense. Meriel told me she felt as though we were trying to quiet a frantic horse, while at the same time keep ourselves from being thrown.

And Doff—Doff. He drove me into frustration and despair. He meant so well, he cared for Charles so deeply, yet his efforts at being the stern nurse drove Charles wild and caused flare-ups between them greater than I had seen before.

"Would it not be better," I suggested quietly to Doff after one such incident, "to do what you can to make his lordship's work easier for him, instead of provoking confrontations?"

Doff wheeled on me. "The way *you're* doing? *You* encour-aged him in these crazy efforts. I told you not to, but you wouldn't listen! Now you're scared of the results, you're trying to back away and make him stop. Let me tell you something, Lady Ransome. If you stop supporting him now, you'll kill him, and the responsibility will be squarely in your hands!"

He had never dared speak to me that way before, as though he were master here, and I the hired assistant. He was trembling with an emotion that was a mirror-image of my own—angry frustration, helplessness, deep concern for the man we all loved. Before I could speak, he turned and bolted back to Charles's study.

The complexity of our relationships stood out for me so sharply now. Myself, Meriel, Lawrence, Doff—we all circled around Charles in a strange intimacy compounded of fascination, frustration, a kind of helpless fury and deep love. At times, hurrying across the Great Hall in one of the long robes Charles had designed for me, my hair unbound, I would find myself glancing round at the shields and banners glimmering in the torchlight. I would be possessed by an uneasy sense of slipping through time, back from the twentieth century into the fifth, as though we were all being moved through patterns we had lived before.

I did not encounter Lawrence much these days. He was working steadily on the tunnel, rarely joining us for meals. Not having his presence beside me at the table removed one great pressure from me. Meriel took up the burden of conversation at tea and at dinner, and that too was a respite. I longed for the abbey ruins and the release of writing in my journal, but was too busy to seek them.

I discarded the idea of having a real party, of inviting Sir Adrian Barker and other guests from our early married days. More and more, Charles had become resistant to suggestions of contact with persons in the world beyond Avalon. This was something I would have to work at, slowly, after the symposium was over; I feared that if I tried to force the issue now my efforts would only increase Charles's tension. So I contented myself, along with buying him the fur-lined cloak, in ordering a splendid dinner. My research in *Sir Gawain and the Green Knight* and *Perceval* had led me to become fascinated by the foods of the period. Hippocras—fine wine warmed and spiced; dates, figs and pomegranates; sorrel soup; fresh ham baked in wine, cinnamon and cloves; spiced partridge—I had devised recipes, consulted with the cook, and decided to prepare a real Arthurian feast for Charles's birthday.

I knew that, for a long time, Charles's birthdays had been ignored. This would be different; it would demonstrate that we all supported him, that we cared.

Keeping knowledge of our plans secret from my husband's notice was not as difficult as I had feared. Charles was engrossed in his own work and thoughts, and on the day itself kept us all very busy making no mention of the day's significance. I was hard put to find time to slip off to add final touches to our plans.

I did not give Charles my felicitations early in the day, nor did the others; we hoped thus to make our honoring him in the evening more of a surprise. "Get Doff to delay Charles in dressing, if he can," I said to Meriel, and she nodded. We would be gathered round the table, our goblets lifted in a toast, when he appeared.

And so it was. The servants, bless them, had worked with silent speed when we had finally gotten Charles off to his room, and the dais resembled a Camelot banquet hall. The refectory table was spread with white brocade and all the splendid archaic gold serving pieces. Our gifts were hidden, ready to be brought forth at the climax of the feast. Even Lawrence had donned correct formal evening clothes; Meriel was like a dark sapphire in midnight blue and I wore my sea-green velvet with my wedding jewels.

And I can remember, in that moment when we waited as we heard the elevator rattle down, how glad I was. Glad that I had been able to create this evening as a gift he would treasure.

The elevator door opened. We stood, poised, our golden goblets high. Doff, in a velvet smoking jacket, his dark hair shining, pushed Charles toward us in his royal chair. "Happy birthday, Charles!" we cried, and, "Happy birthday, milord," the servants murmured deferentially from the shadows.

The flaring torchlight, falling on Charles's face, made him look not of flesh and blood at all, but stone.

For a moment fear touched me; perhaps my surprise would be too great a shock. With Charles's health so precarious, perhaps even joy could impose too great a strain. Then Charles, with visible effort, gathered his strength and nodded acknowledgment. His voice, the strain in it all but concealed, stopped our salutations with a brief inquiry as to whether we could begin our meal, and his hand, reaching for his jeweled cup, was trembling faintly.

Meriel's eyes met mine and with one accord we began talking lightly, gaily, speaking of the birthday as a time to recognize the triumphs of Charles Ransome's life. We were trying to relieve him of the burden of conversation, but he would not have it. He cut us off repeatedly, embarked on monologues about his current work with an obsessive insistence that drained his strength.

He only picked at the exquisite food; when we were half through the cook's triumph, a capon baked in a sheath of real gold leaf, he pushed his plate away. "Can we not have done with this?"

"Yes, of course." I spoke quickly. "Hodge, please clear. We shall have our sweet with coffee, later. Now we have other matters to present."

Meriel signaled the footmen to bring forth the packages. We had rehearsed this carefully—the approach of the serving men one by one, down the whole length of the Great Hall, bearing high our offerings. Lawrence's, Meriel's, mine, a joint tribute from the servants' hall. Only Doff had insisted on presenting his own gift himself, and he slipped off now to fetch it as the first quiet-footed servitor stepped forth.

"More wine," Charles's voice said tautly. Hodge poured for him from a steaming pitcher of hippocras, and the scent of cinnamon and almonds filled the room with a pungent fragrance.

Meriel's gift, an illuminated Book of Hours that was worth a fortune. My fur cloak, which was greeted by Meriel with an exclamation of admiration. Charles's face was pale, and a muscle throbbed in his jaw.

I beckoned to Hodge and whispered, "Bid the men move faster."

Lawrence's gift, a miniature casket duplicating the twelfth-century accounts of Arthur's coffin, its lid adorned with an etched-stone copy of the now-famous marker. "*Hic Iacet Arthurus . . .*"

169

The last man was approaching with the servants' package when Charles's voice struck out. "Enough! Must I endure much more?" There was pain in his voice, and something else, something that made us all stare at him sharply. And I knew with a shock that I had been wrong. The emotion that was overpowering my husband was not joy at all, but rage.

"Incessant reminders of time running out, of death!" He pushed Lawrence's gift away from him with a savage gesture. "Mocking me . . . mocking my studies with these wild parodies! Presuming to claim you know more of the Arthurian Age than I—"

I could not move. Meriel reached out a hand. The servant, approaching, faltered and fell back. And then Doff appeared, eager and all unknowing. Doff, hurrying forward with a great flat rectangle, his face alight. Doff, turning it round before Charles's eyes to reveal a painting.

Painting? Mirror. I heard Lawrence's sharp indrawn breath. Felt suddenly cold. Yet even in that stunned moment there was the realization that this work of Doff's brush, shockingly modern, so different in technique from Charles's, was real art.

Different in technique, but not in subject. Doff had painted a triangle of figures in an ancient hall. This hall; these persons. Deliberately or unwittingly, the forms of Lancelot, Arthur, Guinever bore resemblances to Lawrence, Charles, and me.

"Take that thing away!" Charles's voice was choking. "How dare you come here? Who are you? My dark shadow? My *Doppelgänger*? Go away!"

Incredibly, Charles was pulling himself up, supporting his full weight on hands braced rigidly on the carved arms of his great chair. Then he had balanced himself against the table edge; one hand groped for the jeweled goblet, flung the steaming contents in Doff's face. "I will not have you with me! Get out! *Get out!*"

Doff staring, choking, uttering a wild cry, bolting away. Myself crying out, stunned, "Charles! My dear!" Charles, starting to shudder, staring at me, his eyes dark pools of torture.

"You brought this on! You! I trusted you, and you connived. Enemies! Everywhere about me, enemies—even you! Betrayed—!" His whole stiff body was shaking; as we stood frozen, his arm thrust out wildly. "It's happening again! Meriel!

It's all happening again!" He buckled, toppled sideways like a broken doll.

It was Meriel who caught him, Meriel who got him back into the chair, holding him there tightly as he was wracked by the terrible spasms I had been told of but had never seen. Meriel, snapping out orders to Lawrence, to Hodge, pushing me away. The cortege flew toward the elevator cage, disappeared from sight and I was left among the guttering candles and the ruined feast.

What had happened? Dear God, what was happening to us all? To Charles—why had I not realized that to Charles's feverish obsession, observance of a birthday was like a warning of mortality? What harm had I done him? I shut my eyes, but I could not blot out the vision of Charles in the grip of that terrible pain.

What was happening upstairs? The torches flickered. There was the sound of running feet on the balcony above. A door slammed. I heard Meriel's voice shouting savagely for compresses, for hot water. Then Charles, moaning, sobbing. Charles, who never allowed himself to weep . . .

I ought to be there. It was my husband suffering, and I stood as though I were the one imprisoned by paralysis. I grabbed my velvet skirt, ran up the stairs. The door to Charles's room burst open—Hodge, with a pitcher.

I caught at him. "Hodge, how is he?"

"Don't stop me, my lady, they need hot water." His usually impassive face distraught, compassionate. "My lady, don't go in there." It was Lawrence who stopped me, grabbing my arms and brutally pushing me away. I struck at him, savagely. "Let go of me! My husband needs me—"

"Not now! He doesn't want you there." Lawrence thrust me down into a chair. "Get hold of yourself, and don't go indulging in self-pity. It's the pain talking, you know that. He'll want you again tomorrow, but if you go in now you'll only make him worse."

Beyond the open doorway came a new sound, dark-colored, soothing. Meriel, singing to ease Charles's pain. I took a deep breath, willed my mind calm. "I am all right now. Let go of me, please."

He did so, and stood there contemplating me. "This is hell on you, too, isn't it? I told you that you were committing yourself to more than you understood. Go to bed; get Rose to give you something so you can sleep."

"No."

"I'll bring you news, as soon as I am able. I must get back. Everything will be better in the morning."

If there was a morning. Doff's voice, telling me Charles could die at any time, kept ringing in my brain. *Doff*. Doff was the only one who knew how to nurse Charles through these extremities. Charles needed him. Charles didn't want him, either.

I went down the stairs slowly to the shattering disarray of the Great Hall, and all the past—my own and Guinever's—went with me. All the ghosts of love and loss and loneliness whispered in my ears, stirred before me in the glimmering figures of the tapestries. Arthur, alone, deserted, betrayed by all his knights, disowning Guinever his adored because she had loved elsewhere.

Dear God, I sounded as though I too were going mad.

Mad. It was the first I had allowed that word to cross my conscious mind. That was what I was afraid of, wasn't it? That Charles in his obsession, his desperate search for a reality he could endure, in his pain and tension had crossed that dark divide. And was pulling us, all of us, along with him.

I must not let myself think this way. Whatever happened, Charles would need me strong. Lawrence was right, I could not afford self-pity. He was right, too, that it had been Charles's illness speaking.

The illness, or the medicine. What was that nostrum which he had been taking since the attack while I was up in London?

It was after I had been to London—after I had begun to make a reputation for myself in Charles's work, after I had been drawn to Lawrence—that this distortion in Charles's attitude had begun.

I had wondered before, had I not, about that medicine? Had questioned Charles, been rebuffed, had not pursued it.

I had to know. Those attacks of fevered brightness, of heightened tension, that usually came after Charles's low period in late afternoon, just as he emerged from his study for our tea.

172

I crossed over to the small room, threw open the door. Charles's desk was covered, as always, with manuscripts, galleys, notes. I jerked open drawers, felt among the tangled jumble of their contents. My fingers closed around smooth glass, thrust down deep.

It was the bottle from the chemist's shop. I held it so that I could make out the labeling in the faint light. *80% Laudanum*, and in barely decipherable writing, *Dosage not to exceed three teaspoons a day.*

How much was Charles taking? This bottle was half empty; how many times had the prescription been renewed? Laudanum was tincture of opium, and opium was stimulant, intoxicant, sedative, narcotic. The main cause, to those addicted to it, of hallucinatory dreams.

What happened when laudanum was mixed with brandy? And why in God's name had I not pursued all of this before?

I felt it then, the uneasy stiffening that told me I was not alone. Only my driven search had prevented my realizing it before. Something instinctive made me thrust the bottle back where I had found it, deep beneath papers, made me slide the drawer shut without the slightest sound. My limbs felt again the curious heaviness that impeded movement; I was caught, trapped, by what danger I did not know. Then I heard it, the faint sound that both released me and gave me answer.

Doff was crouched on the floor before the empty fireplace, trying not to cry. He looked so like a kicked dog, huddled there, that I moved toward him instinctively.

"Let me alone!"

His voice was muffled. He reeked of brandy, but he sounded like a very little boy. I sat down on the carved chair where I had so often sat when I worked with Charles.

"Doff . . . Barrett . . . you must not worry. Charles will be all right. He did not mean what he said or did."

"He did. He doesn't give a damn about me any more. Well, I don't give a damn about the whole lot of you!" Doff sat up, wiping his eyes savagely on his sleeve. "How you must be gloating. You've wanted to see me out of here."

"No, I haven't. Charles needs you."

"*He* doesn't think so. Not since you've come. You, and

Lawrence. He's got a better audience now, one that speaks his language. *I* could learn it, but he doesn't want me to."

"You mustn't think that way. It isn't true."

"It is! He just wanted a dog to fawn over him, and fetch and carry, not a . . . I've been a fool. He didn't mean a word of all that talk about making a future for me."

"I'm sure he did. He's been so busy, and not well—you must be patient, give him time."

"Time! That's what we don't have. He may peg off at any moment, don't you understand that? And then what will happen? I've idolized that man since I was fifteen. I really loved him—"

"I know. He knows, too."

Doff shook his head, compulsively, the words rushing out. "He doesn't *care*. He threw me out, as if I was a bone he could pick clean and discard—"

I rose, making my voice calm. "You really must not talk like this. You'll be sorry later. Charles does care about you, how could he help it? You've been so good to him; we all know it. You need some coffee, and some sleep, and in the morning everything will be better."

It was almost the same thing Lawrence had said to me.

I did not want Doff to suffer the servants seeing him so undone. I went to the kitchen myself, heated the coffee that had been brewed for our ill-fated meal. It was helpful to me, too, having something tangible to do. I carried the coffee tray to the study with hands that were still shaking.

In my absence, Doff had found more brandy. He was standing, gulping it morosely, staring at the papers on Charles's desk. I stood for a moment in the doorway, looking at him, troubled, and he raised truculent eyes.

"You don't approve? I should think by now you'd be used to the fumes of the vine. *He* swills enough lately. So I'm only following in his footsteps. There's something significant there somewhere." He set the glass down on the desk, heavily; the brandy sloshed onto the papers. Suddenly, with an oath, he had swept all, papers and glass together, to the ground. "I've made everything worse. That's Doff, who can do nothing right—oh, God, God, God—"

He was down on his knees, rooting clumsily through the papers. I set the tray down swiftly, poured coffee into a cup that clattered. "Let it be. I'll see to all that in the morning. Just drink your coffee."

He scarcely heard; his erratic tidying had turned to shuddering sobs. I knelt beside him, holding out the coffee, reaching out to touch his heaving shoulder. Suddenly, compulsively, he swung round, flung himself into my lap, his arms around me, his face buried in my velvet skirt. The coffee, dark and burning, splashed across us.

I was afraid; half of me was afraid, but the other, maternal part responded instinctively as to a wounded child. My arms went round him, rocking him; I heard my own voice crooning wordless comfort. *Just as Meriel had ministered to Charles . . .*

How long I held him thus, I do not know; time had no meaning. My body was stiff with aching—for Charles, for Doff, for us all. At length Doff's sobs abated; I was able somehow to put him on the study sofa and cover him with a wool throw. He would sleep now; the wreckage of the room could wait till morning. With difficulty I pulled myself to my feet and staggered up the stairs.

The upper level was still. Charles's door was shut, and no sound came from within. In my own chamber, candles flickered; Rose was adamant against burning the gas fixtures any more. My bed was turned down, and in the dressing room Rose had fallen asleep on her own cot. I longed for comfort, but I would not disturb her. And there was much I had to face alone.

Disconnected thoughts circled in my brain, like comets bursting in a blaze of light out of the dark depths of memory and sleep. Like the book outline. Like my dreams. Like that waking vision of the figures on Tintagel's cliffs.

Like those struggling figures, their faces hidden, slowly turning, turning . . . and I fleeing, running from a weight of knowledge that I could not bear.

I had been hovering on the brink of some dark truth. I faced it now. I was the connecting link between all these disparate happenings. My presence. My dreams. And however terrible the knowledge that lurked in the abyss of consciousness, if I was ever to be free I had to *know*.

Like a sleepwalker, I rose, took off the coffee-stained sea-green velvet gown. Put on my white nightdress and a thin white robe. Like a vestal at some pagan temple, like a woman of the Celts at some ancient rite. Then slowly, methodically, scarcely with conscious thought, I took from the chest, where I kept it safe hidden, the golden knife, then crossed to the window table, quietly, so Rose would not hear. Impaled the knife, with one swift thrust into the cleft in the oaken top. Returned to the end of the bed where I had sat before.

I would summon the vision of my dreams again, and this time, whatever it revealed, I would not run away.

The book that told of scrying had said the Grail visions often came while suppliants were reciting the rosary or repeating the prayers of the Mass. My own words shaped themselves into a litany without conscious form. *God, show me the truth. Lord set us free. Show me the truth . . .*

I could feel the throbbing of my heart, then my pulses stilling. My breathing slowed. It was happening again. In the flickering light of the candle flames the knife shimmered, gleamed. The room receded. Nothing *was*, except that glow of light growing ever larger until it filled my eyes.

The sea pounded against Tintagel's cliffs. The seagulls screamed. Dark. Damp. The swirling mist. The abyss, filled with sharp rocks far below. A woman, standing, her back to me, her skirts whipped by wind. Charles's painting; that other painting from the Amherst attic; the same tearing panic ravaged me again. The same figures struggled, locked in a love-death embrace. They grew larger, larger; the heads inexorably turned.

My body was shaking, and there was a pain in my chest so that I could scarcely breathe. The roaring in my ears was deafening. *Look*, screamed the inner voices; *look*, screamed the gulls; *look*, moaned the wind and the crashing spray that chilled me through.

The figures turned, and turned, and now the darkness that had concealed them was no more. The light of recognition blazed, and I knew the truth buried within me, from which I long had fled.

Not Arthur, Lancelot, Guinever. Not Charles, Lawrence, Lydian. This was no new truth but recently set in motion.

Charles, yes, golden and glowing, as I first had seen him, with that aura of familiar intimacy which had told me then we had known each other since the dawn of time. Charles, not the impotent king, but the young usurping lover, blazing bright. The older man, whose struggles were watched by a woman at once familiar and strange, that woman who was and was not I—the older man wore the face of *Ason*.

I was both participant and watcher. I was drawn, nearer and ever nearer, to the threatening cliff-edge; I heard the sea waves crashing on the rocks. A woman was screaming, and it was my own voice that screamed. I was running, stumbling through the dark, as I had run from Tintagel in the storm. Hurtling blindly, my steps impeded by the trailing skirts that tangled in my feet—down and down, lunging against barriers and running on, gasping and sobbing, knowing only that I must get away from the sharp terror rushing at my heels.

I came up against something cold and hard, and I went down, and I could run no more.

Hands were seizing me, dragging me up as from the edge of that haunted precipice. A voice was crying out my name, and it was Lawrence's voice. Lawrence was holding me, shaking me, his face full of fear and anguish and another emotion I had sensed there at Tintagel but had never dared to name. All our past encounters ran before my eyes and merged into one. I was on the floor by the dead firepit in the Great Hall, gazing at my sanctuary, my future and my fate. With a shuddering sob, I flung myself into his arms and was locked in an embrace so tight our souls would never let each other go.

12

"What happened?" Lawrence's voice was insistent against my ear, even as his arms held me in a ring of safety.

"I don't want to talk about it. Please, just hold me . . ."

"I've got you. I won't let harm come to you. Not ever. Don't you know I've been *trying* to protect you? That is why—" He broke off. "Lydian, however painful, you must tell me what it is you're so afraid of. Otherwise I can't help you. Don't you understand I have to know?"

I shook my head against his chest, still struggling back to consciousness. "It's all right. I was only dreaming."

"Dreaming!"

"I have these nightmares . . . long before I came I had them. Of Tintagel. That was why—" I made an inconclusive gesture with my hand, and felt Lawrence nod. "They came again, that time when I was staring at the knife. Somehow, somehow they're the key—to everything that's been happening here. I knew it. I ran from it. But tonight—" I took a deep breath and straightened slightly. "We have to uncover it, don't we? The truth. Or we'll none of us be free. So I tried scrying."

Lawrence's voice was so warm. "What did you find?"

"Something I don't understand. I don't want to talk about it. Not now."

"All right. We have other things to speak of, don't we?" He lifted me onto the firepit ledge, and sat beside me. It was the same place I had so often sat with Charles; the thought struck us both at the same moment. Our eyes met, then turned away. Lawrence crossed the room to the wall torches, and they sprang to fitful life. The opal on my ring finger gleamed.

"Lydian." He had come back to stand regarding me in that pose I knew so well, arms folded. But there was no cynicism in him now. "Lydian, Lydian, Lydian." The breath he drew sounded like a pain. "So it is true, then, and we must deal with it. Otherwise we'll be forever locked in separate cages."

I could not speak, and he sat down again beside me, looking at me in a kind of wonder. "You knew, didn't you? You've known from that day at Tintagel, or even London. I tried to keep you from that. I wanted to protect you. Or myself. There wasn't room in my life for love, especially like this."

"Don't. You mustn't say it."

"Yes, we must. We've gone beyond pretending. I love Lydian Ransome." Lawrence laughed, darkly, to himself. "You are a disturbing woman, Lydian. You make people face all their own pretenses, vulnerabilities and needs. I think that's why we felt such antagonism from the first. You shook my careful image of myself as the detached scientist, autonomous, unsusceptible to love because love, trust, passion lay one so open to being hurt."

"I know. I, too."

Lawrence nodded. "Yes, that's why we understand each other, isn't it? We all have suffered the same scars. You. I. Charles."

Charles.

All at once there was a third presence in the room.

"What are we going to do?" Lawrence demanded, and I said swiftly, "Nothing. We can't. It would be too cruel."

"We must. We have to. Pretense is cruelty, too. It raises false hopes, and it sets up walls, and there are few things worse than impenetrable walls between oneself and those one loves."

"Those one loves. Plural." I looked at him, and though we were so close, we did not touch. "Because *that* is the truth. We both do love Charles, as well as one another."

Lawrence gave me a curious glance. "You have finally said it.

That you love me. I was beginning to wonder if you ever would."

"We can say anything to each other now," I said, and knew that it was true.

"Yes, we unlock each other, don't we? That is another of your powers." Lawrence shook his head. "That's why I've been avoiding you, you know. Ever since Tintagel. I knew in your presence I'd make myself an open book."

"I thought it was because in some way I repelled you."

"No.. Oh, no." He leaned toward me and kissed me, deliberately and hard. When he released me, we both were breathless. "That should settle your mind on that score," he said almost brutally. "If I had any doubts about it, it's settled *mine*. And I say again, what are we going to do?"

"Nothing. We can't."

"We must. None of us can go on much longer living with this sickness here. Least of all Charles. Do you think *he* is happy?"

"He doesn't know. He can't."

"I am not talking just about us," Lawrence said roughly. "I mean this whole unreal world."

"Which I made real."

He looked at me sharply. "What made you say that?"

"It's true, isn't it? Doff said so. Before I came there was Avalon, but it was something Charles had deliberately created. He recognized then that it was artifice. Somehow my coming . . . made him shut the walls around us, made him determined to make this *be* the world." The tears were rolling down my cheeks. "I had hoped—I wanted so much to open doors and windows for him, to make him a part of life. And I've done just the opposite." I was both weeping and laughing; I was trembling uncontrollably and could not stop. "Charles is right, isn't he? My coming was both a blessing and a curse."

Lawrence grabbed me by the shoulders. "Lydian, look at me! How long are you going to allow this to go on? You're letting Charles devour you, just as I warned you. Are you trying to expiate Ason Wentworth, or atone for him, or what?"

"You have no right—"

"Yes, I have, and we both know it. Lydian, Lydian, face reality! Look at this artificial Avalon, and see it as it is! Then either stay, or leave, but with full knowledge, not enchantment."

"Why don't *you* leave?"

"I've tried," Lawrence said. "I will one day, for my sanity or my soul's sake, or both. I was just about to do so, when you came. Now I can't go, leaving you spell-imprisoned." I turned my face away, blindly, and his hands locked on mine. "Lydian, come with me, before it is too late. You love me. We belong together, you cannot deny that."

I could not answer, and my silence was as eloquent as speech.

He put his arms around me then, and held me quietly. "Ah, Lydian, what a tangled pattern we've put in motion. It almost makes me believe in Charles's damned archetypes, eternally tracing their doomed triangle. I am not going to let that happen here. We must break free."

"We can't hurt Charles like that."

"He's hurting himself. We've both tried to give him life. If he's determined to withdraw from it, he has no right to drag others with him. Anyway," Lawrence said brutally, "he has Doff. And Meriel, who would be only too willing to take your place. Lydian, look at the truth and face it plain. If we help him continue in this unreal world of his, aren't we encouraging him in the very thing we think is deeply wrong?"

"How can we stop?" I pulled free to look at him in deep bewilderment. "You saw him tonight. He's ill, and not just physically. We both saw it. The only thing that keeps him going is his quest, his work, his determination to bring it all to fulfillment at the symposium. Oh, Lawrence, if you do love me, don't tempt me to betray everything I believe!"

"Then after the symposium. There must be an end to pretending, for all our sakes. You can get an annulment easily enough. Lydian, look at me!"

I did, and what he saw there drew stillness like a chill veil between us. "I can't," I said. "You understand that, don't you? Because I love him, we both love him, and he needs us. If we took that away it would destroy him."

"Tell me one thing," Lawrence said quietly. "If you were free, would you marry me?"

"Don't ask that. Please don't ask me that."

But he knew the answer. He rose then, drawing me up with

him, and pulled me close. "So we go on together, the three of us, playing out our predestined roles. Because there is, after all, such a thing as honor. And compassion. And may God have mercy on our souls."

I lifted my face to look at him through a blur of tears, and his mouth came down on mine, and when at length we released each other one more truth was graven on my soul. For Charles's sake and for our own we would never dare to touch each other in that way again.

I went to bed and rose in the morning like a woman made of stone. Charles was worse, much worse. Rose, bringing me late breakfast on a tray, looked deeply worried. "His lordship had a second bad attack toward morning, and another since. Ma'am dear, why didn't you wake me?"

"What for?" I said tiredly. "You could have been no use. He did not even want me."

Rose snorted. "It was her ladyship he had nursing him this night. But it's you he's asking for now, and he's afraid you'll not go to him."

"Of course I'll go." I threw back the covers quickly, bid Rose fetch my clothes.

The stench of the sickroom struck me like a blow as I entered Charles's apartment. The August air reeked of medicine, alcohol, disinfectant, and a sick-sweet smell. Gangrene, and the ever-present threat of blood-poisoning and death. Charles looked ghastly, his face bloated, his brow wet with sweat. Meriel was holding him, trying to quiet him, and Lawrence was wringing out cold cloths. But I had eyes only for Charles, who was shaking with fever and crying out my name.

I went straight to him and took his hands. "My dear, it's Lydian. I'm here."

"Lydian . . . I thought you were gone . . . they said you'd been taken from me. Don't leave me. Don't ever leave me."

"I won't. I promised. Hold onto me." His hands were burning, and I looked round wildly. "Where is Doff?"

"No one's seen him. And after that scene last night—"

"He's the only one who can help now. Look in the study! And send for the doctor who was here before!"

"You know how Charles feels about doctors!" That was

182

Meriel, her eyes frantic. "We dare not take responsibility—"

"*I* will take responsibility. Charles could die, don't you know that?" I wheeled on Lawrence fiercely. "Get them!"

Lawrence vanished and returned with Doff, his clothes and hair in disarray but his eyes all on Charles. "Get out, all of you!" he ordered roughly. When I did not respond Lawrence pushed both Meriel and me out of the room.

"Leave Doff alone with him. The doctor will come soon, and I'll stay near in case I'm needed."

"But Charles—"

"I'll fetch you when he calls for you. Do you think I won't? But he's barely conscious now. You can do him no good here, nor yourself either."

Meriel, after a sharp look, left, but I lingered, indecisive. When she had vanished Lawrence took me by the hands and drew me over to the balcony railing. "Lydian, get hold of yourself. You must be strong. And you've known this could happen at any moment."

"But for it to be now, after last night—I meant everything to be so good for him, and it was so wrong—"

"You could not have known that. None of us could. And your intentions were the best. He'll realize that."

"He could die."

Lawrence hesitated. "If it should happen," he said at last, "would it not be for Charles the 'noblest end'? He is a proud man who cannot live with failure and decay. To go now, after his successes live and while he pursues his quest and still believes his dreams—wouldn't that be better for him than to be an Arthur who has lived too long?"

I pulled my hands free to press them against my ears and after a moment, not touching me again, he left.

The day dragged, and Charles's door stayed shut. I longed so for the peace and solitude of the abbey ruins, but I would not leave Avalon. I took the Celtic women manuscript out to the garden and worked mechanically among the dying roses, and presently Meriel joined me with her needlepoint. We spoke but seldom, wrapped in our separate thoughts.

The doctor did not appear until early afternoon, and when he did the house was thrown in an uproar. I could hear him storming in the upstairs corridor as I hurried in. "What have you been giving this man? He's drugged! It has seriously worsened his condition!"

Doff's voice, heatedly: "Nothing but the soothing drops you ordered, and according to directions! He's been in great pain!"

"He nearly reached a permanent end to that condition," the doctor snapped. "Laudanum's an opium derivative. A small quantity more of it would have killed him!"

Then Doff again, frantic and protesting. *He* had not given an overdose. It was not he who wished Charles dead. Charles had suspected some enemies tried to kill him. There had been other attempts. The doctor, snorting, labeled that typical opium fantasy. And I—

I stopped dead halfway up the stairs. Turned, as if I too were drug-compelled, and went straight as one possessed to Charles's study. The room was still a shambles. Charles's book notes, brandy-stained, lay on the floor, and the blanket I had thrown over the sleeping Doff trailed from the sofa where he must have thrown it in his haste to speed to Charles's side. I paid no heed, crossed to the desk, pulled out the side drawer and thrust my hand within.

The glass bottle, which last night had been half full of medicine, was gone.

I leaned against the desk as nausea swept me, but through my faintness certain facts stood clear.

Charles could not have administered the dosage to himself, certainly not from the bottle hidden here.

Those enemies Charles had alluded to so darkly could be real, those occurrences we had labeled accidents not accidental at all. My mind flashed back to that sense of presence in my room, the ivy torn loose outside my window. But the threat, I knew now, came from no outside agency bent on robbery or vengeance—the guards patrolling Avalon's approaches ruled out that illusion. This danger came from within.

The servants. Charles himself. Doff. Meriel. Lawrence.

Doff had had cause to turn on Charles last night. Doff had been in this room alone.

But it was not Doff's shambling form I saw in my mind's eye

as I straightened, gulped air, and automatically commenced
tidying the debris. It was Lawrence, bending over me, saying,
"Would it not be for Charles the 'noblest end'?" Saying,
"If you were free, would you marry me?"

It was impossible. My mind leaped at straws. Lawrence could
not have been behind the "accident," for two of the accidents
had threatened me.

Threatened me, not killed me. "I would have thought that
would have driven you away," Lawrence had said after the
earlier attempt.

I had to keep busy, could not allow myself to think. I worked
doggedly on my manuscript, scarcely took respite when Meriel
insisted that I stop for tea. Lawrence was not there; I could
hardly have borne it if he had been. I could hardly bear it,
either, that he was not. For the first time I could understand
why Charles might resort to brandy and drugs to blot out not
only physical but mental pain.

It was nearly dinner time when Doff came out to us. He
looked exhausted; as though he'd gone through hell.

"He wants *you*."

It was to me Doff spoke. I who sped to my husband's side,
and held his hand all through that endless night and through the
day that followed. Charles alternately clung to me, pleading
with me to stay, and then when fits of irrationality were on him
tossed and moaned, imagining he was that bygone Arthur, crying out that he was invulnerable, that he needed no one. Crying
that he was cursed for some old sin, that Nemesis was drawing
nearer to destroy him. And then, in intervals of lucidity again,
recognizing me as his wife, promising me greatness, murmuring
his gratitude and love. The August heat was heavy in the trees
and I sat like stone, whispering reassurance, whispering peace,
and the thin feverish fingers clutched at mine and dug the opal
ring deep into my flesh. And I knew that what I had said to
Lawrence that disastrous night was irrevocably true: while
Charles lived, I could never leave him. Not if I was ever to
know peace within myself.

Then Charles was better, or he claimed he was, and insisted
on being put in his chair, to resume his driven preparations

for the symposium. "Don't fuss at me," he exclaimed pettishly, when I remonstrated. "I have work to finish. Or do you want to see me fail?" And even worse, when I fought against his continued use of laudanum, "Am I to be condemned to pain and suffering by my own wife? That's it, isn't it? You hope I'll die!"

Oh, Lawrence was right, the air in Avalon was poison, and all of us were growing sick.

September and the symposium were drawing near. Reports came from London of successful sales of paintings and of books. The art exhibit closed and the Arthurian cycle paintings were returned home to Avalon. I could scarcely bear to look at them; they told too much. Charles ignored them; his mind was all on the symposium and the lecture notes he was constantly rewriting. He drove Lawrence to work faster than ever on the tunnel excavation—the missing tomb containing the bones of Arthur and Guinever, the dower gifts, *must* be found.

"What happens if the tunnel doesn't lead to Glastonbury Abbey? If I come to the end and there's no tomb? He has to be prepared for that," Lawrence said to me, and I retorted, "How?" It was one of the few conversations that took place between us.

Then Lawrence stopped working in the tunnel and vanished for two days, murmuring about personal business elsewhere. God help me, with his departure some of the tension within me eased. Because I was not so constantly reminded of our Lancelot-Guinever attraction? Because unconsciously I sensed that Charles was safer in his absence? I would not allow myself to think.

I worked on the Celtic women manuscript, meeting all of us as in a mirror on every page. Whether the writing or scholarship was good or bad, I did not know; it was as if I were drugged. I longed for criticism, but I did not show the work to Charles, not only because I feared material like the Fisher-King myth would hurt him, but because he so clearly did not wish to see. He wanted attention on nothing but his own endeavors. He was taking too much laudanum, too much brandy. He was painting again, far into the night, on canvases he violently refused to share. And at his insistence our midnight tête-à-têtes at the firepit, in a parody of their old spontaneous intimacy, were resumed.

I felt as if I were constantly being forced to play a role and never had a chance to come offstage.

Did it help or hinder, having Meriel there? I could not know. She showed no sign of leaving; she shared with me the burden of keeping Charles in balance. She made me feel as if I must constantly be on my guard.

And behind everything, like a slumbering giant, lay the yet-uncomprehended memory of Tintagel, of my waking dream, my terrifying scrying and the unanswered questions that reverberated in my brain. The gnawing sensation that somewhere, hidden and unrecognized, I held the key to past and to present nagged at me. When Charles released me and I tried to sleep, the night that Lawrence was away, the figures kept appearing and reappearing before my eyes. Figures on a cliff-edge— Arthur, Lancelot, Guinever. Ason, Charles, my mother. Charles, Lawrence, me. Our relationships, our life together, tottered on the edge of the abyss.

"Charles," I asked next morning when we were handling correspondence with the symposium organizers at Winchester, "why did you stop working with my father? Was there real trouble?"

"Why should there be? We had a difference of opinion. And I no longer believed in the direction your father's research took. Don't think of that. It's all dust and ashes now."

"Please, Charles. I need to know. Did you quarrel? Fight?"

Charles laughed shortly. "You knew your father. Do you think that it was possible to fight him? He was pig-headed, arrogant, not caring whom he hurt. But one could not reach him. It must have galled him having research, especially the financing, depend on an assistant. Lydian, is it too much to ask that we let the dead past stay buried and concentrate on getting these letters in the mail? I have no time to waste."

Nor did I have better success with Meriel later, when we sought relief from the late August heat in the dimness of the Great Hall. "Why did Charles and my father give up their search for Arthur, do you know?" I tried to make my voice innocent and casual. "Did they decide it was useless, or was there trouble? What were my parents like?"

"I was only seventeen. I don't remember," Meriel answered shortly. "I never met your mother. Excuse me, but I believe I'll lie down until time for tea. This heat fatigues me."

Perhaps it was that humidity which caused the sense of steadily accelerating tension in me. I worked on doggedly after Meriel left, at once grateful and uneasy in the solitude. Even in summer the Great Hall with its thick walls retained a hint of dampness which was intensified by the air. This room was not at its best by day; it came to life by night when torches and firepit blazed, but now everything lay as in a waiting stupor. The banners on the walls hung limp, and the thin mull of my summer dress clung to my body. I rubbed my arm across my forehead, longing for a glass of American iced tea.

A presence loomed behind me. Doff, bending forward to glance over my shoulder at my work. It was an invasion of privacy that annoyed me, but ever since that night when I had seen him vulnerable, I had endeavored to be kinder in my treatment of him.

"So you're taking over the writing department at Avalon these days," he remarked. "The old order does change."

"I'd scarcely say taking over." I made myself smile pleasantly. "I only hope I can do my husband credit."

"You needn't expect him to *give* credit. He never appreciates anything except what's his, and not always that." There was a strange note in his voice. I glanced at him, and he was grinning painfully. His eyes had moved swiftly to my manuscript. "Impotent king, eh? I shouldn't think *you'd* be wanting to write of that."

The manuscript was open to the legend of the Fisher King. A distorted version of that must not go back to Charles—with one swift movement I moved it away, and Doff's face colored.

"Maybe writing about the situation makes you feel better, does it? Of course, there are other cures for what ails you, aren't there, Lady Ransome?"

The sudden, unexpected animosity in his voice took me by such surprise that there was a moment's shock. In that instant, before I knew what was happening, Doff's arms had gone round me and he was kissing me clumsily. My reaction was immediate and instinctive; my hand came up and struck him hard across the face. "You devil!"

He let go of me and backed away, rubbing his mouth against his arm. "What's the matter, do you think you're too good for me? You'd be surprised!"

He'd been drinking. My voice was shaking, but I willed it low and quiet. "Don't you ever lay a hand on me again."

"Or what? You'll tell your husband? That's a laugh! I thought you were decent, but you're not. You're a trollop just like both the others. What do you think it'd do to *him* if I was to say what I saw by the firepit the night he was so sick? His lady, and his substitute son! That's a laugh, too! The great expert can't tell the difference in value between counterfeit and real!"

"Get out of here!" Lawrence was standing in the doorway. He strode forward, grabbed Doff by the arm. "If you ever threaten her ladyship again, I'll break you in two. Do you understand?" He released Doff roughly and the boy stumbled off, shooting us a black glance of pure hate.

I turned to Lawrence, half dazed, but he did not touch me. "Are you alone? Come outside, quickly. We have to talk." He led the way to the far side of the rose garden. "We won't be heard here. Lydian, you'd better sit down."

"Lawrence, what's the matter?"

Lawrence's mouth twisted. "I've been engaged in research. Into the recent past, not the fifth century. Lydian, has it occurred to you there could be more truth than we thought to Charles's enemy theory? And that as things now stand, it has to be somebody within these walls?"

I prayed Lawrence would take my silence for bewilderment; I could barely breathe.

"It dawned on me that for investigative scholars, there's one unknown quantity we've been taking at face value. Mr. Barrett Doffman. He leads a serf's life here. Did you ever speculate on why?"

My lips were dry. "Charles took him on as a protégé, and educated him, since he was fifteen."

"Yes, but why? Why him? He's scarcely Charles's style. Except in spaniel-like devotion. Charles takes advantage of him, and suffocates his talent. I've often wondered why the youth would want to bury himself here. So on a hunch I paid a visit to Somerset House."

I looked at him blankly.

"The national house of records. Births, deaths, adoptions. That obscure country doctor and his wife weren't our Doff's real parents. He was adopted at birth. And do you know who his mother was? The Lady Meriel Spenser."

There was someone else here besides Lawrence who had a motive for wishing Charles dead. That was the first thing that registered on my dazed brain. Only then was I allowing myself to realize consciously what I had so feared.

"He must have looked up the record sometime, seen a chance to connect himself with wealth and position, and brought himself to the family's attention." Lawrence paused; went on gently. "You realize, don't you, Lydian, where this leads? What is the next, inevitable question?"

But reaction had set in now, and I was stunned. I gazed at Lawrence dumbly, but before he could go on a voice interrupted from the garden entrance. Firm, imperious; Meriel's voice.

"Mr. Stearns, if you will excuse us, I wish to talk to her ladyship alone."

Lawrence hesitated a moment; looked at me; bowed; left.

She's his mother, I thought. Meriel is Doff's mother. Twenty-one years ago; she must have been barely seventeen . . . I wet my lips. "Meriel, forgive me, do sit down. Tea will soon be here."

"I don't want tea. I want you to understand!" Her dark gaze intensified her pallor and the blackness of her hair, and her eyes were flashing. "I warned you I would not allow you to hurt my cousin! I can understand how you may feel a need for an outside life, but you could at least have the decency not to seduce a young man Charles regards almost as a son, and under his very nose!"

I stared at her, then color rushed to my face. "Talking with a professional associate in my own garden can scarcely be called seduction! Lawrence Stearns and I have never been guilty of any impropriety, and we never will. We both care about Charles too deeply. And if you have been made a party to any misrepresentations—"

"Lawrence!" Meriel made a savage gesture. "I'm talking about that disgusting exhibition just now in the Hall with Barrett Doffman!"

My voice was shaking. "If you witnessed that, you ought to know it was not *I* who initiated it!" She was looking through me with those implacable, judging eyes. Meriel, whose own morality had just been exposed to me as a façade. My whole body was trembling, and it was then they burst from me, as from some daemon deep inside, those brutal, damning words. "Is it really Charles you're worried about, Meriel? Or are you afraid I'm going to corrupt your son?"

I would have given some of my own blood to snatch them back. But it was too late. As in slow motion, like a picture under water, Meriel's wrath crumpled, dissolved, was replaced by a numb premonitory bewilderment. "What did you say?"

"That I know Barrett Doffman is your son. Meriel, I'm sorry, I never meant to— *Meriel!"*

For she had sunk down, like a carved figure, on the marble bench, and like marble were the knuckles pressed against her rigid mouth. Only the eyes were alive with torment and a terrible apprehension. I went to her, shaken. "Meriel—oh, dear God, Meriel, did you not *know*?"

Her voice was a dry whisper through her lips. "I never knew . . . what happened to the child. I was ill when it was born, and my parents said it had died. No one would tell me anything."

"Meriel, I am so sorry—"

"He must not know. You have got to promise me that the boy and Charles will never know!"

I could not tell her what I already suspected: that Doff knew, that this was why he'd come, that her son was seeking to profit from her cousin's death. I could only repeat, with a deep pity, "I will not tell. I would never tell."

"Wouldn't you? You go digging into a dead past, waking the forgotten ghosts, and I should *trust* you? You've come here, setting old patterns into motion—" Her strength was returning; she turned on me, her bosom heaving. "You brought that past

to life, against all warning, so you are going to hear it all, *all*. You found out I had a child. Did it occur to you to wonder who was the father? Charles, my dear, your Charles! I gave him a son, which is more than you can ever do."

That was what Lawrence had been about to say, looking down at me with such compassion.

"And do you want to know why?" The words were bursting from her as though a dam had broken at last from the pressure of twenty years of silence. "Your mother! Your predecessor, Charles's daemonic angel . . . she had him in her power, and I tried to rip him free with the only means I knew."

My mother. *To Virgilia, who has all the Gifts.* Charles, Ason, Virgilia in my vision of Tintagel's cliffs.

"Your mother," Meriel repeated quietly. "I never saw your parents, but I heard of them. Endlessly, whenever Charles needed to talk. That was the only way he saw me, as his shadow, his listening ear. I'd hoped for more in time. And then *she* came."

Meriel made the same brutal, cutting gesture I had seen Doff make as at an invisible foe. "The perfect wife. Charles's damnable ideal woman, his Guinever, his Sidh. Virgin, Mother, mistress, nurse—all the things he stopped longing for in the dead years, things he dreamed of again when he saw *you*, her image. What you're writing about in that infernal book—"

I knew. I knew.

Her mouth twisted bitterly. "There was only one flaw in his perfect creature. Unlike Guinever, she would not risk all, would never really give. They were young and warm, your father was cold and cruel. She'd weep to Charles, he'd rail to me. For three years . . . indecisions, uncertainties, Charles growing more and more enthralled." Meriel's voice was vicious. "I knew she'd never leave your father. She was too wary of her reputation. But Charles wouldn't listen. He was throwing his money away on a fool's expedition, being exploited by your parents, wasting his talent and his life."

My voice was a ghost's voice, dry and still. "You can't know for sure."

"*I know*. He was losing his hold on reality then, as now. She'd thrown a spell on him. I loved him, and I had to watch him growing ever more besotted." Meriel drew a deep breath that was like a sob. "I was young, and terrified for him, and a fool. I thought I could break the spell by weaving my own, the only way I knew."

Her hand flickered for a moment at her breast and was still. "One night when she'd repulsed him—he was in a terrible state, distraught, he'd been drinking . . . I kept him with me, and wouldn't let him go. And in the morning, he went from me, to *her* to paint her picture at Tintagel; to fall, or jump with her. I've even wondered sometimes if there was a suicide pact."

"You're mad!"

"I'm not! She'd left word she was going to London; your father went there after her, taking you. It was more than a day before her body was found, lying on the rocks, by Charles—" Her eyes shut tight a moment, but she went steadily on. "Charles was in hospital for two years, he almost died, he buried all of it deep inside. And meanwhile I had a child, and my family . . . disposed of it. To a country doctor, apparently. I didn't know. And I'd never told them who the father was."

I rose slowly, shaking my head. "No. It isn't true. These images you're painting, they're not Charles, not my mother. Charles told me she was everything that is good. They would never—"

"Where are you going?"

"To Charles." I flung it at her blindly, and the tears were streaming down my face. "To Charles, to find out the truth. We have had enough of pretending here. I have to know!"

"No!" She stood before me fiercely. "You'll tell him none of this. It's buried too deep in him, it would destroy him. And destroy *you*. Because there's more. You know that, don't you? And you're afraid to hear. Why do you think I tried to keep you from marrying Charles? What do you think caused that great, final rift between Ason and Charles, Ason and your mother? You've said Ason never loved you; didn't you wonder why? Didn't you realize he came to suspect that he was not your father?"

13

For a moment I could only stare at her. Then, choking and gagging, I was running to the house. To the firepit, to drop onto the cold stone ledge while the world whirled.

Charles's painting of Virgilia, the book inscription; Ason's attitude; the peculiar chemistry of emotions they both felt toward me. My dream vision of my mother, my father and my husband, locked in struggle . . . had I as a child, too young to know, sensed and remembered deep conflict in the air?

Myself as a child . . . the numb horror of Meriel's last allusion broke over me like an engulfing wave and I went down under it. Came up, carried on a sea of pain toward one ray of light. Charles might have buried the memory of those last days with my parents so deep he could not bear them; perhaps even, as she suggested, could not remember. But I had been nearly two years old. Three years those three had worked together, Meriel said. Since before my birth. Charles had to have remembered that; he never would have married me . . . that terrible implication of my parentage that she had flung at me, to keep me silent, could not possibly be true.

But what *was* truth? I had not known my mother. Had never really, I realized now, known my father. What had they been like, Ason, Virgilia and Charles, before—

I was already accepting Meriel's story at face value, when I had no proof.

My mother, my father and my husband. The tragic, doomed pattern repeated again now, myself in my mother's role, Charles no longer the life-restoring lover but the impotent aging husband, the Fisher King. In the myth, the quester changed his role as he grew older, became what he had betrayed.

No. It was too neat, too pat, too coincidental. It could not be true.

What was truth? Truth was that I could not go to Charles, could never ask. To confront him with this web of suspicion and past tragedy at this time and in his condition would destroy him. I could not do it, because—whatever other truths there were—I still loved him. I clung to that known fact as an anchor in the swirling dark.

But I had to find the other, hidden secrets of this place as well. Sanity, even life itself, could depend upon it. The only way to put an end to these sick, recurring patterns was to let in the light of truth. And it was I who must do it. The right questions must be asked if the wasteland was ever to be green again.

The right questions. The question in the myth of the Fisher King had been, "Whom does the Grail serve?" I knew that in the old pre-Christian myths the Grail symbolized woman, the sacramental, healing, life-giving force. Whom does the woman serve? What role had my mother served in that past, now-repeating triangle? Had she been a Guinever, as Charles perceived her—or, as Meriel had portrayed her, a daemonic, corrupting Morgan le Fay, Arthur's sister-mistress, the strange enchantress? What was the role that I should play at Avalon? To conceal, reveal; to give—but what, and how? Those same powers that could heal, could bless, could also, if misused, bring destruction.

I must find the truth about Guinever and her gifts, the truth about my mother, if I was ever to be free to be Lydian. Free to love in sunlight and wholesome air, without fear that my gifts and what I did with them would bring a doom on the house, and those for whom I cared.

Guinever, whose shadow I had become, whose copied jewels

I wore, and who appeared in my place even in my wedding portrait.

Portrait. The word soared upward like a meteor. Charles's paintings, which had, from the first, so disturbed me with their uncanny, pulsing life. Charles's Arthurian cycle, his lifework, which that day in the gallery had drawn me with a kind of threatening fascination, as to a dark mirror. Paintings that were re-created, even before I saw them, in my dreams. Paintings of Tintagel. I remembered Meriel talking about that never-explained accident that had happened at Tintagel.

My mother, Meriel said, falling to her death on the very rocks that had exerted such a sick pull on me. Falling in a way identical to the way I fell in my own dreams. Charles falling, to live on in a suspended life at Avalon, not unlike King Arthur's mythical sleep. Accidents: Charles being gassed, Charles being overdrugged. Myself gassed, trapped by falling stone—were these accidents designed to kill, or to drive me off. "Accident" was another motif in the dark pattern that had woven Charles and me together.

Charles had been painting a picture of my mother just before his accident. I caught my breath. Could *that* have been the Ransome painting I had uncovered in the Massachusetts attic, which had shaken Ason so? But how could it have gotten there, and why would he have kept it?

The thoughts, the questions, ran in erratic circles through my brain. I was pacing back and forth in a square of light on the floor of the Great Hall, jewel-colored light, emerald, sapphire, ruby, falling through the stained glass high above. Charles had had those windows specially made, depicting his obsessive pre-occupation; there was no escaping the prison of those legends here.

"My lady." Hodge was beside me, trying to gain my notice. "My lady, tea is waiting. Does your ladyship wish to have it taken to the garden, or brought in here?"

"Oh—I should like a cup of tea in here, alone. You might serve the others wherever you may find them." I had no wish to encounter anyone now. I sipped the tea slowly, and thought of pictures. Pictures in colored glass, pictures in dreams, pictures on the gallery wall. Why were there blank spaces in the gallery, waiting for missing scenes? What was missing, and why had I, even that first day, sensed in their very absence something wrong?

I set my empty teacup down on the firepit ledge, crossed to the gallery and went in, locking the great carved doors behind me. They stretched before me down both sides of the long corridor, Charles's paintings, almost leaping off the canvas in their throbbing power. They were living presences, lowering over me. I summoned all my own strength, flung it back at them with the force of love and the quest for truth, and they seemed to shimmer, to grow less dynamic, to fall into a kind of sleep. Slowly, deliberately, I made my way along the gallery, searching, analyzing, probing. How much more I saw now, after my delving into the earlier Arthurian sources and the psychological truths behind them; how much I had learned. I recognized early Celtic elements—the symbolism of knife and chalice for man and woman; the union of elements sacred and profane; the meeting of the Real World and the Other in water, twilight, mist, and dawn.

Recognized what was missing, for I knew chapter and verse of the legends so much better now. The tournament in which Lancelot had fought, wearing for the first time Guinever's favor on his lance. Uther Pendragon seducing Ygraine at Tintagel Castle, disguised as her husband. Lancelot and Guinever, entrapped together in her tower room while Arthur was away . . .

All scenes of passion between lovers—and ladies who were not their own.

I moved rapidly now, from one painting to another, swiftly scanning. Understanding, now that my eyes were open, why it was that those figures had troubled me with a nagging sense of familiarity. The woman, who resembled me faintly but was not I, was the woman of my dreams. The young man with his glowing eyes and golden beard . . . the older king, with the suggestive touch of the fanatic, slightly cruel, driven . . .

I slammed a door across the path of my own thoughts, lest racing imagination lead me to fantasy. It was truth I must find, the truth behind Meriel's allegations, the truth behind my dreams.

I left the gallery, locking it again after me, then went to my room and dressed for dinner in one of my flowing gowns. They were undeniably comfortable in summer's heat; they were becoming, too becoming; in them, I was slowly changing to Guinever, as though some subtle poison emanated from their seams.

Lawrence did not appear at dinner but it was a great enough strain sitting at table with Meriel, making small talk, while the memory of our earlier confrontation pulsed between us. If Charles noticed the tension, he gave no sign; he was embarked on one of his feverish monologues. Brighter, if anything, than usual. I wondered if he was in pain, if he was covering it with laudanum. Doff sat in silence, watching us.

Doff could not have told Charles of our own encounter, or of having seen me that night in Lawrence's arms. He would not have dared—not for my sake, I knew that well enough, but for Charles's.

Dessert was served. Demitasse. Brandy. Meriel excused herself; was even her iron control breaking? Charles waved Doff off; talked on.

Charles had come up with yet another theory. He grew excited, expounded; looked at me and broke off, his eyes growing cold. "I am sorry if I bore you. Your mind is on your own writing."

"Oh, my dear, no."

"I saw your look of tolerance."

"I only wondered if you would have time to develop this idea adequately, if you mean to include it in your talk at the symposium."

"Must all of you harp incessantly on the passage of time? Work on your book. I am going to paint."

Though he drained all pleasure from my newfound ability to write, I brought out my manuscript dutifully, for the deadline was drawing near. Charles wheeled himself into his studio, slamming and bolting the heavy door behind him. The hours passed. My manuscript did not progress; every note I read sent my mind rushing down dark paths. It was nearly midnight when Charles reappeared, bade me ring for Hodge to bring the brandy and our usual supper.

The savory tasted like sawdust; I drank two cups of black, bitter coffee, and when Charles quaffed as much of brandy I did not interfere. He glanced at me sharply, over the rim of the gold-crusted glass. It seemed an interminable time before he summoned Doff to take him to bed.

I went to my room, undressed, said good night to Rose and lay awake in the darkness after the sound of her soft breathing told me she was asleep. The night sounds were magnified outside my window, or perhaps it was only that my nerves, tautened by caffeine, vibrated like a violin string at every sound. An hour I waited, two, until I was sure laudanum and brandy had Charles deep in slumber. Then, cautiously, I swung my feet out of bed.

At the window, the eerie sounds of dying summer assailed my ears. No glow of light emanated from any of the windows. I dressed silently, in a dark waist and skirt, thrusting my feet into slippers that would make no sound. The door of my bedroom creaked as I opened it; I froze. Rose had not been disturbed. I eased myself out, drew the door shut behind me, inch by inch. The black darkness of the upper hall swallowed me.

Eight feet over and I would reach the rail; follow the railing between the high-reaching pillars to the headpost of the stair. Then down, down, each step like a plunge into the abyss. My fingers gripped the banister, my toes in their soft slippers like cat's feet on the treads. All my life's panic, all the terror of precipice, nightmare, falling stones and poisoned air crashed over me like waves upon a rock. Then there was level ground beneath me, the slate floor of the Great Hall.

Wait. Listen. Search for bearings from the faint gleam like a North Star through one high window. I groped in my pocket for the candle and matches I had secreted there, but dared not light them. My fingers closed around the hairpin and the slender metal manicure implement I had taken from my dresser. I glided through the dark to the carved door that was a duplicate of the gallery's. It was the door to the studio, forbidden ground, repository of secrets like Merlin's cave. Slowly, carefully, deliberately, I picked the lock.

The tumblers turned. I eased the heavy handle. Soundlessly,

199

the door swung open and closed at my fingers' bidding. I was engulfed again in blackness. Now, at last, with shaking hands, I struck a match.

The corridor sprang to life, distorted in the flickering light. *Here* were pictures. They reached out to me with their daemonic pull from every space of wall. Familiar landscape, rooms, their techniques developing, changing—he must have worked on them over the whole sweep of twenty years. Here they all hung, the missing paintings from the Arthurian cycle, so like the others yet touched with a macabre, Bosch-like horror. Scenes of threatening danger, dark enchantment, forbidden love. Meriel's voice, Charles's voice and that of Ason all echoed like sounds from the underworld in my ears. For there was no evasion now, no careful, faint disguise. Arthur's face, Lancelot's, Guinever's. I knew them as I knew my own, even though they had grown younger by twenty years, even though one was known to me only in my dreams. My father's face, my husband's, and my mother's.

It had been true, the unbelievable allegation Meriel had flung at me. Virgilia, who had all the gifts; who had loved, as I. Ason the aging Arthur, Charles the young Lancelot, the protégé, the son-figure. I recoiled from a painting of my mother in Charles's arms, her hair cascading like gold down her bare back, swung round to confront a towering painting on the easel.

The paint was still wet, it had been slashed on with savage strokes. Like the others, yet not like. Lancelot and Guinever, locked in passionate embrace in the Great Hall. Not Charles and Virgilia. Lawrence and myself.

He knew. He knew. Charles, the Lancelot lover-figure in my parents' tragedy; now, in bitter reversal, the Arthur to his own protégé's Lancelot—and with my mother's daughter.

I was going to faint. Caution flew; I reeled to the studio door, flung it open, stumbled out of it to be caught and locked in Lawrence's arms.

I did not wonder why he was there; how I could be so sure that it was he. I *knew* him, even in blackness—his touch, the faint scent of the clothes he wore, his presence. I had wanted him, though I had not even known it till that moment, and he had come. It was enough. I clung to him as to a lifeline.

"Lydian, what in God's name has happened?" His voice was a harsh whisper against my ear, but his arms were strong. I shook my head, trying to blot out memory.

"I had to find out—I had to know—"

"Know what?"

"My mother; Charles and my mother—"

"*What?*" Lawrence came to a swift decision. "No. Not here." Before I knew what was happening, he had scooped me up, was running with me in stealthy silence.

"Where are we going?"

"Don't speak." We stopped; there was the barest creak of metal. The elevator—opening to admit us, shutting again, descending.

"Lawrence—"

His hand across my mouth cut off speech. The elevator stopped. He set me on my feet, propelled me out; the door behind us closed. Lawrence struck a match, set it to a wall sconce, and his laboratory workroom sprang to life. White, orderly, sane, like a safe haven. I whirled on Lawrence, and he said, "Not yet. We'd better go into the tunnel proper." He took me by the hand, pulled me after him through the warren of rooms to the vault door, spun the dials. And I went after him, unquestioning. Later, that was what was to seem so curious; I felt no fear, no wonder, just followed where he led.

The tunnel seemed strange. The artifacts were gone, and there was only stone corridor, stone blocks, rubble and dust of stone, gold and copper-toned and white in the light of the gas jets Lawrence turned up high. The sense of threat and terror the tunnel once had held for me was no more. Now it seemed like a safe haven, and it was the swirling mists, the dark secrets and locked rooms of Avalon that filled me with horror and with fear. How ironic. I started to laugh and could not stop.

"Steady." Lawrence's fingers closed around my wrist, and my pulse stilled. "Sit down. I apologize for my peremptory treatment, but this is the only place where there's guaranteed privacy to talk. I'm beginning to feel as if nowadays the walls upstairs *do* have ears."

"That is just what I was thinking. Ears, hands of entrapment, evil souls—we're all of us getting sucked into fantasy, and who's to know any more which is the fantasy, and which the real?" I started to laugh again, hysterically, and checked myself.

"What were you doing in Charles's workroom?" I did not answer, and Lawrence looked at me. "You were going to tell me, just now, when I had to stop you. Tell me now."

My voice was dry, mechanical, its ordinariness belying the shudder that ran through me. "I had to know the truth. Meriel told me Charles and my mother had been lovers."

"Meriel would tell you anything if she believed it would in some way help Charles."

"But it's true. We may lie in our words, but not in our work. Painting, writing . . . truth surfaces there, whether we wish it or not. Lawrence, you know that." He nodded, and I swallowed, willing myself on. "That's why I broke in. He's never let me in there; I should have known that there was something I was not supposed to see." I began shaking uncontrollably. "They're all there. The missing paintings. My husband, my father, my mother. Lancelot, Arthur, Guinever. We're not the first to repeat that triangle, you see. And we're damned, damned to keep walking through the pattern, on and on."

Lawrence's hand struck my face sharply. "Lydian, stop it!" He looked at me, breathing hard. "I seem destined to keep being brutal to you for your own sake. I'm sorry. There's more, isn't there? Tell me."

I could not look up. "Meriel said the reason Ason never loved me was that he always had doubts about whether he was my father."

There was a silence. "She used every weapon that came to hand, didn't she?" Lawrence said slowly. "Real or imagined."

"I can't blame her. I'd just told her I knew Doff was her son."

"You told her?" Lawrence demanded sharply.

"I didn't mean to. I shouldn't have, but when she kept hammering at those terrible things— Lawrence, she *didn't know*! She says she didn't know, and I believe her. The child had been put out for adoption." I shook my head dazedly. "It's all so impossible, more like myth than reality. Doff's her son. *Charles's* son," I added, and Lawrence started. "But none of them knowing . . . Doff came here just by chance."

"I doubt that." Lawrence's mouth twisted. "As you say, it's hard to discern truth from fantasy while in the vortex of the storm. But, as I told you, I suspect Doff paid a visit to Somerset House himself one time. He's the type to feed on boyish dreams of being a changeling, an aristocrat not belonging to the common herd. How convenient for him to unearth illustrious parentage, however unblessed, and how easy to write a fan letter, insinuate oneself, feed on dreams of revealing one's true identity at a propitious moment. Perhaps he's already tried it, and been rebuffed. It would explain some of Charles's outburst on his birthday. I've wondered why he's been so callous toward Doff of late."

"Meriel swears neither Charles nor Doff could possibly know. She begged me to keep the secret from them."

Lawrence's eyes were skeptical. "Charles, perhaps. But Doff? He's certainly seen himself as Charles's closest devotee and certain heir. How distressing for him when the unexpected happened and Charles took a wife."

Charles took a wife. The shaking began again, and Lawrence saw it. "As for what Meriel implied about your parentage," Lawrence said steadily, "she's suggesting incest, shall we say it plain? It's not true, Lydian. First, do you think Charles would ever have married you if there had been the faintest grounds for such suspicion? Second, I've always known there was a great lost love in Charles's life. I had no idea that it was your mother, but he told me himself, with no reason to lie, that the relationship was totally platonic. That was, for Charles, part of the tragedy: he never really was a Lancelot, or she a Guinever. And all chance of more ended when the accident occurred."

"Not accident," I said dully. "A suicide pact. They fell together, and my mother died." I drew a wondering, painful breath. "That was it, wasn't it?" I said slowly. "When I came here, and we fell in love, it seemed too incredible, too rapid to be real. Charles wasn't really marrying *me* at all, was he? Just trying to live out what never happened with my mother. To make me become her. And it wasn't truly Charles at all. The magic that drew me, the being accepted unquestioningly, being protected, loved . . . I was trying to find in him the father I always wanted and never had."

"Then you're free of each other, aren't you?" Lawrence said quietly. "You married ghosts, not each other. So you're free to leave. And, to be painfully blunt again, your own marriage was never consummated either. It's all over, my dear."

"How can I? Charles has pinned his whole life on me and on his work. And he's so ill." I turned to Lawrence, my eyes bright with tears. "He *matters*, Lawrence. To both of us. We can't destroy him. We've hurt him enough already. He knows; he's done a picture of us. Together. What do you think that must have cost him?"

"He's sicker than we realized, is what I think." Lawrence stood over me, his face grave. "Lydian, don't you see? We must get off the carousel, before it's too late. Charles can't stop it, so we must for all our sakes. What was that?"

"What?"

"I heard something. Someone."

Faint as the rustle of a mouse tail it had been. So small, so slight, so insignificant. The sound of a door closing.

Lawrence was to it in the instant, throwing his weight against it. But the only response was one that even I could hear. The dials on the vault door being whirled.

We were caught, trapped, locked into the tunnel. And by no accident.

"It's the only way out, isn't it?" I asked, calmly. "Of course. So we wait here, until we're found. Or until we run out of oxygen and die."

"We're not going to die," Lawrence said grimly. "Do you think I've found you only to lose you? We're going to get out of here, and live. Together. Come on."

"Where?"

He looked at me as though I were a fool. "This tunnel is supposed to lead to Glastonbury, isn't it? We can't get out this way, so we dig through the other end." He began to run down the long corridor, only pausing to make sure that I was close behind.

It was impossible. It was absurd. Lawrence had been digging in this tunnel for months, and it had led nowhere. He had said the end must be in sight; that sheer factual measurements indicated he was now deep under Glastonbury ground. Concentrate on that; concentrate on known truth and the task at hand. Be grateful that the tools for digging had been left carelessly where his day's work had ceased, instead of being hung carefully away on the other side of that impassable vault door.

Don't think about that door. Don't think about its closing, or wonder at whose hand. Don't think that this was real, irrefutable; attempted murder. None of the things that had happened had been accidents. Someone wanted us dead. Wanted me dead.

"Take the shovel," Lawrence ordered roughly. "Clear away the rocks as I knock them loose." He swung the pickaxe, and stones hurtled down.

Time had no meaning. Minutes were hours, endless, the rhythm of routine, of working in unison. There was no sound except the falling of the stones. We hoarded our energy, hoarded breath.

We were penetrating deeper and deeper into the dark earth, leaving those wall installations many yards behind.

"Careful!" Lawrence's voice was sharp. "Don't *throw* the rocks behind you, *set* them down. You could precipitate a slide." He was opening, now, only the narrowest of apertures, barely wide enough to struggle through. What was removed must all be placed behind us; we could so easily bury ourselves alive.

"It's going nowhere, isn't it?" I said suddenly. "This tunnel: like all the illusions of Avalon, it's just one more fantasy. One more dream that never can be real." I stumbled against him. Lawrence, his arm with the pickaxe in midair, was thrown off balance. He fell forward heavily; pulled himself up, cursing. The pickaxe had imbedded itself between blocks of stone in the side wall. He pulled at its handle; pulled again with all his strength.

The rocks gave way.

There was no time for him to shout. Lawrence flung himself at me and knocked me down. I think I screamed. Then rocks fell all around us, sharp as the hail of the Tintagel storm monstrously magnified. I was conscious of nothing but the rocks and of the full weight of Lawrence's body on me.

The rockslide stopped. I dared not move. Then there was Lawrence's voice, in a tone that I had never heard. "Lydian. Lydian, Lydian, Lydian, open your eyes!"

Directly before us, beyond the opening left by the stones, there was a room. So low, so small, so very old. The walls were of carefully chiseled blocks. A remnant of ancient Celtic subterranean worship. At the time of the dissolution of Glastonbury Abbey the monks must have used this as an improvised storeroom to hide their treasure from the king's agents. Eucharistic vessels, ancient crosses, objects I could not name lay piled as though by frantic hands. And to one side . . .

"I read of this when I was a boy," Lawrence said in a strange voice. "Exactly like this."

A colossal coffin, hollowed out of an oaken log. Our search for the tomb of the possible Arthur was at an end.

Our bruises, our danger were forgotten. We squeezed ourselves through the child-sized opening into the room, stood by the coffin. Slowly, with an instinctive reverence, Lawrence raised the heavy lid.

The faint light from far behind us illuminated the heap of bones so carefully, so poignantly reinterred—just as in the old stories. My eyes stung with tears. The man's, giant-sized; the woman's, delicate and small. The covering of fine velvet had been laid there, it was said, by Edward I and his queen. And at the foot—involuntarily, even after the splendor of my own wedding gifts, I gasped at this blaze of gold. The chalice, jewel-encrusted, stood within the gleaming circlet of an intricate torque. Guinever's dower gifts.

My own thoughts tumbled one upon the other. Awe. Humility. A deep pity that Charles was not here. A sense of journey's end.

Journey's end. Here, in this sealed, subterranean room. Such as, in the old days, were often used for tombs. I felt, rather than heard, Lawrence's indrawn breath; knew he was realizing, as was I, that this might be end to search but there was yet no freedom. Still no way out.

And at that moment, we were plunged suddenly into blackness.

14

"Get them!" Lawrence's voice gasped at me through the dark.

"What?"

"The gifts. Hurry! I can't hold this lid much longer!"

My hands searched, hurried over bones and velvet, snatched. "All right. I've got them."

The lid slammed down.

"What the matter?" I demanded.

Lawrence cut in swiftly. "Gas flame's gone out. Or been cut."

"You mean there's gas escaping again—"

"I don't *know!* We've got to get out of here, quickly. I'm going back for the tools."

I felt as well as heard him leave me. Then he was back, his hand closing around mine, his voice deliberately calm. "There appeared to be a sealed door in the far right corner beyond the coffin. Get your bearings from that, and follow me."

I groped my way after him, stumbling over the monastery treasure pieces, clutching Guinever's own golden talismans tightly to me. As I lifted my skirt with my free hand, I felt the bulge of pocket, and remembered. "I have matches. Is it safe to light them?"

"Yes," Lawrence ordered. "Better—" He did not finish what

I had already thought: better the immediate oblivion of explosion than the slow death of burial alive.

I had never realized before how finite, how frail a thing was the flame of a kitchen match. I struck one, held it till my fingers burned as Lawrence sighted on the outline of stone-sealed door and swung his axe. The match went out; again and again he swung; still blackness.

"Do you want me to clear—"

"Stay *back*! I can't control where the rocks may fly."

The clank of metal on stone, the rattle of rock. The sound of our own breathing. "Door frame's clear," Lawrence said at last. "There's a corridor."

"Cemented—?"

"I don't know. Strike a match."

At least there was no gas escaping; we knew that now. But the passageway was filled with rocks and rubble, tightly packed.

"No masonry. Thank God for that," Lawrence ejaculated as the match went out. Then again, the sound of tools in darkness, the dust of the dead past stopping up our lungs. So it went, groping with our fingers, fearful of dislodging another avalanche that would engulf us, never daring to lose touch with one another. At intervals, a match. Time was endless; the tiny store of matches in my hand grew smaller.

Lawrence was tiring; he did not say it but I could tell. I was afraid, so afraid, and he must have sensed it, for suddenly, in the darkness, he had flung down his tools and swept me tightly into his arms. "We are going to get out of here, Lydian Wentworth, and we are going to live. Together." He released me, his voice became brisk again. "Strike another match."

"There's just one left."

"Strike it."

The swift, abrasive sound of phosphorous in the blackness; the sudden flash of flame, casting a feeble aura around the tomblike passage. Then the match went out.

"Why did you blow it out?" Lawrence shouted.

"I didn't. It just—blew. As though a draft—"

As though a draft . . . Air. From somewhere, unseen but close at hand, a tiny current of fresh air was flowing.

There was no stopping us then. No more weariness, no discouragement, no fear. We groped, skinned our fingers, tore our nails. The stream of air grew stronger, and then there were ribbons of pale light. The stones became damp; there was lichen among the rock. "Look," I said giddily, and pointed. The beginning of a staircase lay beneath our feet.

We came up into the ruins of one of the Glastonbury outbuildings as the shell of the abbey was silhouetted against the first flush of dawn. We had escaped death, we were together; and the tomb of Arthur, the passage to Glastonbury were realities. They had not been a dream.

I looked down at the golden treasure in my arms, and up at the broken arches, and we were no longer two but three. The thought of Charles was a tangible ghost between us.

Lawrence knew it at once. He had begun to take me in his arms, but now he stopped. "Face it, Lydian. You can't go back to him. Not after all you've learned tonight."

"We must."

"Not I. Oh, no, not I," Lawrence said firmly. "There have been enough accidents. Do you want to go on until one of them succeeds? It could be Charles, you know."

"Could be what? Charles as perpetrator, or as victim?"

"Either. Both! We can't help him this way! If we've any sense at all, we go straight from here to the railway station and up to London. Take those objects for validation at the British Museum, and have the whole of this out in the open air. No more secrecy, no more conspiracy, no more danger."

"You said 'if.' "

"Damn it, I can't go off and leave you here," Lawrence said angrily. "You've just escaped being buried alive in one way. Do you honestly mean to submit to it in another?"

"Only until it is right for us to leave."

"When?" Lawrence demanded inexorably. "After the symposium? When Charles's next book is finished? When he's dead —or we are?"

"But don't you see, it's different now! We've found his proof. Charles will have Guinever's gifts, he'll have established incontrovertibly there *was* an Arthur."

"A pre-Saxon leader," Lawrence said flatly. "Not the mythic hero, not the immortal. And when you come down to it, *he* hasn't proved that fact. *We* have. We found the coffin, in land that doesn't belong to any of us, while in the process of escaping an attempt upon our lives."

But I knew he could not have claimed the treasure trove for himself, any more than I could have. He looked at me, and his voice was heavy. "All right. I'll take you back. Us. That ancient code of loyalty still is potent, isn't it, even in this modern age? I will bide my time, for his sake, and yours, until after the symposium. Until his lifework is validated, and he has the recognition he does deserve. After that, he is no longer our responsibility. We leave him to Meriel and Doff—and to himself. He is a man, however sick, and he would not appreciate being someone else's charge, however strong the ties of love and duty."

I knew. Honor, and self-respect—it was what I wanted for him, too. What I wanted for us all. I could not speak; Lawrence saw and understood, and bent and kissed me. And we turned back toward Avalon's guarded gates in the flooding dawn.

Curiously, what we experienced as we walked together was a kind of peace. The die was cast. Reality had been faced. The quest was over. What remained was the time of waiting, of revelation, of weaving the disparate threads together into new and stronger patterns. I looked down at the torque and chalice in my arms, the goblet, symbol of woman, of Guinever; symbol also of the divine—a reality that inspired dreams of a better life, but which must be sought and followed; which could be drunk from but never owned. The torque collar—a circle, symbol of infinity, but an open circle, signifying freedom, the responsibility for the binding or loosing of one's own self. Above our heads, the sky was bright blue, and the dawn mist associated with the Celtic Otherworld veiled the hills. The birds rehearsed their morning chorus in the apple trees as we walked along.

The wrought-iron gates of Avalon stood open.

Lawrence frowned. "Strange. They're never unlocked this early. And why aren't those guards patrolling, as they should be?"

We quickened our steps. The long window from the morning room to my side garden was ajar, and together we ran swiftly toward it. A strange tableau presented itself to our startled eyes. All the servants, mustered, including Lawrence's gardener-disguised guards, confronted by one of the latter and by Hodge. Something was very wrong. As we stepped through the window, Rose pivoted, looked at me, and burst into tears.

"Oh, ma'am, dear ma'am, I knew it wasn't true!"

"What wasn't true? Rose, get hold of yourself and tell me!"

"Mr. Doffman said—his lordship was taken bad sick, and you two was gone—"

It was the "you two" that told me. I flung an anguished look toward Lawrence, but he was already demanding explanations of the head guard.

"—what I'm trying to ascertain, sir, myself. Apparently his lordship was taken by a bad seizure in the night and wished to see his wife. Her maid discovered the bed not slept in, and raised the alarm. Then you were discovered absent also, and it was suggested—"

"I understand," Lawrence said shortly. "And his lordship?"

"Looks in great pain, sir, but not so much as to be incapable of blistering our hides. We were brought in by young Mr. Doffman, accused of loitering with criminal intent. Begging your pardon, sir, I was obliged to reveal the terms of our employment, and his lordship fell into a fury."

"I can well imagine." Lawrence's face was grim. "Very well, Thompson, you men can go. Get yourself some tea or a pint; you've earned it. I have matters to discuss with you quite shortly. Rose, take care of Lady Ransome. She's been through a grueling ordeal."

"No." I pulled myself from Rose's well-intentioned arms. "Before anything, we have to talk to Charles."

"I will. You need not subject yourself to that."

"I do." I took a deep breath and said quietly, "Don't try to protect me from the responsibility of being who I am." Our eyes met, and after a moment Lawrence's jaw eased and he nodded.

"Charles was right in what he saw in you, wasn't he? And no one has the right to hold you back from entering into your inheritance. Hodge, tell his lordship we wait upon him as soon as he is well enough to see us."

Hodge bowed deferentially and vanished. The servants, at my

signal, all dispersed. I went upstairs to bathe and dress, for as Rose pointed out in maternal outrage, I looked "a fair mess."

"Like a street sweep out of the East End," she scolded, shutting the bedroom door behind me. "That lovely skirt all ripped, and your poor hands torn. Oh, ma'am dear, it give me such a turn to find you gone. Are you hurt? Why didn't you take me with you? You know I'd have gone with you wherever you've been!"

"I couldn't," I said tiredly. "I'll explain later, what I can, but I'm all right." I dropped my burden on the bed and Rose regarded the priceless objects with disfavor.

"Was that what you were up to, getting more gaudy gewgaws? Well, at least that may mollify his lordship some."

"Rose, is he very bad?"

Our eyes met. "Not to say bad like the last time," Rose said uneasily. "Seemed like it was more the pain that was in his mind. Her ladyship and Mr. Doff were with him, and there was such a row. We could hear him all the way down in the Great Hall. Like he was screaming in his sleep and seeing things."

Meriel and Doff here; Lawrence and I both gone. What poison had they added to that already in his mind?

There was no point in speculating. It was time to have done with fantasy feeding on sick surmise. It was time for truth. All of it? About my mother's death, Charles's accident? About our marriage, about Lawrence and myself? About Doff?

If truth could free, could too much truth, too late, also kill?

I bathed, drank black and bitter tea, brushed up my hair, put on the clothes that Rose laid out. The same white shirtwaist and pale-gray skirt I had worn when first I came to Avalon, so many worlds ago.

There was a soft knock on the door. "He's waiting for us," Lawrence said. "In the study."

How like Charles, despite his burden of pain, to be determined to be seen on his own ground, clothed and erect in his chair, not the helpless invalid in bed. I was half surprised he had not chosen to receive us like a king in the Great Hall.

Lawrence and I went down the wide stairs together, I carrying in my arms Guinever's golden treasure. So had Lancelot and Guinever, in that doomed confrontation that ended their shared world, been taken before Arthur. Before Arthur, who had spent the night of their fatal assignation under the spell of Morgan le Fay. Charles had spent his hour of torment last night with Meriel. What had she told him? Meriel, who as a young and frightened girl, too much in love, had tried to weave a Morgan-spell to break Charles free from my mother's thrall.

Charles was sitting in his carved throne-chair, his great desk like a barrier between us. Even in late August, the walls of Avalon still held a morning chill, and the dark fur cloak rested on his knees. The sun, slanting through the open doors to my rose garden, aureoled his hair and threw his features into cruel relief. This was the reality of Arthur—an old, still proud lion, wracked with pain and despair.

His voice was the voice of power, strong and cold. "To what do we owe this unexpected return from your elopement?"

"You mean from our attempted murder," Lawrence said brutally. "Whose attempt was it, Charles? Yours? Meriel's? Doff's? I imagine someone is surprised to have us reappear."

Charles rapped the words out harshly. "What do you mean?"

"I mean we were locked in the tunnel. Deliberately. Someone slammed the vault door on us and spun the dials. Someone must have claimed to have searched for us down there, and lied. Who was it, Charles?"

Charles was shaken; we both knew he was shaken. He passed his hand heavily across his brow. "Doff said, Meriel said, you had gone off together. It was, after all, not implausible. If you were shut in the tunnel, how did you get out?"

"Through Glastonbury," I said swiftly. "Out through the abbey, just the way you'd dreamed. Your quest is fulfilled, do you understand? Oh, my dear, look."

I set the precious objects down on the desk. In the light emanating from the golden chalice, still encompassed by its circlet, we all fell silent. There *was* strong magic here, and it stilled, reduced to insignificance, the bitter entanglement of our lives.

Charles lifted his hand, then let it fall. "If I were to have chosen out of all the world, one man, one woman about whom I could truly care . . . but no matter."

"I know. Oh, my dear, I know." I moved toward him instinctively, tears starting in my eyes, but Charles turned his proud face away.

"Is a cuckolded husband allowed to ask what you intend doing now? Claim these discoveries as your own? Float off as romantic lovers on a cloud of notoriety and scandal?" His effort at bravura quickly ceased. Somehow, in the presence of those two solemn, magical objects none of us were able to continue play-acting.

"Of course we can't claim the discovery," I said quickly. "It was your belief, your vision that led to it. We were only your instruments."

"Instruments," Charles repeated slowly. "We're all instruments, aren't we? Of something. Fate. Justice. Perhaps they're both the same. What were you doing in the tunnel at that hour?"

"Talking," Lawrence answered tersely, and Charles frowned. And I burst out, "No. We have to have truth out at last, don't we? For all our sakes. I went to your workroom, Charles. To find out if it was true, what Meriel had told me—that you and my mother had been lovers. Oh, Charles, why did you let me believe it was I you loved, and not a ghost?"

Charles closed his eyes. "It was you. Is you. And she—you two became one."

"As you became for me the Ason I had never known."

Oh, truth can wound. The very bones in Charles's face grew white. "I was afraid it was like that. I would not let myself confront it. And when, after learning the truth, you said you'd stay, I let myself believe—"

"I never learned all the truth."

"Perhaps no one can. Perhaps when we do, we die." Charles shifted with difficulty, looked at me directly. "Whatever you may have been told, your mother and I were never lovers. *She* was a faithful wife. So much so, that when she could live with your father's destructive influence no longer, she was going to take you and go back to America, to leave us both, so that she would not be tempted to snatch at happiness with me. Ason's suspicions about her infidelity were completely groundless."

Just as yours were of mine, I thought. But I could not say it, and Charles went on, laboriously, "She was incapable of evil, an angel of light."

214

His head dropped before he rallied again and went on. "As for her death, it was an accident. You must believe that. Neither of us meant . . . We were going to separate; she insisted on it, and I understood. But I begged her for one more sitting for her portrait at Tintagel, to let me finish it so I would at least have that. And she agreed. If only she had not . . . It was an accident! She fell; I fell; one trying to save the other. It happened so fast. When I recovered consciousness, she was gone, and nothing ever again would be the same. The light had gone out of the world. And then you came. And now," he said carefully, precisely, "you go. It happens all over again."

There was a silence. I heard my own voice saying, "I don't know what I'm going to do. I can promise nothing. We dug into the past and found it was not dead; we set old patterns in motion. But we don't have to allow them to have control. This isn't the fifth century. We care about each other, we care about our work. It's important and not finished. My book. The symposium. Publishing your discoveries. They're too important to be damaged because three persons cannot act like civilized adults."

Charles looked at us, wryly. "So we go on together, do we? Arthur, Lancelot, Guinever, before their shared secret was discovered by the destructive world?"

"As *ourselves*. No more playing roles. We're safe now that we've faced the truth."

"Someone tried to kill us," Lawrence said inexorably. "All of us, at one time or another. Unless one of those 'accidents' was a ruse to remove suspicion from the perpetrator."

His words hung heavily. I said again, "Until the symposium. It was one of us five, we know that now. No robbery, no outside danger. Nothing will change if we go on for a month or more." Suddenly, my eyes were brimming, and I reached out to both men blindly. "Please. Finding Arthur's tomb is so important. *I* caused this trouble, coming here; I don't want to be the cause of more. Can't we work together, as we've been doing, until the discovery and its significance are properly known?"

And may God have mercy on our souls.

We did all three love each other, that was what made it possible to go on. A kind of complex emotional blackmail bound us. September came; we moved through these final weeks as though we were indeed imprisoned by a spell, going through the proper motions, saving one another's public reputations as our final acts of love.

Correspondence passed daily between Charles and the symposium organizers in Winchester. It was a delicate task, apprising them of the nature and significance of the information he would present, without making any premature revelations. "Surely you can trust the facts to *them*," I protested, but Charles trusted no one.

Lawrence widened our passage to the tomb room, took photographs and detailed notes, walled up the subterranean chamber and our tunnel to it. We had no legal right of ownership; to leave it open would have made it prey to souvenir-seekers or worse. I worked steadily upon my book. The medieval gown Charles had designed for me to wear to the symposium was delivered from the London dressmakers.

I was to wear it, with Guinever's own torque, when I read Charles's speech at the symposium. Charles had insisted on my doing so; after the way his health had failed this summer he would not risk being scheduled to appear and then not being able. I could understand, I thought, watching him grow day by day more worn and remembering the radiant youth of his own self-portraits. Besides, "You have been my partner in greatness," Charles said; "it is right that your contribution to the work be recognized."

That was one great good that had happened since the tomb of Arthur and Guinever had been found. Charles was more nearly the old Charles again, magnanimous in his power, and able to share. No longer suspicious, threatened, needing to possess. I was able, at last, to discuss my writing with him, and he consulted me constantly on the preparation of the speech. But we had no more midnight tête-à-têtes, nor did Lawrence and I meet each other even by chance in the rose garden.

Noblesse oblige, going through the proper motions, but always accompanied by a servant, always on guard. For Meriel and Doff were also there, revolving in the background in their own troubled orbits. Doff angry, sullen, more protective than ever of Charles, looking at Lawrence and me as though indeed he easily could kill. Meriel grown suddenly older, avoiding me, avoiding Doff, burying in herself the devastating truth that I had flung at her in pain and rage.

It could have been any of them who had tried to kill; that was one of the truths I had to face. We were so intricately intertwined by the two-sided bond of hate and love. Love grown daemonic can kill in order to protect what matters more than life. Even in Lawrence. He had wanted from the beginning to drive me off from Avalon; he could have devised those first "accidents" with that aim in mind. And the attempt on Charles . . . had I not said then I would not leave him in his life? There was no reason that our burial in the tunnel was perpetrated by the same person responsible for those other, earlier events.

When I thought this way I ended with a raging headache, my mind racing in convoluted circles like those endless lines in Celtic drawings. And as the time passed, we grew thin and tense, as though Avalon were being wound around us like a watch spring tighter, tighter.

Two weeks before the symposium, the storm broke.

I was in the rose garden, working on the last chapter of my manuscript, when Lawrence came rapidly toward me through the glowing morning. It was the first time we had allowed ourselves to be alone together; I was startled, swept by memories and longing, then stunned by a cold fear as Lawrence flung a London newspaper into my lap.

The news of our discovery of the tomb and its treasures had leaked out. And what was more—"Oh, no. Oh, dear God, no," I whispered, staring at the headline. *"Recluse Archaeologist Discovers Both Missing Treasure and Missing Son."*

"I've let nothing slip," Lawrence said swiftly, before I could even ask. "But the guards were here when we came in with the torque and chalice. There are always reporters loitering round Somerset House. I could have been recognized there; my connection with Charles is known. Someone must have followed it up."

"Charles mustn't see this. Not now." The same thought struck both of us at once—the morning papers were always

217

delivered to him on his breakfast tray. Together Lawrence and I raced for the stairs. Hodge was just disappearing through the doorway.

"I'll get it, somehow," Lawrence said, plunging after him. But it was too late. There was a shout of rage, then crystal and porcelain crashing to the floor as Charles gave a shattering cry of pain.

It was the beginning of the worst attack of illness I had witnessed yet. I need not recount it—the raging fever, the muscle spasms, the periods of delirium. And between them, a terrible cold lucidity that was even worse. For Charles accused us all of vileness, lies, betrayal. Rationality was gone, perhaps forever.

Meriel, ashen-faced, told Charles all that she had told me. Doff tried to win Charles's recognition and acceptance, but in vain. In vain, too, Lawrence and I protested we had let no news of the tomb discovery escape. We had to have, Charles insisted; the information could have come from no one else. As for that cruel accusation of his having fathered an illegitimate son—he turned even on Meriel then, accusing her of a middle-aged spinster's fantasies. He had never touched her, had always been true, till my coming, to his one chaste love. When Doff, trembling and shaking, tried to approach him, he was driven off with oaths.

Then came pain and delirium. Taking turns staying with him through the night, working together, never one of us alone, for we all knew murder had been attempted in the past and might be again. Lawrence came on me one afternoon, just after Meriel had relieved me in the sickroom, as I leaned against a pillar of the upstairs hall. I was too wrung out even for tears; I had rested my face against the coolness of the stone and my whole body trembled. He put his arms around me and when I instinctively responded he turned me to face him.

"Why do you put yourself through this? You have done all and more than anyone could ask. Hire nurses and come away."

"Don't even say that to me. The symposium's only a week and a half away."

"Do you honestly feel you can go through with that? In the face of this circus of publicity and scandal?"

"I can. I must. Whatever he is now, Charles was—magnificent, towering; he must go out in a blaze of glory, not like a circus sideshow. Oh, darling, please, help me. Don't tempt me to go against my conscience. I'm too vulnerable, I can feel myself being pulled closer and closer to the abyss, like my mother at Tintagel, and I could so easily go over."

Lawrence rubbed my shoulders. "You're still afraid of that, aren't you?"

"I think I always will be. I believed for a while in the illusion of invulnerability. But I'm not one of the Sidh; I'm only human."

"Perhaps that's what the Sidh were," Lawrence said gently. "Persons who weren't afraid to be totally human. You'll have to go back to Tintagel someday, you know, and face those old ghosts down."

"No. I don't ever want to see that place again." We were already living a nightmare; to voluntarily walk into that old one was more than I could trust myself to bear.

When I was not in the sickroom, I disciplined myself to the routine of normal life. There were symposium details to attend to, notes to go over, arrangements to complete for Charles's speech. I finished my first draft of *Woman in Celtic Myth* and mailed it off to Charles's publisher.

An announcement that I would present my husband's address was carried with dignified formality by the London *Times*. The more sensational press made this an excuse to rake up the recent revelations, but at least Charles on his sickbed was spared the knowledge. Poor Charles, I thought with bitter anger. What did they hope to gain, other than the ridicule and degradation of a splendid, brilliant man? Perhaps the trouble was that the world could not cope with brilliance and splendor; it was too disturbing.

And then, like a miracle, Charles's fever broke. The outbursts of anger ceased, and he seemed, to my longing anxiety, to be again on the mend and in control. He was even able to discuss, quietly, what he hoped I could accomplish at the symposium. An unnatural, early autumn calm hung over Avalon like an invisible veil.

The symposium was just three days away when, without foreboding, trusting too much in the healing I wanted to be true, I ran up to Charles's room to join him for his tea. Entered, unsuspecting, to find the eyes that turned to mine were my husband's eyes no longer, but a stranger's. The stranger, irrational, distorted, who had accused me of usurping, destruction, vileness. I stared at him, shaken, and before either of us could speak I saw it, lying in a thousand pieces across the bed. My manuscript. The first draft of the manuscript I had sent, with his blessing, to his publisher the week before. Returned, addressed to him; torn up by him, and scattered like the pieces of a myriad broken dreams.

"Charles, what is it?"

His pathological jealousy had returned, focused now upon my work, my gifts.

"I will not have you rise like the phoenix from my ashes! This is what you've wanted, isn't it, from the first? *Your* name, *your* discoveries, *your* work! You've come here like a daemon wearing my love's face, to suck my blood, devour me, usurp my dreams! You won't succeed, I won't allow it! No symposium! The treasure will stay here, with me! I'll destroy it, before I allow you to usurp it."

I could not listen. I pulled the bell-cord for Doff and ran shuddering to the sanctuary of my own room. When Lawrence found me, an hour later in the rose garden, I was still shaking.

He had taken me in his arms, but now he drew away. "It's come again, hasn't it, that veil between us? Separating us. Are you going to allow it to stay, or will you tear it down?"

We gazed at each other across that deep but narrow gulf, not touching, and I told him. The accusations, the torn manuscript, the threats.

"He's insane," Lawrence said flatly. "Lydian, face it!"

"I have. At least, I know that wasn't really Charles who was talking."

"What are you going to do?"

"Go to the symposium. Rewrite the book. I have the original manuscript; that was only a clean copy." I drew a ragged breath. "I took the torque and chalice, and put them in my room. So at least Charles can't carry out that threat."

"What you ought to do," Lawrence said to me roughly, "is

walk out of here right now. With the manuscript. With the treasure. Publish in your own right. Get out of this sickness before it is too late. I told you that before, and you should have listened."

"It's not possible."

We stared at each other across a gulf that suddenly was alive with dragons.

I put my hand out impulsively. "Lawrence, please! I asked you before. Don't tempt me, help me! I have to do this for Charles. It's what I want for us, what he would want if he were truly himself."

Lawrence moved ever so slightly, just beyond my reach. "We loved Charles, but the Charles we loved is dead. I love a woman, a woman who is alive and real, or would be if she'd find the courage to bury the dead past. I'm leaving, Lydian. I hope to God you will come with me. I won't force you; it wouldn't do any good. Unless you are able, yourself, to look your nightmares in the face and not flee from them."

"That is exactly what I'm doing."

"No, you are not. You're fleeing into an alternate nightmare, here at Avalon, just as Charles has done. What you had with Charles here was illusion. When you can accept that, and the truth about your mother and yourself, and not flinch from it— when you're able to be a person in your own right, and not Charles's or Ason's shadow, *then* you'll be free. Till then it's like what you said about Tintagel, Lydian; you're both terrified and yet attracted to the abyss of nothingness, nonbeing."

We stood up, then, and the air between us was electric with our waiting. But it was he who turned at last, and left. And I walked back, through the gathering twilight, into Avalon's walls, which closed like a shell around me. I was numb as I dressed for dinner, numb as I sat in that strained silence which was now habitual with Meriel and Doff. Charles did not come down. Charles did not want to see me, nor I him. Just until the symposium, I told myself; just until that was over, a few days hence. But would Lawrence still be waiting? He had left the house, Rose told me as she helped me undress that night. He had packed a valise and departed in the direction of the railway station.

I was going to speak at the symposium in two days. That was the one rock I had to stand on. I would present my husband's speech, unveil the torque and chalice, hear his lifelong search at last recognized and vindicated. Then, whatever happened, I would know I had at least given him that much.

I slept at last, and I dreamed of my mother's death.

Again the mist. Cliffs. Storm. The seagulls screaming and the waves crashing on the rocks. The fingers of remembered nightmare, remembered reality reached out like seaweed to twist around me and drag me down. I was again both watcher and watched. Saw two men struggle, saw them turn toward me—my husband's face, and Ason's. I was running, stumbling, falling. Down from the precipice, down toward the knife-sharp rocks. The abyss yawned, magnetic, beckoning. An end to fear, to anguish, to feeling. I fell, and fell, and then there were no rocks, but something, someone, in the mist, enfolding and upholding. A light broke through the darkness and in the light I saw it, luminous and glowing—the golden chalice, surrounded by its golden ring. Guinever's gifts.

I woke, and I was sitting bolt upright in bed; the first faint light of dawn was silvering the sky. The vision of the torque and chalice still possessed me, still beckoned. My eyes focused, and a strange fear gripped me. The gifts were gone. I was out of bed, to the window table where I had left them, but there was nothing there. Nothing but the mirror, and the candles. And a note.

A note, scribbled hastily on a scrap of paper. One word, in Lawrence's hand.

Tintagel.

15

My first reaction was rage. Rage that Lawrence had so diabolically forced my hand. He wanted me out of here, wanted me to have credit for the tomb discoveries, wanted me to confront once and for all the ghosts of the past that held me. And he had accomplished it all in one stroke, for he knew I could not speak at the symposium without the evidence of torque and chalice. And he had taken them to Tintagel, forcing me to follow, as he knew I would.

Then realization swept down on me, chill and cold. *He* had been in my room, to take the gifts while I slept. Just as someone, on that other night, had been in my room, unnoticed, to turn on the lethal gas.

It had not been Lawrence. *Could* not have been Lawrence. But why was I so sure? The gas had not killed me, any more than that other gas in the tunnel had killed me. It might not have been meant to kill me.

I was up against a closed door which I refused to open.

And I was confronted by the fact that *it did not matter*, not so far as my feelings toward Lawrence were concerned. They were what they were, it was as simple as that. Even if he had endangered me, even if he had tried to kill Charles, as long as he remained the person he was I loved him. Just as, no matter what, my feelings toward Charles—the man he had been, the

223

memory of what he was no more—would never change. I could not judge Lawrence's actions, any more than I could judge Charles's—any more than I could judge my own.

It did not matter if we had not "played fair." I realized now that when one was fiercely trying to protect someone one deeply loved, "playing fair" was the last thing that mattered. Justice mattered, and mercy. But at times what was merciful and just to one person hurt another. That was the way of it. And who could know what was right? We had to keep trying, keep on loving the wisest way we could.

And now, as he had known I would, I had to go to Tintagel. Not to go away with him, but to get back Guinever's gifts. To bring him back if I could, but in any event to make him know that if I did not speak at the symposium, did not give Charles that last gift, whatever he had now become I myself would be no more the person Lawrence loved.

Dawn was breaking as I dressed swiftly. I was just fastening the wrists of my shirtwaist when I heard a voice, grimly accusing.

"Ma'am dear, whatever are you doing?" Rose had awakened and was contemplating me sternly, hands on hips.

"I have to go out. Don't try to stop me, and don't ask me why."

"I *will* ask." Rose planted herself firmly before the door. "Haven't we had enough queer things happening? Not one step you're stirring away from here without me."

The clock already stood at half-past six. How many hours had it been since Lawrence left? How many hours would it take to drive to Tintagel and back again? How long could we keep Charles from knowing that the gifts were gone?

"You can't come, Rose, and you must not tell anyone. I'll be with Mr. Stearns, so I'll be all right."

Rose took a step forward. "I'm coming with you, it'll look better. And high time you went—"

"It's not that." I looked at her, made a swift gamble. "Mr. Stearns has taken away the treasure. Just for a time, to make me leave. He's left word for me to meet him at Tintagel to get them back. No one must know, do you understand? Neither that they're gone, nor where I am. Tell them anything, that I've gone up to town, that I've taken the treasure to the bank vault for safekeeping. Lord Ransome must not know, not in his condition. Swear it!"

Rose swore, grudgingly. The sun was rising now. I snatched my purse, glad of the bank notes it contained, slipped catlike down the stairway.

I would not risk the heavy door; Hodge might be stirring and hear. I went through the study windows into my own rose garden; waited among the shrubbery till the guard had passed. How easy it was, I thought, running soundlessly into the orchard opposite, to avoid detection! Just so could a cautious intruder gain access to Avalon.

I had brought with me a cloak of some dark linen stuff; I had coiled my hair after a different fashion. When I emerged from the abbey orchard to walk down Glastonbury's street toward the livery stable, I hoped no one could recognize me as Lady Ransome. I hired an auto, and if the stable hand had any questions about a strange woman appearing with such request at this early hour, they were stilled by the bank notes I pressed into his hand. I took precaution of asking directions for the road toward Bath. If any inquiries were made later that day for Lady Ransome, he would not be able to give away my true destination. For all our sakes, no one must ever know Lawrence had taken Guinever's gifts to Tintagel.

Thank God, Lawrence had given me driving lessons during that other journey, that I had practiced since. I maneuvered the auto from the stable without undue difficulty, rolled down the street, and when well out of the stableman's vision turned around and headed back the other way. Toward the southwest, toward Cornwall and Tintagel.

The streets were deserted at this early hour. The hills of Glastonbury glowed greenly in the early light, and the sun gilded the remains of St. Michael's Chapel on the Tor. Mile after mile I drove, through open country; no need to shift, to tamper with clutch or throttle, just hold the steering bar and maintain an even flow of power. I sidled through sleepy towns without coming to a stop. Then at last I was out upon the rolling moors.

Mile after mile—green hills, gray stone, the dull gray-white of sheep. The gorse was golden but the heather was dried and brown. The road was a ribbon, dipping and rising, running steadily on. I drove, my eyes fixed on that endless streamer, but the ghosts rode with me.

I passed the inn where Lawrence had bought our picnic lunch. The sun was high, the sun began to sink. I felt a faintness in me, but I would not stop, could not, till I was approaching Tintagel's cliffs. Thank God for memory, telling me at which crossroad to turn and head toward the sea. The land grew flat, the grasses in the fields were high. I rolled through hedgerows, too intent to be afraid. What time was it now, three? Four? We had reached Tintagel, that other day, just in time for tea. Could I reach there now, drive home again in a single day? Would I be able to manipulate the auto after dark?

The thought of the moors, alone and in darkness, would terrify me. The thought of Tintagel ought to terrify me, but did not. Nothing mattered, nothing was real but the fact that Lawrence had the gifts, and I must get them back. Lawrence was at Tintagel, waiting for me, That was what drew me on.

The sky was darkening already, and I had not noticed. It could not be that late. It was a storm. Another storm upon Tintagel's cliffs. That would not matter. I was nearly there, now. I turned out of the wheatfield onto the road that ran along by the sea, and now I could smell the salt tang in the air. I rolled into the town, came to the cottage where we had had our tea. I would leave the car here; I could never negotiate those steep and narrow twisting turns. Explain to the woman later, I thought, grinding to a halt in her yard and jumping out. I had thought for nothing but to reach the castle ruins before the storm should break.

I ran there first, to the lofty headland and the narrow spit from which rose the stark remains of monastery and Ygraine's castle. Up, and up, the stones skipping and sheering off into nothingness under my running feet. No terror, no panic, nothing but the compulsive anxiety that drove me on. I wasted such time, climbing, making my perilous way up that steep path and those tortuous steps. Then I was at the top and there was nothing. No one. No nightmare. No panic. No ghostly visions, and no Lawrence.

Of course, I thought bemusedly. For it was not here that my terror of the past was focused. There, *there*, over on the far plateau, on the gargoyle head of rock staring at the sea. It was there he meant to force me to confront my ghosts, there I must confront him with the necessity to do what I must do.

How I got down from the ruins I do not even know. I was there; I was below, running along the path on the narrow spit of land. Running up the slope on the far side, toward memory, toward nightmare, toward the gargoyle head. And now all once and future memories raced with me. Charles had fallen here. My mother died here. But I went on and on, triumphing over my irrational panic. I went to where Lawrence waited, where Lawrence had called me, where I must go of my own volition if I was ever to repossess Guinever's gifts.

I came out at last onto that high plateau, sweeping unbroken toward the precipice and the sea. Rain spattered, striking against my face. I was in the void, alone with the mist and spray and the seagulls crying. "Lawrence!" I called, and the wind carried the faint murmur back to me: "Here . . .!"

Nearer I went to the precipice, and nearer, each step a decision taken. The ghosts crowded round me and I fought them back, thinking of Lawrence, thinking of the torque and chalice and all they meant. Then I was at the edge, looking downward at the rocks and the turbulent sea. Alone. Alone with the drumming in my ears and the roar of the sea and the whisper of a taunting voice that called my name.

It was not Lawrence's voice. I knew that at once, and in that same instant I knew the truth, even before I saw the figure, as yet a dark blur, emerging from over the edge of rock. A figure clutching two golden objects and a gun.

Doff. It had been Doff who was behind everything that had happened, Doff who was insane. I who had been so quick to catch the signs of irrationality in Charles, why had I been blind to the taint of it in Charles's son? Why had I not realized how narrow, and how deep, was that knife-edge gap between health and sickness, and how easily the raging torment of rejected love could push the sensitive over the brink?

It was Charles who had been Doff's intended victim. Not through his dying, but through the death of his dreams, the death of those he loved. Doff meant to kill me, I had no doubt of that. He'd trapped me in a cat-and-mouse game. He meant to kill me, throw the treasure over the cliff-edge where it would be lost forever in the waves. And then Doff's voice, exulting, "You came! I knew you'd come! I was clever, wasn't I, coming into your room along the ledge, leaving that message I'd ripped out of Stearns's notebook?"

Doff. Modred, Arthur's daemonic offspring, his other half. Modred, his dark shadow, the proof, if proof were needed, that though man may be a little lower than the angels, he can, too, be little higher than the devils. The terror of Tintagel, the terror of my dreams, the terror I had felt in Avalon's mysterious threatening dark places coalesced and swelled into heart-bursting fear. Yet even as it was happening came that overpowering sense of déjà vu—as though the nighmares, scrying visions, even this, were but re-creations of what had already been.

It was so strong in me, the presence of the lost, panicking child Lydian, feet weighted as with cement, horror pulling her ever nearer to the brink of death. Yet even as those dark passions warred within me, the other Lydian I had become was speaking. Quietly, calmly, as I had learned to do with Charles when he was in one of his irrational passions. I heard myself saying, rationally, soothingly, "Why, Doff? You have a whole life before you, you have such gifts. Why is it necessary for you to take this way?"

I must do as I had so often done with Charles—keep him talking, sanely, focused on reality; keep the precarious balance on the tightrope. And concentrate, *concentrate*; careful, careful, that not a word nor gesture convey a threat; strain every nerve so that the rope stay taut.

"*Gifts!*" Doff burst out. "He doesn't want my gifts! He took from me in the old days. Like a king, like it was his due. I thought it was, too—I thought he was a god. Then Stearns came, with his fancy learning, his archaeological education!" He spat each separate syllable out like a poisoned bullet. "*He* was going to send me to Oxford, was going to train me so I could work with him. But why waste the time and money, why part for three years with a serf who gave him coolie labor, when there was just the kind of colleague he wanted already to hand?

The kind of son he wanted!" Doff laughed, a bitter gloating. "He found out, didn't he? The son he chose served him just as he'd served your father! Seduced his lady! Oh, yes, I know all about past history! I've been in and out of that secret gallery of his a hundred times, and he's never known it. That shows he's the fool, not I. Just as he's been a fool about not seeing the difference in value between his real and his counterfeit son!"

If I could get a little closer, I might be able to grab that gun.

"He hadn't known you were his son," I said reasonably. "How could he? You were put out for adoption when you were born, while he was ill. He was never told." Slide one foot forward, cautiously; keep talking, and then surreptitiously shift weight. "When it came out in the papers it was a terrible shock; Charles had been under great strain; he couldn't comprehend—"

"He didn't *want* to comprehend! He didn't want me as a son, not any more! He would have once. He liked me," Doff said, with a pathos that tore my heart. "Then Stearns came. And you. He didn't want me as a colleague, as a painter—anything but a serf. You saw him at the birthday party!"

"But there was so much more involved in that than you! He couldn't bear getting old—"

"He couldn't bear that I'd inherited his talent! I have, you know. And he can't bear rivals. Or truth! That's what I gave him in that picture, the truth about himself, his wife, his counterfeit son! None of the rest of you cared enough about him to tell the truth. Just lies to protect him, to encourage him, to protect yourselves. Even Lady Meriel, his dear cousin—she never even told him he had a son! Well, he's found out now! You've all found out!"

An extraordinary look crossed his face and I said quickly, "It was you, wasn't it? You've known the truth about your parents all along. You leaked those stories to the papers. About yourself, about the discovered treasure. That was one of the ways that you've been clever!"

"You saw that, did you?" Doff nodded, his eyes gleaming. Like a small boy whose mischief is perceived as brightness. "Yes, I knew. I always suspected the dull, respected Reverend Doffman was not my rightful parent. After he died I found some papers in a strongbox I went through. *I* visited Somerset House, too. Then it was easy. Write the right sort of letter, be properly ingratiating and attentive. *That* wasn't hard. I ought to serve him; he's a genius; I've known that, better than you all. I knew quite quickly, too, he had to be my father. He'd have recognized it in time. We're so much alike. Everything went so well!"

"But then Lawrence came, and took Charles's attention from you. I came, and took his love." Slide another foot forward; imperceptibly move. "So you stirred things up. You gave those stories to the papers."

"I did many things. Discredited you and your paramour, for who else would have given away the secret? Made Charles see he could trust nobody, he must go back to living as he had before, just him and me. Made him realize he had a son." His visage darkened. "But he wouldn't face it. Couldn't bear to face it! He didn't want me, any more than he wants my gifts!"

"It isn't the gifts you give as presents that are important. It's the gifts you have. You've such real skill at nursing. And you *are* an artist. That painting you did was magnificent, fully as powerful as Charles's—"

"It's his own talent. In *me*. That's what he can't bear. I told you, he doesn't like anyone else having power. I have it, though, haven't I?" His eyes again took on that mulish, gloating look. "I can paint. I can make things happen, just as he can. I can re-create the past. It was Charles who set the triangle in motion. Arthur, Lancelot, Guinever! But it was I, wasn't it, who kept it going? Lawrence and Lydian, getting scared, taking refuge in each other's arms! Lawrence and Lydian, having assignations in the tunnel!"

He was wrapped in his own brilliance, his eyes on mine. My gaze never wavered. My foot risked another forward glide.

"It really didn't matter," Doff said thoughtfully, "that those experiments of mine with the gas and the keystone failed. A word here; a word there. Lawrence and Lydian together. Lawrence and Lydian doing what Charles could not. Lydian, writing what had been Charles's book. You never suspected it was I, did you, fiddling with the gas mains, doping him with laudanum, altering Charles's mind!"

The sky was very black now, and lightning crackled, sending a gleam of silver across the barrel of Doff's gun. If it grew darker and the mist became thicker I might be able to throw myself down and roll to hiding. "It was very clever of you," I remarked, "to have trapped us that night in the tunnel."

"That should have been the end!" Doff was perspiring; for the first time I recognized what a tremendous strain he was laboring under. Not the cold, Olympian detachment of the psychotic; this was the madness of all-possessing love, the madness of desperation. Madness of an overpowering hunger to be needed, appreciated, recognized as a person—the same madness that had touched us all. "It should have been stopped then. Charles understood; he saw the harm he'd done in bringing you and Stearns there together; he *accepted* he was meant to be alone. With me! And then you came back! With the treasure!"

The mist was clearing. My eyes risked, measured the distance to shelter on either side. Doff saw. The arm that held the gun came up more firmly.

"Then I understood! I saw how he reacted. And I knew what we must do. Play out the pattern! Not Lancelot and Guinever only, but the other! It had to happen *here*."

I had to keep him talking. "Why here?" I asked, and he looked at me pityingly.

"Don't you *know*? Even after you finally had the wit to get into the secret gallery? Or do you, like Charles, run from the ultimate truth? Don't you really know what's in your heritage? Lust, betrayal, murder. Just as in Arthur's. Just as in mine!"

Doff dropped the torque and chalice he had held clutched to him. And my attention was suddenly possessed by the other objects that he held, the two rolls that he now snapped out, awkwardly, the pistol never wavering in his grip. The lightning above us flared on the vivid colors as he flung them at my feet.

Pictures. Charles's pictures. Secret pictures, two of them, which I had not seen because before reaching them I had reeled in horror from the truth-mirror painting of myself in Lawrence's arms.

Tintagel. Arthur, Lancelot and Guinever. Ason, Charles and Virgilia. *This* was the missing piece, *this* the truth beyond what

I had seen in memory, nightmares, scrying. This was what I had fled from knowing; what told me now that if I lived, I need never again have to flee.

Charles and Ason struggling, and my mother, Virgilia, trying desperately to separate her husband and her love, she and Charles together teetering on the brink of this very cliff, and Ason, my father, forcing himself against them with all his weight. Not accident. Not suicide. A life-death struggle, and perhaps a murder.

And the other picture. My eyes closed for a brief instant in pain and horror. A view of the cliff, not from above but from below. As Charles must have seen it, lying in terrible conscious agony on the rocks. Virgilia, the hand that wore her wedding ring outflung, her golden hair cascading; a broken doll. Charles bent backward, his blue eyes filled with torment and accusation, gazing upward. And above, on the cliff, Ason—cold, emotionless, austere, looking down. And in his arms, a golden-haired child.

I had been there. I had been there, and I had seen it all. That was why the nightmares, the sense of déjà vu and panic. Not possession by my mother's spirit. Not insanity. Memory, buried deep because it was too painful to be borne. Memory which, seen at last, could set me free.

"And now," Doff said quietly, conversationally, "now I am going to kill you, Lydian."

A kind of strength had come to me in those few minutes. A strength from my mother? The Sidh? My own inner self, from having faced the truth at last? "No," I said calmly, serenely, and I was smiling. "No, Doff, because it isn't right. You're not a murderer. And it's not me you hate anyway, is it? It's your father. And most of all, because this isn't the way it's meant to be. You're trying to re-create a pattern, and this one's wrong. It's not supposed to be Lydian and Doff here, but Lydian and Lawrence."

A cold smile curled Doff's lips. "It wouldn't matter, would it? The story says King Arthur's lady and the knight that was like his son. I *am* his son. It could have been you and I—and then none of this would have needed to happen. I could have liked you, but I wasn't good enough, was I? The night of the birthday you were so kind to me I almost gave up the plan. But you went from me to *him*."

His weight shifted, balanced; his grip tightened on the pistol handle. "Which shall it be, Lydian? The cliff, or the bullet? It doesn't matter either way, you see, because this is Stearns's gun. That's where I've been clever. I'm wearing gloves, I'll leave no fingerprints. You and he stole the paintings and the dower gifts, there was a lovers' quarrel, and you went over the edge. The whole old scandal, happening again. And Charles will know that I'm the only one he can trust."

"It won't work," I said. "Because it's only me alone. Lawrence isn't here."

"Ah, but that's where I have been clever!" Doff laughed, a peculiar shrill laugh that sent a shudder up my spine. "I fooled you, didn't I? I left that note for you, in Stearns's hand. I left a message for Stearns, too. I knew he couldn't leave Glastonbury last night, there were no trains. So I called round till I found where he was staying, and I left him word he was to meet you here today. He'll come, won't he? He's so anxious to take you away from the danger he thinks is Charles, at Avalon! Even if he comes too late, he'll have been here, it will be his gun, his fingerprints! He'll pay. He'll have betrayed Charles, just as Charles betrayed your father, betrayed me!"

He was insane, and I could understand now why the insane could be dangerous if they cared less for their own safety than for what they meant to do. He was coming toward me now, grimly, his eyes glittering. It was futile for me to try to run; I had all my dreams, all my experience to tell me that was no use. He would shoot if he had to, but he did not want to shoot; he wanted me over the cliff, unblemished, repeating my mother's terrible fate. There would be a moment when he would have to drop the pistol to seize me with both hands to force me over. If in that moment, before he grabbed me, I could throw him off balance and get the gun— I braced myself, waiting.

Nearer he came, and nearer, and our gaze never wavered. And then from behind me came Lawrence's voice. Lawrence had come, just as Doff had predicted, and now the pattern was irrevocably changed. No chance, now, for the momentary shift of focus in which I could have gained command. Doff had lunged at me, and the muzzle of the pistol was pressed against my breast.

"Don't come any nearer," Doff yelled, "or I'll kill her, right in front of you!"

"That would be your way, wouldn't it!" Lawrence's tone was superior, insolent. Without daring to turn my head, in my mind's eye I could see him standing motionless, his arms folded in a familiar, measuring way. "You *boy!* You've nothing against her; I'm the one you want. I'm the one who took your rightful place. You're not man enough to fight me for it, are you?"

His contempt made a tremor run through Doff. "I'm a man! I'm more a man than *he's* ever been!"

Doff's arm was around me, clutching me close, the cold iron of the gun digging painfully into my bosom. He shifted our position so I could see Lawrence now, shaking his head slowly.

"Oh, no. Impotent, in his wheelchair, your father's more man than you can ever be. Do you think he'd own a son doing what you do now? Would he ever hide behind a woman's skirts?"

Doff's body shuddered as though from ague; I braced myself, wondering if I dared try to snatch the gun from him.

"Let her go," Lawrence ordered. "*I'm* your rival. Fight *me*, if you really want to prove your honor!"

Doff took a step back. For a moment we teetered, there on the sheer edge. Then with a savage oath he flung me from him. I fell, but down the grass slope and not toward the sea. Fell, rolled, the sharp stones scraping, my own brain whirling. Beyond me, far below, I could hear the pounding of the sea, the seagulls screaming against the darkling sky; and there was another sound, incongruous, alien. What it was I could not know, and neither could I bring myself to think of it. I pulled myself back up and circled in the dimness, trying to keep myself from Doff's range of vision. Watching for an opening . . .

Doff had dropped the gun; had grabbed the golden chalice as a club and was charging. Lawrence was braced, a coiled spring, gauging the distance, waiting for the moment at which he could launch himself at Doff and bring him down. The past was repeating—all my old nightmares, Charles's paintings were coming to life, only the protagonists wearing different faces.

234

Lawrence's body leaping forward, the two of them going down. Rolling, struggling. Coming up, locked in mortal combat. Doff with insane, inhuman strength battering with the golden chalice at Lawrence's face, his head. Lawrence, fastening an iron grip upon Doff's wrist. The two of them, outstretched arms rigid, trying to break each other's grasp, their bodies locked together in a dance that carried them nearer and nearer to the edge.

I could not stand there and do nothing. I ran toward the precipice that so long had beckoned me with its fatal fascination. Flung myself at the combatants; clawed, grappled, trying to separate that deathly mating. And all the while a terrible futility engulfed me. This was what Doff had wanted. This, the inevitable, macabre re-creation of my mother's death. He did not even care if he fell too, not if he could bring down on Charles's head the horror of a dead past come to life.

It was Charles who was Doff's real victim. The old scandal would all come out, and Charles would live with it all his remaining days, in a life that would for him be worse than any death.

I screamed, and incredibly, an answering cry came back to me. A voice that could not possibly be there, but was. My husband's voice. I was startled, thrown off balance, fell; rolled away from the struggling figures and found myself caught in a grip of iron. Meriel's grip; Meriel dragging me away from the edge, away from the others, her hand clamped across my mouth so that I could not speak.

But I could see, could hear. Charles in his wheelchair, his Arthurian cloak flying, was propelling himself forward up the bank of grass. Charles's great hypnotic voice was ringing out in the way I had not heard in months.

Charles saying, "Barrett! Listen to me! *Son!*"

Doff, still struggling with Lawrence, still so near the edge, yet hearing, flinging back, "I won't be your son! You didn't want me as a son!"

"I didn't know! Can't you understand that? Not till today, when I found you gone, and missed you, and your mother told me all the truth!"

Clever Charles, even in the pain and torture that must now

possess him, skillfully weaving that image of the happy family Doff had so longed for. The old Charles, seeing truth, not shrinking from it but making magic with it. Charles, restored for this shining moment to all his power. "Let them go, son! They don't matter! This is between you and me, it always has been between you and me, and it is we who must resolve it!"

Doff stood for a moment irresolute, then flung Lawrence from him so that he rolled, like me, powerless down the slope.

For a moment son and father faced each other against the electric sky. Then Doff, with an oath, flung the chalice from him over the cliff-edge into the sea below. "Arthur and Modred? The last battle! Oh, no! I want you living. You can hurt more, living. I want you hurting, the way you've hurt me! Loving, with no love in return!"

Before any of us understood what was happening, he bent and scooped up the forgotten pistol—to point it straight at me.

In that instant, my husband charged: Charles, his pain transcended, his power restored, a king such as Arthur, larger than life, surging toward his Modred-son on the wheels of his royal chair. His proud face like an eagle's, his golden hair streaming in the light of the hunter's moon. The great throne-chair, with Charles in it, rammed straight at Doff, there on the precipice. And they both went down, in a great cry of pain and triumph, over the cliffs and into the pounding sea.

16

"Don't look!" Lawrence lunged after me as I ran to the sheer edge. He caught me in his arms, forcing my head away. It was too late, but that did not matter. In the discovery that I had actually witnessed, not only dreamed, my mother's death the horrible power the cliffs had had to draw me toward my own falling was now gone. The two figures motionless and mangled on the rocks below resembled Charles's own dreadful painting more than something real.

I pressed my hand against my mouth; my eyes filled with tears. Lawrence led me back from the edge. "There's no place for you to sit. The ground is soaking."

"It doesn't matter. Go to them. Quickly!"

His eyes searched me, and then he was gone, clambering down over the face of the rocks to where the still figures waited. Fast as he was, Meriel had been swifter. We had not even seen her vanish, after her first cry. Yet now, as I ran back to the precipice, watching, praying, I saw her already far below, running heedless of danger along the spit of rock. Grabbing up her sodden skirts, plunging directly into the surf to reach Charles's side. Her hand touched his breast, his brow. She straightened, and I knew. Knew even before Lawrence was beside her, turning to fling the words up to me on the keening wind.

"Gone. Instantly."

237

"Doff?" I shouted, and Meriel was already moving toward him. I thought I saw the faintest movement. Then she was wedging herself, kneeling, among the rocks, bracing herself against the buffeting spray, pressing Doff's hand against her heart.

"Alive. Barely. Are you all right? I have to go for help."

"Stay with them, Lawrence. *I'll* go!" I was running over the level plain, skidding down the slate path. Across the narrow strip of land, up the steep slope to the tiny village. The shops were already closed. Along the street, deserted now, finally at the cottage where I had left the car. I pounded at the door, sobbing out my cry for help to the startled woman who threw it open.

I was drawn in, wrapped in a shawl, pulled to where a fire burned cheerfully on the hearth. Already the householder and his two stalwart sons were plunging out into the mist. I ran after them, thrusting off attempts to make me stay. They knew a short cut to the sea; one turned to the village for police and doctor while the others went directly to the rocks, with me running after. Meriel was still by Doff, but Lawrence came to meet me, shaking his head.

"Gone. And it's probably a blessing. Come away; we can do nothing here and are only in the way. Lydian, where are you going?"

Like one possessed I was clambering up the rocks to the level plain, to the cliff-edge where Doff and I had struggled, where my mother and now my husband too had died. I heard Lawrence's voice calling me, but there was no time now to answer.

The rain had ceased, the mist dissolved and far off in the western sky was the red glow of the dying sun. Its rays lingered on Meriel, bent over Doff. Four villagers stood at Charles's head and feet. And on the ground before me I saw it. Knelt and lifted it from where it lay, half hidden in the grass where it had been flung.

Guinever's torque. A split circle, the open-ended symbol of infinity.

Lawrence came up behind me and took me in his arms.

"Charles died instantly. He felt no pain; remember that." Lawrence kept repeating it, far into the night, rubbing my hands as I sat before the cottage fire, shivering as though I would never again be warm.

He could not say that of Doff, though. We did not speak of Doff's dying, in deference to Meriel, who sat across from us, a still, dark figure. She had refused the housewife's offer of clothes and let her own dry on her, wrinkled, their beauty gone. She had aged; she looked haggard, but in her face too there was a kind of peace.

She felt my gaze on her now, and looked up somberly. "You needn't be tactful. Ask your questions. You know you need to."

"Haven't we talked enough?" Lawrence asked, for it was now near midnight and we had been questioned already, endlessly, by doctor and by local constable and ultimately by the chief constable himself.

I shook my head. "No. Meriel's right. We have to know." I turned to her. "How? How did you come? How did you *know* to come?"

It was Lawrence who answered. "Rose. It was Rose, wasn't it?" he said, and Meriel nodded.

"But how? I made her promise—"

"Apparently Rose's concern for you is more important to her than her word. And it's a good thing," Lawrence added grimly.

"You talked to her? I thought you'd gone to London!"

"No train till morning. Apparently Doff knew that. Apparently he knew a great deal more than we gave him credit for," he said, and I nodded slowly. "I found a message waiting when I came down to breakfast this morning at the inn, The George and Pilgrims. Lady Ransome requested me to meet her at Tintagel. That seemed a strange message from Lady Ransome, all things considered, so I just stepped round to Avalon and had a word with Rose. When she found out I hadn't been in contact with you, she had more than a few words for me." He turned to Meriel. "I still do not understand how you and Charles came into it."

"Rose again. She had an intuition, that girl, and once she learned of that false message you'd received, she was more than ever worried. So she came to me."

Yes, I thought, Rose would do that; she'd have recognized

Meriel's strength. Of all of us, Meriel had perhaps always been the most clear-seeing.

"Then we discovered that Doff was missing." Meriel's voice faltered; strengthened. "*I* went to Charles. Thank God, it was one of his good days—neither the pain nor the laudanum yet started. We finally could talk about everything that had been happening. Too many accidents, I never could quite believe in them. Neither could Charles, not really. Not when his head was clear." She looked at Lawrence, her mouth twisting. "One thing we were sure of, whatever you might have intended happening to Charles, you never would have endangered Lydian. So, once we had cleared each other of misdeeds, that left—Doff."

Doff.

For several minutes there was no sound but the crackling of the flames.

"I think we've both always felt something there was not quite right. Perhaps that was why neither of us could ever really warm— Why, after that dreadful newspaper story, Charles had to strike out, to destroy." Meriel's eyes were on her hands but she went on evenly. "Today, for the first time, Charles wanted to know the truth. And so I told him. He really hadn't known. Those last terrible days when he fell, when your mother died, something in his mind had made him blot everything out. Just as something made him set all the old pattern in motion again when you came."

"To punish himself," I said slowly, and Meriel nodded.

"Call it expiation. He really loved your mother, he couldn't bear to believe he'd been unfaithful to her with me. Just as he couldn't bear knowing he'd betrayed Ason Wentworth's trust. Whatever he said about your father, Lydian, he nearly worshiped him."

Just as Lawrence had loved and respected Charles. I could not look at him.

"And then you came," Meriel said, her voice hardening. "Poor Charles, he was pulled so obsessively in opposite directions. To make you your mother's surrogate. To bring justice on himself for his past sins, for your father's suffering, your mother's death. He, who had been the Lancelot in that earlier triangle, must now play the Arthur. I saw him forcing the two of you into those roles and I was powerless to stop it. And then— Doff."

"I was responsible there, too, wasn't I?" I said. "Doff might have gone on, biding his time in the hope of winning Charles's respect, his affection. But I became the love, the wife, the heir."

The heir. *I* must now be the custodian of Avalon and all its treasures. Just as I was already the custodian of Charles's dreams.

"I think we have gone quite far enough with this," Lawrence interrupted firmly. "Of course, we each have sins of omission and commission. But there's no point flagellating ourselves with the past. Otherwise we'll become—"

He broke off; the unspoken words hovered in the air. Become like Charles, like Doff; unbalanced, doomed continually to re-create our own sick fantasies and dreams.

"We have heard more than we need to hear," he said, "about powers without and within. About being forced to become what we are not; about the *geis*. Our *geis*, our fate, if you want to call it that, is our own nature. And that, thank heavens, can be changed."

The gifts, the responsibility, the destiny. I thought a lot about that as I lay awake in the dark cottage bedroom with Meriel probably equally wakeful in the bed across the room. I thought about them the next day when, as the widowed Lady Ransome, I gave my evidence to the coroner, gave instructions on transferring the bodies back to Avalon, wrote an obituary for the London papers, sent a telegram to the Winchester symposium explaining why I might not come. Then, at last, we were free to go, and Lawrence drove Meriel and me back to Glastonbury.

We still did not understand how Charles and Meriel had made that incredible journey. But after we had driven an hour or more in silence, Meriel began to tell us. How Charles, once convinced of Doff's parentage, had been filled with a terrible apprehension.

"He had, I think," Meriel said starkly, "a strange belief that, having been the author of Doff's life, he now was responsible for whatever was evil in that life."

241

Yes, that was true to the Arthurian code; so had Arthur himself come in time to feel toward Modred.

"Don't try to speak of it," I said compassionately; Meriel shook her head and, as the miles along the moors flew by, her voice went on. Somehow, with Hodge's help, she had gotten Charles into the car. Somehow, Charles had endured that terrible ride, allowing himself just enough laudanum to dull the pain, to pacify the addiction, without blurring the brilliant mind. "It was something he had to do," Meriel said, and Lawrence and I could understand.

That was how I would always remember him, with love and gratitude and a deep tenderness. Charles, noble and radiant in his wheeled chariot riding to save my life. One last grand gesture and then a valiant death, surrounded by loved ones, at the peak of power.

It was a king's funeral we gave him; a fifth-century king's. I was set upon it, and Meriel agreed. He lay in state in the Great Hall, in his purple velvet cloak, covered with his fur robes, the golden torque like a crown upon his pillow. Torches burned at the four corners of his bier, and priests from the church prayed a night and a day beside him, and Lawrence and Meriel and I kept watch, I in my wedding jewels and the now-ruined velvet gown. We buried him in a specially made coffin, a hollowed-out section of a giant oak like the one we found Arthur's bones in, and we laid him to rest in one of the walled-up crypts opening off the subterranean tunnel.

The great and near-great of aristocracy, society, archaeology, the arts flocked to his funeral. Doff's body lay like that of a prince beside him, separated by a gulf as narrow and as deep as that which had separated them in life. But only Lawrence and Meriel and I witnessed Charles's interment, and only Meriel, at her own request, attended Doff's.

I came up from the tunnel into the quiet of Avalon at late afternoon. Already Hodge, with silent efficiency, had removed the torches and the bier. The Great Hall was still, deserted, peopled only by the figures glowing in the stained glass overhead. I went up the long stairs and Rose came to help me out of my velvet gown. I would never wear it again.

I put on a thin white muslin, for though it was September the day was warm as midsummer. Like distant music I could hear Charles's voice, that first evening long ago, saying, "You are not wearing black, I see. You're wise."

Black had been my mother's color. It was not mine. I had been my mother's shadow long enough.

Rose hooked me up silently and then as silently, impulsively, hugged me. I kissed her and went downstairs, went out through the study and the rose garden into the golden glory of the afternoon.

It was no conscious thought, but instinct deep within me that drew me from Avalon through the orchard, over the low wall, into the abbey grounds. The apple trees were heavy with fruit, the grass was green, and the flowers of late summer still foamed over the abbey's steps and stones. All the soaring window frames, the walls, the arches were serene and glowing in the peaceful light. I sat in my familiar place on the sunken wall, and the restoring magic of Glastonbury enfolded me with comfort and with peace.

A shadow fell before me, and my love was there. Lawrence, my love. I was free to love him now. Free not just because Charles was dead, but because of the nature of his dying, and of my living. What had Lawrence said, that short eternity of days ago? We were free to change our natures. And they had changed, Lawrence's and Charles's and mine, for the better. It was, finally, what Charles would have wanted.

"I knew you would be here," Lawrence said, as I rose to meet him.

I nodded. "This place has magic for me."

" 'Strong magic.' Charles used to say that, didn't he? I think that is one of the things he found so frustrating, that there was a magic he could not duplicate. Or own."

Already we could speak of Charles easily, with a kind of bittersweet tenderness.

"Your kind of magic," Lawrence said, referring back to Glastonbury's special peace.

I shook my head slowly. "I don't know. I thought so, once, but then it vanished."

"It has come again. That was the effect of Avalon. Avalon's own peculiar power is a kind of quicksilver, and it holds no peace."

Lawrence looked at me. "What will you do with it? Avalon? You are its mistress; will you still live here?"

I shuddered faintly. "No. Never again. I think perhaps it should be a museum. To King Arthur, and to Charles. His work is important; it must go on, it must be shared. Avalon always has been a museum, hasn't it? Only now its doors, instead of shutting out the world, can let it in."

Lawrence nodded. "And you will go on with the work, of course? Not only his, but yours. Writing. Researching. Speaking."

"Yes. I did not tell you; I've changed my mind. I am going to Winchester tomorrow. To give the address, and present the evidence of the tomb. Please don't try to stop me; it may not seem proper, but it is a thing I have to do."

To my astonishment, Lawrence began to grin, and his eyes, no longer opaque, were filled with laughter. "Lady, I wouldn't dare stand in your way. I can only hope that as co-discoverer, I may be permitted to come along. Those blessed Sidh of Charles's must be roaring with amusement at the sight of us. I never thought to take a wife at all; now I'll have one capable of fighting me tooth and nail on my own ground, and winning."

"Why does one person have to win and another lose?" I stopped, flushing. "Anyway, no one's talking about marriage."

"Yes, we are," Lawrence said quietly. "And we both know it. Oh, it may not be proper yet, as you said. But do you know something? I don't think old Charles would mind."

For a moment the image of the old Charles Ransome, magnanimous, beneficent, shimmered in the air.

"Lawrence," I said suddenly, "what happened to the chalice?"

"It fell into the water, and was washed away. We'll have to send divers after it, of course." He looked at me thoughtfully. "Will it matter to you, very much, if it should not be found? After all, according to the myths, grails were never meant for anyone's possessing. And you have the torque."

And Guinever's gifts, I thought. The real ones. Serenity.

Compassion. Wholeness. The ability to love. And by some blessed miracle I'd found someone grown strong enough himself not to be threatened by them.

I put out my hands to Lawrence. "No. It will not matter."

We walked side by side, through the joyous stillness of the abbey ruins. And Glastonbury's special healing peace, that once and future magic, was all around us.

About the Author

NICOLE ST. JOHN wrote her first book when she was twelve and has continued writing ever since, throughout various careers in fashion, teaching, theater and publishing. Of her Anglophilia she says, "I draw my strength from England, though my ancestors were Dutch."

She is the author of *The Medici Ring* and *Wychwood*, and lives in Wyckoff, New Jersey.